Bitter RETREAT

BITTERROOT MONTANA VETERANS
BOOK 2

ANNE M. SCOTT

To survivors of all kinds. Living well is
the best revenge.

Cover designed by Mibl
Developmental Editing by Lia Huni
Proofreading by Paula Lester, Polaris Editing

Anne M. Scott
Visit my website at www.amscottwrites.com/romance

First Printing: August 2022 as Love, Computers & Cows
Second Printing: January 2023
Version 2.0
Lightwave Publishing LLC

Author's Note and Trigger Warnings

Trigger Warnings: The main female character in this novel is a survivor of military sexual assault. Details are minimal, but her terrible trauma, recovery, and her attacker are integral to her character. Some readers may think her reactions are unrealistic, but every survivor's coping mechanisms are different, and they are all equally valid.

This novel also contains gun violence.

If you are a US military sexual assault survivor, I hope you are getting the support you need. The Veteran's Administration is finally taking the issue seriously. If your branch of the VA isn't, complain to your congressional representatives. If you feel unsafe at your local VA, call and ask for an escort before your appointment. You earned your benefits, and you deserve them. If you're not in the US, I know many countries have hotlines and organizations to help; I hope you find one.

For every sexual assault survivor, reaching out for help is brave, not weak! I hope each and every one of you receives the help you need. In the US, RAINN is one of the largest; call their hotline at 1-800-655-4673 (HOPE). There are similar organizations in many countries. Get help now; don't wait, please.

Same with anyone struggling with trauma, physical and/or emotional, depression, or any mental health struggle. We need you here—please ask for help. In the US, call 988 for help, today. Don't wait.

This novel was previously published as Love, Computers & Cows. The title and cover have changed, but the story remains the same.

Chapter 1

TOM

Tom Borde almost ran from the ranch house living room, clenching his fists as tightly as his mouth. If he stayed, he'd say something unforgivable.

"Tom! Thomas Pierre Borde, don't you walk away from me! I'm talking to you! Tom—" Dad's voice stopped with the bang of the ancient back-door screen. His anger-fueled steps ate the hundred yards to the barn. He had to get away from his father's stubborn insistence on business as usual and incessant badgering. He should have stayed in New York City for so many reasons. Number one on that list was his dad treating him like he was still a sixteen-year-old boy, instead of forty-two with a professional career behind him.

He stopped at the paddock fence. Horses trotted to him, looking for a treat. All of them needed exercise, but he hadn't ridden the new one yet, a palomino named Strawberry. A neighbor couldn't afford her care and begged Dad to take her. Of course, Dad couldn't say no; that's why they had a corral full of horses they didn't need. And a ridiculously high monthly vet bill, even though they administered all the routine medications themselves.

He grabbed Strawberry's saddle and bridle from the barn and took them to the paddock fence. At least Dad got Strawberry's tack along with the horse. She tried to avoid him, but with his long strides and a treat, he caught her and got her tacked up. Grabbing a pair of saddlebags pre-stocked with a first aid kit and a water bottle, he filled the water bottle and fastened the bags and a holstered rifle to the saddle. He mounted and turned Strawberry up the long dirt road heading up into the Sapphire Mountains on the east side of the Bitterroot Valley.

He'd ride up the crest trail and let his father cool his heels for a while. And maybe Tom's temper would cool too. Generally, it took a lot to get him upset, but Dad pushed all his buttons. Plus, the man just couldn't see that times were changing and Tom had changed, too. He wasn't a teenager, and he didn't live on ranching; he had money to invest in the business, but only if they were modernizing. If they remained stuck in the past, they'd get run over and lose the business and the land. Marcus didn't need another "gentleman's ranch," barely used by a multimillionaire twice a year, and America still needed good cattle ranchers. The problem was agreeing on what "good" meant.

The morning was brighter than his mood. Sunny but cool; September in Montana was his favorite time of year. Strawberry was a nervy, jumpy ride, doing her best to prevent him from enjoying the fall colors. "Well, horse, you're in for a surprise." He patted her neck and controlled her gently but firmly, letting her know he was in command.

Once she was warmed up a bit, Tom moved her into a canter up the increasingly steep road. If she didn't want to settle down, well, fine, she'd work—hard. Her former owner probably hadn't ridden enough and spoiled her. Since Tom was six-four and strong from hefting hay bales, she was carrying more weight than she was probably used to, and he wouldn't put up with bad behavior. Near the top end of the road, he slowed to let her rest and get a better look at the huge timber-frame mansion that finally sold after many years on the market. He'd heard rumors about the work being done on the place, and seen lots of construction trucks going up and down the road, but hadn't had the time to check it out.

Strawberry sidled and turned, keeping his attention mostly on her, but the glimpses he caught were certainly different. The new owner must be seriously worried about something to surround the majestic three-story stone and wood house with a high, ugly chain-link fence, including razor wire at the top, a big solid metal gate across the driveway, and no trespassing signs warning about surveillance in use every fifty feet. Tom hadn't worried that much in the middle of NYC, let alone Marcus, but to each his own. Or her own, since he'd been told the owner was a woman. With that kind of security, maybe she was a mob boss or drug cartel leader. Or a famous actress. Whatever she did, neither his dad nor their neighbors had met her yet; she kept to herself.

He clucked at Strawberry, urging her into a trot, then slowed to a walk once they reached the lightly used, rather rough feeder trail. Dense groves of aspen and birch crowded the trail, their branches making Strawberry jump. They passed the Bitterroot National Forest sign, and the trees thinned, turning to ponderosa pine. She still wasn't very happy about the trail, shying at rocks and brush. Probably an arena queen, used for show only. To be fair, the trail needed some clearing; he'd bring a pair of loppers on his next ride.

He'd probably be smarter to take her back and trade her out for a trained trail horse. But he was a good rider and well used to training horses; the experience and work would be good for her and take his mind off his problems. After they turned onto the Sapphire crest trail and the terrain opened into rock and sagebrush with the occasional ponderosa pine, she settled a bit. He'd ride to the high point, and then they'd turn around.

They reached the point without any real problems, Strawberry jumping at the occasional wind-tossed bush but easily controlled. At the top, Tom twisted, reached into his saddle bag, grabbed his water bottle, and drank, taking in the green and gold expanse of the Bitterroot Valley and the stunning, rugged mountains beyond. In the midst of the quiet beauty, his mood settled and his determination hardened. He'd find another way to explain his plans for the ranch and bring Dad into the modern world.

He turned Strawberry back toward the ranch, keeping her to a slow walk down the rough, rocky, single-track trail. She seemed steadier; the miles up the crest worked the nervous energy out of her. Not bothering to stop, he twisted in the saddle, opening the saddle bag to return the water bottle.

He went airborne, Strawberry bucking and spinning beneath him. He clamped his legs tight, but saddle leather slid under his jeans. He sailed through the air and hit the ground hard. "Oof!" He rolled up, grabbing for the reins but missing.

Strawberry ran down the trail, blowing, neighing, and bucking like the drama queen she was. He blew out an exasperated breath. Stupid horse and stupid him to trust a new horse.

He stood, brushed himself off, and followed the horse down the trail, water bottle in hand. A long hike in city-style cowboy boots, but at least he had water. He'd enjoy the lovely day, since he didn't have to worry about controlling Strawberry. Ridiculous, spoiled horse. He strolled, taking in the sights and appreciating the quiet for one mile, then two. On a steeper slope, his foot slid, and he scrambled to stay upright, but his heel jammed into a hole. Suddenly, he was on the ground on his smarting backside again. "Ow!"

He got to one knee and put his foot down. "Ah!" He must have twisted his ankle when he stepped in the hole. *Great.* Nobody knew where he was, his horse probably hadn't been on the ranch long enough to know her way home, he had half a bottle of water and—he pulled his cell phone out of his back pocket— a broken cell phone. *Double great.*

And his first aid kit and rifle were on the saddle too.

He sighed and shook his head at his own stupidity. Ten feet off the trail, a group of boulders were stacked twenty feet high, a single pine growing near them. He could hobble to the rocks, and when it got hot later, use them for shade. Until then, he'd put his leg up. Rest, ice, compression, elevation—two out of four was the best he could do. He crab-walked his way over to the rocks, using both hands and his right leg. At least he'd been wearing gloves, and he was in good shape, so it wasn't impossible. He turned on his butt, put his leg up on the rock, and lay down, putting his gloves under his head. There wasn't much else he could do right now, so he might as well take advantage of the warming day and take a nap. He pulled his hat over his face so he wouldn't get burned and closed his eyes.

Tom started awake and sat up, his hat flying off his face and landing in his lap, and his legs thwacking on the ground. *Ow*. Oh, yeah, he'd twisted his ankle. The sun was higher in the sky, the air temperature warmer, but that didn't wake him. Hooves plodding on rock did. Strawberry coming back didn't seem very likely. But sure enough, Strawberry trod toward him, but not by herself.

Nope, she was being led. A fairly short person, judging by Strawberry's height. He waited until they got closer and then waved his arms. "Hey, over here!"

The person raised a hand in acknowledgment and kept moving up the trail. With the big pack, floppy hat, and baggy clothes, he couldn't tell if his rescuer was male or female. As they led Strawberry closer, uncertainty and unease made the back of his neck crawl. He might have been better off waiting for Dad to call out Search and Rescue. The person leading his horse was heavily armed.

A semi-automatic pistol was strapped to the right thigh, bear spray on the other, over desert camouflage pants. A backpack dwarfed the person's frame, with several knives fastened to the hip strap and a couple more on each arm. Another canister of bear spray hung from a shoulder strap. They wore a loose, long-sleeve T-shirt in a dull brown and a floppy military-style hat. Dark hair might be under the hat, but it was either very short or pulled back tight. He could only see a slightly pointed chin below the hat. No sign of a beard, so possible a woman or a younger boy.

They stopped a good twenty-five feet away. "This your horse?" The voice was even, without any emotion, and not pitched high or low enough to indicate gender.

He smoothed his frown. "Yes, that's Strawberry. She threw me, and then I twisted my ankle. Can you help me get back up on her?"

The person stood silent for a moment. "Maybe. Can you get up on the rock? You're too big to lift." Again, the tone was flat and matter-of-fact.

Well, whoever they were, they were willing to help, and that was good enough. "Probably. Hold on." Tom spun on his backside, putting his back to the rock, then used his good leg to press up. He shoved his body on top of the four-foot-high rock, then pushed on his good leg again, so he stood on the rock. "If you can bring her over, I can probably get on her from here."

With a tongue-click, his rescuer led the horse to him. While he'd been clambering up the rock, the person had taken off their pack and pulled his rifle from Strawberry's holster. The tension at the back of his neck tightened. All those weapons, and they wanted his, too. He didn't like the picture, but they were helping, so he couldn't complain. His rescuer led Strawberry up to the rock, with her right side toward him; but the horse was too skittish to try new and different techniques. "Excuse me, but do you know anything about horses?"

"No."

"This one's nervy and not very well-trained. Can you turn her around so her left side faces me please? The left side is where you normally mount."

The hat tilted to one side, followed by a single nod. "Okay." They turned Strawberry around.

He wasn't going to be able to mount on Strawberry's left because he couldn't push off his throbbing left foot. Well, that was stupid. "Uh, I'm really sorry, but I just realized I can't mount from this side."

"I know." They looked up at him, but the hat still hid everything but the chin. A fairly observant or smart person; they'd figured out the mounting issue before he did. Most people would have laughed. Before he could say anything more, they spoke. "Before you get on the horse, do you want me to splint and wrap that ankle? I have a medical kit."

Since he stood upright, it had thumped painfully. With the swelling it had undoubtedly done, the boot might be enough to hold it in place, but maybe not; cowboy boots were kind of loose. "It would probably be smart of me to take you up on that offer. Thank you."

The person led Strawberry over to the side of the rock and tied her reins to the tree, far away enough that Strawberry couldn't kick either one of them. Whoever they were, they were a smart cookie. They walked back to the backpack and pulled out a large, military-looking bag. From their stride, he was ninety percent sure his rescuer was a woman. A few feet away from the rock, she put the kit down and opened it. "Are you armed?"

Interesting question. "No, you've got my rifle. I've got a multitool on my belt if that counts."

"Please leave it in the holster and sit."

A very cautious individual; paranoid, even. He'd do his best not to rouse any suspicion or fears. "Sure. I'm Tom, Tom Borde." He carefully lowered himself to sit on top of the rock. "Will you tell me your name, please? I'd like to know who to thank."

"Wiz."

"Wiz? As in short for Wizard?" What an odd name; it must be a nickname. Perhaps earned in video games or D&D? It didn't help him decide on a pronoun.

"Yes." They pulled out a large pair of shears, an Ace bandage, and a rectangular formable splint and pulled on nitrile gloves.

Wow, they were prepared. "It's nice to meet you, Wiz. Thanks for rescuing me."

"You're welcome. Do you think it's sprained or

broken?"

"I don't know for sure, but I couldn't put much weight on it, and I figured I wasn't going to try. Someone would come looking for me sooner or later." If Strawberry was still missing by supper time, Dad would ride out to look. Probably.

They grabbed the shears and slowly moved toward him. He kept his hands flat on his thighs in plain view, trying not to make the person more nervous. Small, delicate fingers cased in dark blue grasped the bottom of his left pants leg, then sliced straight to his knee. He bit back his protest; jeans were cheap in comparison to the donation he'd owe Search and Rescue if they got called out. After pulling the material away, a whole-body sigh followed, the first expression of emotion he'd seen. "I'm guessing these are expensive." A gloved finger tapped his boot.

The tiny hands were either a woman's or a boy too young to be out here on his own, armed like that. Almost certainly a woman. "Yes, they are." He hadn't planned on riding when he got dressed. He should have changed, but he'd just wanted to get away from the house and his dad before he said something he couldn't unsay.

Wiz grasped the boot at the heel and toe. "I can yank it off if there hasn't been too much swelling, but that could damage your ankle more. Or I can cut it like I did your jeans."

"You didn't ask about the jeans." He smirked.

Another head tilt. "Did you want to ride in your underwear?"

He sputtered a laugh. "No, I guess not. You're smarter than me by a long shot." She didn't say a thing or laugh, but his certainty grew. "Okay. I don't think it's broken, and I raised it while I was resting, so it shouldn't be too swollen. Try yanking first, please."

"Okay." Wiz sounded a little skeptical. She grabbed his boot and yanked, nearly pulling him off the rock, but the boot came off.

He gritted his teeth to hold back a scream. "Holy hanna that hurt." Wiz put the boot down and waited. He slowed his panting, trying to control the pain. "I know, my own fault. Please continue."

Wiz quickly shaped the thin, foam-coated aluminum splint into an "L" shape, then gently raised his calf and placed it on the splint. Putting a small rock under the splint near the top, she wrapped it with the Ace bandage.

"Tell me if it feels too tight." She wriggled a finger under a couple of the wraps, testing it.

Tom unclenched his jaw. She was trying to be gentle, but every movement was painful. "It's okay. It needs to be tight because it will be well below my heart." In a stirrup, his ankle would swell fast, but better than trying to hobble on a steep, rocky trail.

Wiz finished the wrapping and fastened it. "Still okay?"

Grimacing, he nodded. "Yeah, sure. Shall we see if I can mount now? You'll have to hold Strawberry firmly, if you don't mind, please."

She picked up his boot and jammed it into his open saddle bag. The shaft stuck out, but she buckled it tight. Then she led Strawberry to him, with her right side facing. She stood at Strawberry's head, and gripped the reins behind the bit, her other hand on the cheek strap. For someone who knew little about horses, she was doing everything right.

"Okay, Strawberry, I know you're probably not gonna like this but..." he said in a soft voice as he slid over to her. He leaned over and grabbed the saddle horn. "Here we go, hold tight." He pushed up on his right leg and pulled his body across the saddle, his left leg swinging high behind him. He plopped into the saddle, putting his right foot in the stirrup. When Strawberry sidled, Wiz pulled her head down.

He maneuvered his bad foot into the left stirrup. He'd better hope Strawberry didn't try anything because his splinted foot could slip through, hanging up in the stirrup, and she'd drag him to death or break his ankle completely or both. He took a deep breath and, feeling like a greenhorn, didn't let go of the saddle horn. Better to look ridiculous but give himself a chance to recover if—when—Strawberry shied. "Okay. Thanks, Wiz. I really appreciate the save."

She nodded. "I'm not sure it's safe for you to ride like that by yourself. Which way are you going?"

"North, then down the feeder trail that goes to MPG Ranch's south gate." Their ranch was lower down the hill, below the big timber frame mansion, and spread across part of the valley floor.

Wiz released the tight grip on Strawberry's bridle, letting her hands slide down the reins. "There's no legal public access on that road."

Interesting she knew that. "I'm not public. I live on the Rocking B Ranch." For some reason, he didn't tell her he was part owner.

"Okay. That's the way I'm headed. Why didn't you call for help? There's cell service up here." Wiz patted the horse's neck a little gingerly.

He chuckled. "Broke my cell in the fall."

"You don't carry a backup method of communication?"

That would take more smarts than he had. "No, never had any problems before. You do?"

"Yes. I have my cell, a satellite phone, and a SPOT emergency beacon." She tied Strawberry back to the tree, yanked off the medical gloves, and pulled on her pack. Carrying his rifle, she returned, undid the reins, and led Strawberry to the trail.

He reached out. "Uh, do you want me to put the rifle in the holster? It will get heavy, fast."

"No." She didn't turn, just kept walking.

Usually, people trusted him. Her suspicion made his neck tighten again. "Your pack must be awfully heavy. That's a really impressive medical kit. Are you a medic?"

"No."

Something in her bearing and her no-nonsense attitude reminded him of his dad. "You were in the Service?"

"Yes."

Not a very talkative type. "Which one?"

"Air Force."

"And what did you do?"

"I'd rather not say."

"Okay. Sorry." So much for conversation. So strange. Most people were happy to talk when they met someone new, especially around these parts, where there weren't a whole lot of people, period. She didn't say anything else, but she kept glancing back at him, making Strawberry jerk. She'd tighten the reins, Strawberry jerked, and the cycle got worse. He had to stop both of them, or he'd be on his backside again. "Hey, Wiz, uh, I really hate to say anything, since you're saving me here, but those quick head movements are making Strawberry nervous and jumpy. I promise that I won't do anything back here except sit and hang on. Unless you want me to talk. Or do something else. Just let me know."

"You can tell me about your ranch." She didn't turn to face him.

"Sure." Relieved to do something to ease her tension, he told the story. "My family homesteaded the Rocking B back in 1884. We've been raising cattle and hay ever since. It used to have more trees, but after a disastrous couple of years, the family sold them to Marcus Daly to shore up the tunnels in his copper mines. That's where the majority of the trees in this entire area went to, and after the cattle came in, the trees never came back, since they would have been trampled before they got very big. Anyway, it's been in the family forever, and now my dad runs it. But he's getting older and needed some help, even though he didn't ask or admit it, so I came back a couple of years ago."

He took a deep breath. "But that's not working out all that well. Dad wants to keep doing things the same old way, and while you can make money ranching the old-fashioned way, it's pretty tough on the environment. I'm trying to get him to change a few things, but he's not very receptive. We fight a lot. That's why I'm out here. We had another argument, and I figured it was just better to leave for a while and let things cool off. But I should have changed into work boots at least." He laughed. He'd been dumb, and he used to know better.

"You should carry more safety gear. And carry it on your person, not fastened to your saddle. Animals are unreliable."

"Strawberry is. She's new to us, and I shouldn't have taken her out on a trail ride by myself. I let my temper get the better of me, and that was stupid."

"Yes."

He blinked at the back of her head, then chuckled. "Wow. Way to put me in my place. Most people would have said 'no, you weren't. It was understandable.'"

"I'm not most people."

No kidding. "I can see that. Can I ask your preferred pronoun?"

Wiz's shoulders tightened, then relaxed. "She/her, thank you."

Tom smiled. He'd been correct, but he should have asked earlier. Wiz was an interesting person. The only emotion she'd displayed was wariness. Granted, she was a short, slight woman, and he was a big guy, but she was armed and he wasn't. His position behind her, out of sight, was obviously nerve-racking for her. Something must have happened to make her wary. Was it him, or his size, or everyone? He had no way to know. Maybe she'd had a bad experience in the military. Post-traumatic stress, perhaps.

The throbbing in his ankle increased in intensity. He gritted his teeth until it was nearly unbearable. "Would you mind stopping for a minute?" Wiz stopped and turned toward him, holding Strawberry firmly. "I'm going to put my left leg over Strawberry's neck and see if that will help." She nodded. He carefully drew his left foot out of the stirrup, leaned backward, and clamped the back of the saddle while he moved his foot up and over Strawberry's neck, laying the side of his calf on her neck in front of the saddle horn. The horse shivered, but Wiz didn't let her toss her head.

"Okay, I think I'm set." Not sure the position helped a lot, but it was better than it was. "Wow, this is awkward. How in the world did women do this in skirts for all those years?"

Wiz didn't say anything, just shook her head. "Not very talkative, are you?" She just shook her head again. So, what non-threatening thing could he talk about? She knew the road was private; she might be the new owner of the recently sold house. The forbidding security fence would match the person he saw in front of him. "I'm guessing you're the new owner of the big house at the top of our road, right?"

She looked back at him sharply, and Strawberry shied again. He clenched the saddle horn. Wiz grasped the reins right behind the bit, keeping her under control. For somebody who didn't know horses, she had some good moves. "Thanks. I really didn't want to end up thrown again today." He gentled his voice as if he were talking to a foal. "I'm sorry if I startled you."

She looked up, and her hood fell back, fully revealing her face. Wide set gray eyes with thick, dark lashes and black eyebrows slashed across a heart-shaped face, her skin a few shades darker and warmer than his pasty white. No makeup, but she didn't need it. She was pretty in a fierce way, reminding him of a manga warrior princess. She'd be stunning if she smiled, but she carried sadness along with the caution. "Why do you think I must be the new owner?"

Tom shrugged. "Marcus is a pretty safe place, but there's a brand-new chain-link fence around the house, and from the looks of all the hardware you're packing, I'm guessing you take security seriously. You match the house rather well." He smiled, trying to reassure her, but he was pretty sure it didn't help.

"Yes. It's mine." Her frown smoothed.

"Then you're new in the area?"

"Yes."

"I could tell you something about the area if you'd like?" Hopefully, she'd feel safer if he talked, and he really wanted to put her at ease.

"Thank you." She turned away and stepped forward, but stopped. Strawberry didn't want to move.

He nudged the stubborn horse with his right heel. She blew out a big sigh and plodded ahead. He told Wiz about the Bitterroot Valley and the history of the area, then about nearby trails and the trails on the west side in the mountains. Then he started on the West Fork of the Bitterroot River, Nez Perce Pass, and the Magruder Corridor, and by then, they were at her house. "I think you're probably safe to leave me here. I can get back down to the ranch on my own."

She looked at his ankle and frowned. "I didn't like the looks of that ankle. You need an x-ray." She handed him her cell phone. "Call. Make sure someone can take you."

He dialed the ranch number, but no one answered. Then he called his dad's cell, but he didn't answer either. But Dad left his cell at home most of the time, the source of another argument. It wasn't safe for the older man, or anyone, to be out on the ranch without a means of communication; he'd just proven that. "Shoot, I can't get a hold of anyone."

"I'll take you to the hospital. We can leave the horse in the fenced area." She walked down her driveway, Strawberry's hooves clip-clopping on the asphalt.

Didn't look like he had a say in the matter. "Uh, okay. You don't have to do that."

"I know."

At the outer horse fence, she entered a code into a lock on a big green metal ranch gate, and it swung open soundlessly. Strawberry tried to jump again, but Wiz must have anticipated her reaction because she had a firm grip on the reins. They continued down the drive, and she opened a metal box mounted on the fence post and punched in a code. The chain-link gate slid out of the way with a rattling jerk, but the mechanism was surprisingly quiet. "You must have really top-notch installers."

"Yes."

Tom wondered what she'd done in the military.

She led Strawberry to the side of the house. The garage held four post-and-beam style wood garage doors with matching human entry doors on both ends. She entered a code on yet another panel, and the first garage door opened to reveal the rear doors of a tall white panel van.

Huh. Not what he would have expected. She should have a fully armored Humvee.

Wiz pulled a set of keys out of her pocket, and the van beeped. Strawberry tried to jump again, but Wiz controlled her and led her to the back of the van and opened the back doors. The right side held a long bench seat with a thick cushion, a metal shelf above holding plastic boxes and a shorter, fold-down metal bench on the other side with a sink and stove above additional shelves holding more plastic crates. All of the supports were plain, dark metal, shiny on the corners where welds had been smoothed. A homemade RV? Very interesting. The woman was interesting, period.

"I think you'll be able to step off of the horse and lie down on the bench."

"I think you're right. But then, I'm beginning to learn you usually are." She led Strawberry in a circle, around to the end of the van, but the horse didn't want to get close to the scary vehicle. "Use your knee or elbow, and jab it up into her side a little."

He hung on to the saddle horn, and she goosed

Strawberry. Sure enough, she sidled over, snorting a bit. He took his right foot out of the stirrup and twisted, sitting sideways on the saddle. He slid off, landing on his right foot. Hanging on the doorframe, he turned on his toe and collapsed on the seat. *Whew.* "If you put Strawberry's reins over her neck and loop them loosely around the saddle horn, so they can't come down and trip her, you could set her loose in the horse fenced area. I can send someone up to get her later."

"It may be a while. Would it be better to take the gear off?"

Strawberry would be more comfortable, but wearing the saddle wouldn't hurt her. "Yes, but I don't want to trouble you."

Wiz led Strawberry to the chain-link fence. She opened the gate again and walked up the drive. After a quick look under the horse, she raised the stirrup, unbuckled the saddle, and put it on the fence rail next to the gate. Then she unfastened the bridle and hung it over the saddle. Extremely efficient for a novice.

Strawberry put her head down and grazed, undoubtedly thrilled to have a big pasture to herself with lots of fresh grass. Wiz returned, her short but quick strides closing the distance fast, and closed the van's back doors. She hopped into the driver's seat. She must have left her backpack, and his rifle, in the garage. She backed the van out and drove steadily up the drive. She didn't click standard garage door openers or use her phone for the garage door or the fence; she must have an automatic door opener in the van.

The RV was a great setup. His bench obviously met the fold-down on the other side to make a bed. A dorm-size refrigerator nestled below the sink. A tall enclosure at the end of his bench probably held a bathroom. A folding partition was secured between the camper area and the front seats. It was perfect for one or two people, although the benches were barely long enough for him.

Before long, they reached the hospital. Wiz stood, moving behind the seat, and unstrapped her weapon holsters. Kneeling, she opened a cupboard below his bench and metal snicked. The door blocked his view, but the gun and the knives were gone when she got back up. Then she edged past him and opened the doors at the back.

"Hey, Wiz, did you do the work on this?"

"No."

"Somebody local?"

"The design, I got online. Erin at Coffee and Cars did the metal work. Wait here. Please don't touch anything, and I'll get a wheelchair." She hopped down and disappeared before he could say anything, and returned with a woman in scrubs pushing a wheelchair.

He hopped down the steps on his right foot and ungracefully squeezed into the chair, which was too short for his frame. "Wiz, thanks very much. I really appreciate you doing all of this. If you'll give me a number, I'll have someone from the ranch call and get Strawberry. And my rifle."

She pulled a wallet out of her pocket, opened it, and handed him a card. Without another word, she hopped in the van, closed the van doors, and was gone before he made it through the hospital doors. She didn't waste time, that was for sure.

The aide wheeled him into the lobby. The card read *Victory Cyber Security*, with an email address and a phone number. There wasn't anything else, not even a website, which seemed odd for a cyber security company. But then, she was odd.

After a few minutes, the aide wheeled him into the business area. "Can I get your name and insurance information?"

He grabbed his wallet, pulling cards and reeling off information on auto-pilot. His mind was on Wiz and the puzzle she presented. Now that he had a little time to think, he was reminded of abused horses they'd fostered. While she'd obviously acted from a sense of duty, he got the impression of someone who cared deeply and wanted to show compassion but couldn't leave herself vulnerable. Somebody had hurt that woman badly, and he'd sure like to hurt them back.

Hopefully, she'd let him say thanks in more than words, but he'd have to think carefully about how and what. He obviously made her very nervous, especially when he stood. Not surprising, since he was a giant next to her—she was easily a foot shorter, thin and wiry. Well, thinking about an appropriate gift would keep him busy while he waited for x-rays. He sighed. And while he tried to call Dad.

Chapter 2
Wiz

Wiz locked the doors and pulled out of the hospital parking lot as fast as she safely could, relief coursing through her entire body like a waterfall. Finally, nobody lurked behind her. Finally, she could get away from *him* and all these people. Her relief was tempered by vulnerability; she'd forgotten to rearm. She pulled into the back of a grocery store parking lot, retrieving her pistol and knives from the hidden safe. Once she strapped on her forty-five, she breathed another sigh of relief. *Much better.* Not that she'd been naked; her backup pistol was on her ankle, and she kept a fighting knife under her long sleeve, but those were emergency fail-safes. She stared out the windshield and breathed, blanking her mind, regaining her equilibrium. Then she let herself remember the hike.

It had started so well. A beautiful fall weekday, with no one on the trails. Once she got above the tree line, no one could lie in wait or sneak up on her, and she could enjoy the colors, the bright sun, and the cool breeze. Then she found the horse; a saddled horse with no rider. She had to find the rider; she'd never abandon someone in need. Not when she'd been left behind so many times. But the rider, the man she'd found, was huge. She shuddered. The man, no, wait, what was his name? Tom. Thomas Borde, of the Rocking B Ranch, the working cattle ranch bordering her property. Before she bought the place, she'd checked all the neighboring ranches and found nothing suspicious or even odd.

But local cattle ranchers didn't buy fancy custom cowboy boots. And he'd worn designer jeans, not work wear. Plus, he'd said he came *back* to help his dad, which implied he'd been somewhere else. She'd have to do a little more research. She shivered and realized her shirt was drenched with sweat. She unbuckled, returned to the back, and slipped a fresh one on. Then she put the van in drive and got on the highway north.

Tom was clearly an intelligent man and maybe a kind one. He'd noticed right away that she was nervous and had done his best to put her at ease. But there were a lot of evil people who were good at hiding what they were. Facades were easy. Predators were good at them, especially sexual predators. Look at how many hid in the military, masquerading as upstanding members. She knew, for a fact, that at least one of those deployed with her was as rotten as they come.

No, it was better to just avoid people, unless you knew for sure that they weren't a risk. She probably shouldn't have given him her business card, either. But she'd wanted to get away so badly, she had done the fastest thing, if not the wisest.

The bright orange, pink, and teal of Ryan and Erin's Coffee & Cars sign stood out among the green and beige along the highway. They were safe, and she had this strange need to share her story. Maybe an iced mocha would be refreshing after the unexpected drama. She pulled into the parking lot, and her shoulders relaxed. No other cars were parked in front. That didn't mean the shop was empty, but the chances were better. She backed the van in, parked, locked, and entered the coffee shop, stepping to the side of the door and surveying the room, the scent of dark roasted coffee overwhelming her for a moment.

Ryan stood behind the espresso machine, his long, caramel-colored hair pulled back from his slightly scarred face. "Wiz! Surprised to see you here!" His eyebrows rose, then he grinned.

No one sat at any of the tables in the long room. "Ryan. How are you?" She sat at the table in the corner farthest from the front door, where she could see the door into the garage behind Ryan.

"I'm good. What can I get you and how are you?" He lifted an espresso cup in his grasping prosthesis.

The dining room was just a little too long to watch everything without turning her head. "I'm okay. Can I get a medium iced mocha?"

"Sure. Whatcha doing today?" He flicked a lever and packed espresso into the filter.

"I was out hiking earlier."

"Really? Great day for it. Where?" The espresso machine squealed.

"Sapphires. Crest Trail."

"Cool. Haven't been up there recently." Ryan turned away when the door to the garage opened. "Hey, babe. Look who came to visit."

Wiz rose slightly. Erin entered, her long, curly red hair bobbing in a ponytail. She squeezed Ryan's shoulder. "Wiz! Been a while. How are you settling in?" Smiling, she walked closer and sat on a stool behind the counter halfway between Ryan and Wiz.

Wiz relaxed into the chair. Erin understood how she felt without needing tedious explanations. Or digging into her psyche. "Good. Everything is finally done and in place." It was such a relief to have all the construction finished, the furnishings delivered, the security measures completely activated, and all those strangers out of her house. "Thanks again for your help with everything."

Erin waved a hand while Ryan scooped ice into a glass. "Babe, Wiz hiked the Sapphire Crest trail today." He handed the mocha to Erin, and she placed it on the counter. "How was it?"

Wiz took the glass and sipped. "Delicious." She raised the glass to Ryan, and he bowed.

Erin laughed. "Do tell. I need a vicarious wilderness experience today."

Wiz took another drink, the smooth, milky chocolate and coffee mix cool and refreshing. "It was very nice to start, but it got... interesting." She couldn't find a better way to describe the experience.

"Oh?" Erin's eyebrows rose.

"I found a horse. A horse with a saddle and a bridle. So, I caught it, which wasn't hard, and continued up the trail, and I found the owner. The horse had bucked him off, and then he twisted his ankle. I splinted his ankle, got him back on the saddle, and led the horse back down to my house, loaded him in my van, and took him to the hospital. Then I was driving by here and thought a mocha would taste good."

Erin and Ryan both just stared at her for a minute, then at each other and back at her. It was kind of funny, but she didn't smile. She wasn't sure she remembered how.

Erin blinked. "Really? You didn't just call out Search and Rescue?"

"No. Why would I do that when I had the capability to help him myself? That would be a waste of taxpayer dollars, and those people are volunteers." It was funny that they were so amazed, but then she'd shocked herself. Probably why she felt the need to stop here and share. The whole day was unusual and well outside her normal routine.

"Good for you. What did you do with the horse?" Ryan put away the milk.

"Took off the saddle and bridle and left it in my outer perimeter. He said he'd send someone from the ranch to pick it up." She hoped it was soon because she didn't have a water bucket out there. An irrigation ditch ran through part of the field, though. The horse could probably find it.

"Ranch? Which ranch?" Erin asked.

"The Rocking B Ranch, which borders my property to the west."

"Oh! So you met the neighbors. Good for you." Erin's grin grew. "What's his name, anyway? Maybe we know him."

"Thomas Borde. His dad owns the ranch, and he

said he came 'back' to help him. He didn't specify back from where." But she'd find out. Which made it even stranger that she stopped for a drink; she should be desperately searching through databases. She should call her therapist.

Erin nodded. "The Borde family has been here forever. I think there were Bordes ahead of me in school, but there weren't any in my class. I'm not sure where Thomas fell in the age range."

"I will look him up. I looked at his father and his ranch hands and there was nothing troubling in his background. The father has been a rancher here his whole life except one tour in Vietnam." Her shoulders tightened, and she rolled them back.

"What do you define as trouble?" Ryan wiped the counter.

"Arrests, financial trouble, suspicion of things like arson, assault, sex crimes, domestic abuse, those kinds of things." Anything that meant a threat to her or her house. Her sanctuary.

Erin shrugged. "That's a good definition of trouble. You haven't found anything on anyone in your area, have you?"

"No." Or she wouldn't have bought the house. It was too big for her but the best available. She hadn't wanted to take a year to build a custom home, either.

"Good." Erin tapped on the counter. "You know, you're always welcome to hike with us if you want to."

Wiz shivered. "You go on the weekends, and it's crowded then."

"Good point. Still, what if you get in trouble?"

"I have my cell phone, a satellite phone, and an emergency beacon."

Erin and Ryan both laughed. "Keep us on speed dial. We'll come rescue you if you ever need it."

"I think calling Tom Borde might be more practical. He has horses to carry me back." She wouldn't, but she wanted to see their reactions.

They both laughed again but looked at each other with eyebrows raised in obvious surprise. Erin turned back to her and frowned. "You trust this guy?"

Too big, too scary. "No. Not really." She couldn't hold back a shudder. "But he seemed to be very intelligent, and he now owes me a favor."

"Yeah, a big one." Ryan chuckled.

"I also took his rifle before I led his horse back."

Ryan snorted. "There's the Wiz I know. I thought this story sounded a little incomplete."

"It wasn't a very comfortable experience because I had to lead the horse. Tom said it was new and not well-trained. Even without a gun, it was...nerve racking having him right behind and above me. He's a very large man. If his ankle hadn't been so badly damaged, I couldn't have done it." She hadn't been in close proximity to a man for that long since her lousy ex left.

"But you did, Wiz." Ryan's voice was soft and sincere.

"I did." Telling them even that much was almost as scary as leading Tom down the hill. But Erin and Ryan were good friends, and she trusted both of them.

Ryan raised a brow. "You can live your entire life locked away by yourself, but I'm not sure it's living.

Sometimes you have to take a chance. Sometimes you get lucky." Ryan smiled at Erin, who returned his sweet smile. Ryan turned back to her. "I'm glad you did."

She'd been lucky, but all too often, chances resulted in catastrophe. Look at how her marriage had turned out. Jeff was a disaster, even before her assault, but she'd put up with him. After, he was worse, and his friends had made her life miserable. Almost as miserable as those idiots who protected the identity of the man who'd assaulted her downrange. But she'd gotten her revenge on all of them. Wiz shook the gloom away, brought her empty glass to the counter, and pulled out her wallet.

Erin held up her hand. "Oh, no. Your money is *never* good here. I know what you did for me is worth way more than I could ever afford. And you saved Ryan's life, which is priceless. And don't you dare use this as an excuse to not come here, you hear me? I want to see you at least once a week, preferably every day."

Wiz almost smiled but couldn't. "Yes, Mom."

Erin laughed. "Good. And I want you to come over for dinner on Friday night. Yes?"

She took a deep breath. Erin and Ryan were safe. She could stand it. "Okay. I'll come Friday night. Should I bring something?"

Erin waved her away. "Nope. I got it. Just bring yourself."

"Thanks. I'll see you then." She walked toward the door of coffee shop, but she couldn't turn her back completely. So she strode along the side of the room, looking between Erin, Ryan, and the door.

Ryan stood behind Erin with his arms wrapped around her waist, his chin on her shoulder. "See you Friday."

Wiz waved, left the building, climbed into her van, locked the doors, pulled out, and drove up the highway. Ryan and Erin were so lucky. Being in love was the most wonderful feeling in the world, even better than being loved, especially when the person you were in love with meant everything.

But betrayal was agonizing and the death of love like bleeding from a thousand cuts.

Later that afternoon, Wiz had fifteen tabs open on her browser. Article after article on Thomas Borde, Wall Street analyst, with a tall, beautiful blonde on his arm at one charity event or another. The earlier articles showed a variety of women, but for a period of three years or so, there was only the blonde, a fashion model named Evon. Her real name was Alice Walters, from a small town near Charleston, South Carolina. Mediocre school record, did well at finishing school, and then got picked up as a model in NYC for one of the mid-level firms, where she made a steady, if unspectacular, living as a model. She had dated quite a few mid-level celebrities early in her career, but her career and tabloid appearances had slowed just before she started dating Tom.

Thomas Pierre Borde was more interesting. Very good grades here in Marcus, good grades at University of Montana, resulting in a degree in Economics in three years, and a scholarship to Columbia University to get his Masters in Economics. Internships with J.P. Morgan and Goldman Sachs got him a very good job with Bear Sterns in their analysis division. He focused on fossil fuels, with a particular emphasis on the Northern Tier in Alaska and Canada.

He kept his nose clean, using a blind trust for his investments. Still, he did very, very well, becoming quite wealthy. Then suddenly, all the articles and society page gossip just stopped. She dug a little deeper.

Ah-ha. A little note in the business pages saying Thomas Borde had resigned from his position with Bear Sterns. And a month later, the blonde started showing up on other men's arms. It didn't take her long to move on.

Maybe the local papers would have more. She changed her search terms and found an article about the Borde family applying for a conservation easement, and subsequent articles about the approval, and more about a cooperative agreement with some local conservancy organizations. The Rocking B continued as a working cattle ranch, but the land couldn't be broken up for subdivisions. It could only be sold in a single, large parcel. Which was one of the factors she'd considered when buying her house. More recent articles showcased their involvement in research on cattle grazing and the environment.

Tom had said his dad wanted to keep ranching the old way, but it was tough on the environment. Maybe he was trying to move them toward grass-fed-only methods? Some Montana ranchers had done that, but it was a niche market and required a lot of advertising. The production side was harder, too. She looked up some of the bigger ranches using natural and organic methods. Natural wasn't a regulated term like organic was but generally seemed to mean mostly or all grass-fed, but the ranches could still use pesticides for weed control.

Some ranches went further and tried to use intensive grazing in small areas, the cattle moving from pasture to pasture rather than producing hay for winter feeding. But that took a lot of land, and Montana winters were pretty tough, so it wasn't always practical.

It was interesting, and some claimed there were health benefits. She would have to order some meat from several different ranchers and do comparative taste tests. Maybe she would invite Ryan and Erin over to help. They'd done so much to help her with the house, but she'd never had them to dinner. That wasn't very friendly. She couldn't let her issues control her life to the point of being a bad friend.

Stretching, Wiz rose from her desk and walked to the windows facing the driveway. As her security system told her, Strawberry and her saddle were still there. Well, it had only been a couple of hours. But if the horse remained in the morning, she'd have to be more proactive.

Returning to her computer, she pulled the best society photo back up. The same man she'd met today but at first glance, it was hard to tell. The man in the society pages had a neat, fashionable cut, with his dark brown bangs falling just short of his deep, dark chocolate eyes. His face was a little rounder, and while the body under the very expensive designer suit was in good shape, he was slimmer. Probably spent a lot of time in a gym and ate a careful diet.

The man she'd found on the trail had longer hair, like he hadn't made the time to get it cut, and several days of beard. His face had sharper planes, a few more lines around the eyes and mouth, and the body of a man who worked for a living—broad-shouldered and powerful, built by tossing hay bales and shoveling stalls. Which was interesting because they had workers. Or did they still call them ranch hands? And they had a tractor and other heavy machinery, too. But maybe he liked to do things the old way. Or maybe more of that was necessary than she knew, which was more than possible, since she knew nothing about ranching.

Both versions of Thomas Borde were striking, and both versions showed a man who appeared to be genuinely happy. He wasn't pretty like a male model, or handsome like a Clooney, but he had something. Maybe it was his personality in concert with the looks; he exuded a kind of strength and confidence that not many men, or women, had. Not the overconfidence of youth or the super-rich who knew they could buy their way out of things, no, it was confidence in his own abilities and maybe a... moral compass. The vast majority of those society page pictures were at charity events. Evon/Alice showed up at clubs and parties but rarely with Tom. Unless his company sponsored the event.

She found a few more recent pictures, in and around Marcus, again at charity events. Mostly with his father, although there were one or two with her lawyer, Samantha Kerr. Interesting. They made a lovely couple. Wiz had met with Sam to incorporate her company in Montana and get a recommendation for a local financial adviser to act as her registered business agent. For a fee, of course. The majority of her investments and banking, she left in their existing institutions, but it was always a good idea to have assets and connections locally. And a lawyer. Strange things happened, and bad things more often. Locals could connect with locals, and negotiate rather than threaten legal action.

Tom's latest picture was from the local youth home gala. Sam wore a lovely scarlet gown with high heels. Tom wore a designer suit with shiny cowboy boots, amusing her. Despite the constant invitations, Wiz had a very hard time picturing herself at such an event. Knives and guns weren't generally acceptable at black tie galas, although this was Montana, so it could happen. She snorted. Why in the world would she picture herself at such an event, especially with Thomas Borde? She'd met the man once. *Oh, and you were pretty much terrified, remember that part?*

She shivered and walked to the window again. The horse was still munching away. She didn't know anything about them, but she figured it would be okay for the night. She would have to program in an exception for the detection systems. Hmm, maybe she could modify the deer program, without the bounding and bouncing. Either way, that was a potentially valuable addition. Plenty of wealthy folks had horses, although they probably didn't allow them around their houses. Maybe racehorse stable owners? She'd have a whole new demographic. She made a note to include that in her next report to the installers she worked with.

Well, that could be done later. Time for some food and blowing away zombies. Then she'd get back to work and forget all about Thomas Borde.

But his kind expression lingered.

Chapter 3

TOM

Tom released his jaw. "Yes, Dad, as you've now said for about the tenth time, it was stupid to take a new horse out on the trail by myself. You are right. I was stupid. Can we move on?" Despite the drugs, his ankle throbbed. Not enough room in the old truck to stretch out and raise his foot.

Dad grimaced. "Sorry, son, but I worry."

"Yeah. I got that." He clenched his teeth to keep from saying more.

"How'd you get to the hospital anyway?" He glanced at Tom's foot, propped on top of his other knee, then checked his mirrors.

"Now he asks." Tom held up his hand. If he didn't want to be treated like a child, he shouldn't act like one. "Sorry. Anyway, our new neighbor, believe it or not."

"The one with the big fence?"

"Yep."

"Hmm. Nobody's seen him." Dad pushed his hat back.

"Her." He wouldn't forget that worried, pretty, elfin face anytime soon.

"Really?"

"Yep."

Dad shot him an annoyed glance. "Am I going to have to drag it out of you one word at a time, or are you just going to tell me?"

Tom chuckled. "All right, I'll tell you." He shifted in his seat. The ankle pulsed painfully. "So, there I was, resting with my feet up on a rock, hoping that you would miss me before dark, and I see my horse being led by someone short and slim. As she got closer, my first thought was that I wished she hadn't found me."

"Oh?"

He shook his head, still unable to believe how much the compact woman was packing. "You wouldn't believe the hardware." He described Wiz's appearance. "Even though she's tiny, she was pretty intimidating. At first, I thought she was a short man or boy. Even her voice was kind of low, so I wasn't sure until she got closer." He shrugged. "Anyway, she's a smart one. Brought Strawberry around for me to mount on the right, because of my ankle, so of course I asked her to turn her to the left, and then I figured out I couldn't mount that way. When I said that, she just said, 'I know. Do you want the ankle splinted?' No laughing at me or teasing like I would have expected."

"Huh."

He told his father the rest of the story.

"She does seem like a smart cookie." Dad nodded thoughtfully.

"Yeah, and she told me she didn't know anything about horses. Which became crystal clear on the way to her house. She kept glancing back at me, whipping her head back. She really didn't like the fact that I was behind her. Even though I hated to, I had to tell her she was making the horse nervous. Once I told her that, she quit moving so quickly, but she still couldn't stop looking back at me. Oh, and she took the rifle off the saddle and carried it the whole way." He scowled for a moment. "Somebody hurt that girl badly at some point."

"What's her name, anyway?"

"Wiz." It didn't sound right to him.

"Wiz?" Dad sounded a little incredulous.

"Yeah. She told me she'd been in the Air Force but wouldn't tell me anything about it, not even what she did while she was in. Which seems strange. Most military folks seem to be okay talking about their careers once it's clear you're actually interested."

"No last name?"

"Nope. She did give me her card. The business name is Victory Cyber Security."

"Maybe she did a bunch of super-secret stuff and that's why she wouldn't tell you what she did. Easier to just not answer questions from the get-go." He shrugged.

"Maybe. I got the feeling that she just didn't like people knowing anything about her. She's smart and efficient, but if I hadn't been injured, she wouldn't have come near me. It was clear that I scared her to death, and I was trying my best to be friendly."

"Well, you can charm the birds off the trees when you want to, so I'm guessing you're right, she's taken some damage at some point. Awful lot of these kids coming back hurt, inside and out. It's a cryin' shame. Think we would have learned our lesson after 'Nam, but guess not." His mouth twisted. "Where's Strawberry?"

"At her place. She took her tack off; it's on the fence. But she's still got the rifle. And we'll have to call her to get in the horse fence anyway. She's got some sort of fancy security system with automatic gates."

"Hmm. Well, I'll drop you off at home. You can make the call, and I'll get one of the hands to take me up there. Maybe she won't be so scared of an old man."

"You're hardly ancient, Dad." He looked over at his father. Sure, he'd been eligible for Social Security for quite a while, but he wasn't old. His dark brown hair was streaked with gray, lines bracketed his mouth and eyes, and a few age spots stood out on his face, but that was from being outdoors all the time. Mostly without sunscreen. He still had his full height and could buck bales with the strongest of them.

"I'm not old, but this morning, I was a fossil? Huh." His mouth twisted.

"You're not old physically, just in attitude." Tom kept his voice light.

"Just because I like making money ranching?"

"No, because you won't even try something new."

Dad frowned. "I'm more than happy to try something new. I'm *not* willing to go into debt to do it."

"It would be short-term. You'd be making more money in the end, and the land would be healthier."

He scowled. "So you keep saying, but you don't

know that. I'd be in debt."

"No, I'd be in debt. I'll take out the loans personally." It wasn't a big deal. He had more than enough investments to cover the whole thing.

"Then I'd be in debt to you. I'd rather be in debt to the bank. Business should be separate from family." He stabbed a knurled finger at Tom.

"Dad..."

"We've been over and over this. I'm not doing it."

Tom held back his sigh. "Will you at least talk to some of the ranchers who have? You might be surprised."

"I'm always happy to compare notes."

"Yeah, sure you are. Just not today. Or tomorrow or this week."

Dad shrugged. "Plenty of time later."

Tom gritted his teeth. At this point, he'd need dentures well before retirement age. He'd have to figure out a different way to explain, but he wasn't giving up.

They pulled into the driveway and up to their house. A typical homesteader's two-story ranch house; not very big, the white paint needed a new coat, and they probably needed a new roof soon, too. An addition had been slapped on without any care for the style of the house in the seventies. Nobody cared about that stuff back then. It was a long way from Wiz's fancy timber-framed mansion or the high rises in NYC, but it had been home his whole life.

Using his new crutch, he hobbled up the steps and in the door. Good thing the ankle was only badly sprained, not broken, but he'd be stuck on the couch for a few weeks. Which didn't make him happy at all. Probably wouldn't make Dad happy either. He fumbled into the kitchen and collapsed into one of the chairs there, scooting another around to put his foot on.

Dad followed him in. "I'll go find George or Hank." He handed Tom the house phone. "You want to give her a call and let her know?" At the sink, he poured a glass of water, putting it down in front of Tom on the table.

"Yeah. Thanks, Dad."

"Sure. See you in a bit." Dad walked out the door.

Tom pulled the card out of his wallet and dialed. It went straight to voice mail, a male voice announcing he'd reached Victory Cyber Security. "Wiz, this is Tom Borde, the guy you rescued today. Thanks again. Anyway, my dad is headed up to get Strawberry. Could you let him in the gate please, and give him the rifle too? Thanks a lot. And if you ever want to see the area from horseback, let me know. I'll be happy to take you on a trail ride. Or anything else you ever need or want. Anything at all. Thanks."

He shook his head. That sounded pretty lame for a guy known as a smooth talker. But she probably wouldn't appreciate pretty words. No, she seemed like a person who would only deal with straight shooters.

Who was the man on the voice mail? If there was a man in her life, why would she be out hiking alone? Well, she had a company. She probably employed a lot of people. For all he knew, she had a whole bunch of folks up there at that big house. There was plenty of room, and she'd had a bunch of work done on it, that was for sure. There had been truck after truck going up and down the road, and most of them hadn't been local folks.

Which hadn't endeared her to the valley's businesses, but when the finish work and furniture had all been sourced locally, everybody forgot about the strangers. Gossips chattered about new people, but that wasn't all that unusual anymore. Lots of rich people with second, third, or fourth homes, although a good number of them were at the exclusive golf clubs or down on the river rather than up in the foothills of the Sapphire Mountains. And none of them put up giant chain link fences screaming "stay away!" Nope, he was pretty sure she lived there alone.

He drank his water, then pulled out the instructions the doc gave him. One week, no weight at all and gradually increasing after that, then some physical therapy to help him recover his strength without straining the tendons. Lots of mobility exercises while he was resting. No cast, but a fancy splint with metal braces and enough Velcro straps for NASA. Good thing he'd upgraded the satellite internet when he moved back here. And brought his gaming systems with him. Tom got up, but trying to put his glass in the sink was more than he could do. Maneuvering crutches with something in his hand was going to take practice. And he'd better practice with something other than glass.

He hopped and shuffled over to the refrigerator,

pulled out a plastic bottle of water, and shoved it in his shirt pocket. He tried not to use these things, but they came in handy occasionally. He returned to the living room. The sofa was probably the best; he could put his foot up on the coffee table or the couch. Good thing Mom couldn't see him. She'd pitch a fit about feet on the furniture. Once he was down, he put a couple of throw pillows under his feet on the coffee table. He grinned for a moment. Well, no, she wouldn't have gotten upset. She would have scolded him for pulling a stupid stunt, just like Dad, and then put him in this same position herself. He still missed her so much. Probably not as much as Dad did. Well, no, that wasn't true either. It was just a different kind of heartache. He clicked on the TV and surfed until his dad returned. "You got Strawberry?"

"Yup. The gate opened as I got close, and the rifle was in the saddle holster, so I just threw it all in the back of the four-wheeler, waved at the house, then walked her back next to the ORV. She wasn't real happy about that, but that's too bad. We'll have to teach her some manners, then see if we can't find somebody with a kid who needs a horse." Dad shook his head regretfully. "She's too nervy for ranch work."

"Yeah, and some little girl would love to have a pretty palomino. But she definitely needs some manners. I think she's been spoiled." He shook his head. "No Wiz?"

"Nope. I think she was watching though." Dad's shoulders rose toward his ears. "Got that itchy feeling on the back of my neck. Don't much care for that." He plopped into his recliner.

Tom winced. Dad had done a long tour in Vietnam, courtesy of the draft, but he'd never told Tom or Mom about it, other than occasional off-hand comments. He talked with his buddies at the VFW, but they probably weren't talking about their feelings or discussing post-traumatic stress.

Despite the attitude changes regarding the military since the 1960s, most Americans still didn't care about the impacts of war, especially on individuals. Oh sure, they were upset after 9/11, and they'd get upset again around the anniversary, but it didn't impact most people's lives directly, so it didn't really matter to them. That wasn't true of anyone who lived in NYC during the attacks. The smoke and dust everywhere, the missing people, the heroic rescues, and the horrific loses made it impossible to forget. And it shouldn't be forgotten. Ever.

He hadn't been in his NYC office during the attacks. He'd been at a conference in Los Angles, but he'd done what he could after he got back. He hadn't lost any really close friends, but he knew quite a few of the people who'd been killed in the towers. Some of them he'd talked to on a regular basis, and every time there was a terror alert, he remembered the fear of that day and thanked God he'd taken the opportunity to move back to Montana. He just wished he'd done it sooner and had more time with Mom.

He didn't need to be thinking such grim thoughts. Maybe the stupid pain pills had weird side effects.

Dad also seemed lost in thought. It wouldn't be

good if the new neighbor was constantly making Dad think of bad times in Vietnam. Hmm. An idea was churning in the back of his brain. What if they could help each other? Horses were used in therapy all the time these days. Heck, he'd just seen a piece on the local news about the VA using horses in conjunction with mental health counseling, so maybe if he could get his dad, who might be less threatening, to teach Wiz horsemanship... He'd have to think about that a little more.

Of course, first he'd have to talk to her. Maybe email? Well, whatever he was going to do, it wasn't going to be this evening, all fuzzy from pain medications. He was smarter than that. But he could set the seed in his dad's mind a little. And apologize. He sighed. "Hey, Dad?" Dad looked up, inquiringly. "Thanks for picking me up and getting Strawberry back. Sorry I put you to all the trouble."

Dad shrugged. "That's what family is for."

"Yeah. Still, I don't want you to think I take it for granted. I'm pretty sure our neighbor up the hill is by herself, and while she's clearly got the money to hire help, it's not the same as family. Thanks."

His dad smiled. A genuine smile, the kind he hadn't seen for a while. He'd been pushing too hard, and he needed to back off. He smiled back.

Dad pushed up and out of the chair. "What do you want for dinner? Getting to be about that time."

"Anything's fine with me. I just need to make sure I've got something in my stomach for the next set of pain pills. I really hate the things."

"Yeah, me too. They give you cotton mouth and all kinds of other fun side effects, and they don't ever seem to work that good." He crossed to the kitchen.

"Yep. I'll take them tonight and switch to over-the-counter stuff tomorrow. Dad?" He turned back toward Tom. "Can you grab me an ice pack?"

"Sure. Be right back." The freezer opened, and packages rattled.

He really was lucky to have family who loved and supported him. He'd be luckier if he had his own as well, but that wasn't going to happen anytime soon. Putting his head back on the couch, he pictured her pretty but haunted gray eyes. Maybe they could be family for her. She needed somebody, that was sure. And he needed a project for the next couple of weeks on the couch, so... He'd figure it out tomorrow. A nap seemed like a good idea right now. He closed his eyes, falling into swirling, deep pools of gray.

Chapter 4

Wiz listened to her voice mail. Another "thank you" from Tom Borde, offering to take her on yet another activity. Why didn't he get the clue and leave her alone? He was too big and pushy. Wiz shivered. Scary, even. Ryan and Erin were hard enough in person, and they were so clearly in love with each other it was ridiculous. And they didn't care if she was armed to the teeth. Most people weren't so accommodating.

If he'd just quit already, she'd settle back into her nice, normal, safe, solitary life and forget all about him. But he seemed determined. In a day, she'd get an email with the same message. And then three days from now, it would be another voice mail with some other activity. She'd written back the first couple of times saying she appreciated the unnecessary offer, but she was busy. Which was true. She had more offers of work than she could possibly take on, and those she accepted got done at the last second. There weren't enough hours in the day. Maybe she should block his number and email. But she couldn't, in case of local emergencies, like a wildfire.

She accepted Erin and Ryan's dinner invites, even when her insecurities flared. She treasured their friendship. She had plenty of friends online, but nobody she trusted in real life like Erin and Ryan. After talking to her therapist, she'd taken the next step and invited them to her house for dinner; they were due any minute now. For a main course, she'd ordered rib eye steaks from four different producers; they'd cook them all at the same time, in the same way, and compare. She also had salad, flatbread, roasted veggies with garlic and olive oil, and cupcakes from Deb's Bakery for dessert. Ryan said they'd bring beer and wine. Which was good, since she didn't have any alcohol. She stuck with water mostly, except the occasional cup of cocoa in the winter. And a morning espresso.

Her outdoor patio, designed with Erin's as a model, was the perfect spot for a dinner party. Which was one of the reasons her therapist pushed her to take this step; why build a gathering place that won't be used? She put in the same pizza oven Erin had, but as part of a full outdoor kitchen with running water and a refrigerator. Rather than a fireplace below the oven, she had a double-sided fireplace on the other side of the thirty-foot wide patio, the far side open to the sky, while a roof covered the rest. The roof kept it cooler in the summer, and she could use it all year. If it got too cool during their dinner, they'd move indoors to her gourmet kitchen. She wasn't a great cook, but her tools would never hold her back.

Her cell buzzed with a text from Ryan asking for entry. She checked, then entered the code for the outer gate and jogged through the house to greet them. After the outer gate closed, she let them through the security portal, and they pulled up under the ridiculously ostentatious timber-framed portico. Erin drove Smoky, her classic car, and they both hopped out. Ryan ducked into the back seat, retrieving a six-pack and a bottle, then they trod up the wide, natural stone steps, both smiling.

The corners of Wiz's mouth stretched up a little in response. Huh. That's what it felt like to smile. It had been a long time.

"Wiz! Good to see you!" Erin reached out her arms but dropped them quickly.

Wiz almost accepted Erin's hug, but she couldn't make her arms move. But that was okay. She was taking a big step inviting them to her house; asking for more wasn't necessary. "Hi. Thanks for coming. Come in." She backed toward the door, which she'd left open. Inside the entry room, she pointed at the hooks mounted on the wall. "You can hang your jackets there if you want."

Ryan closed the outer door with his shoulder, and she locked it, then led them into the great room. She let them go by, then closed the inner security door, too.

"Wow, this place looks awesome!" Ryan turned and twisted.

Erin did the same. "You've made it feel cozy even though it's huge. Nice."

"Thanks. A lot of that was hiring the right interior decorator." She let them examine the cavernous, open-plan living area. Leather couches and chairs faced the big windows showcasing her view of the Bitterroot

Mountains, while a gigantic screen, surrounded by smaller screens, was the focal point of her gaming area on the side of the house facing into the hillside. Native American rugs softened the slate floors, and baskets and pots provided a homey feel. "Come on back to the patio, and I'll show you what I had done to the rest of the place."

She pointed, then followed them past the natural rock double-sided fireplace rising to the roof, separating the living area from the dining area and kitchen, to the back door and out to the covered patio. "Ryan, there's a fridge in the bar over there for the beer and a wine rack on top."

Erin grinned. "This is super nice. Outclasses my little outdoor kitchen by a long shot."

"I had to do something that fit the scale of the house. I'd rather have your house, with a few modifications, rather than this huge showplace, but all in all, it's worked out pretty well." She turned to Ryan, who stood by the fridge.

"This is really cool." Ryan popped the top off a beer, putting it between his knees rather than trying to use his grasper on something large, round, and potentially slippery.

Wiz shrugged. She had nothing to do with the original construction and only gave her designers ideas, so she couldn't take credit for any of it. She crossed the rest of the patio, stopping in front of the two-bedroom guest house. "I didn't do much to the guest house, just had it painted and added more lighting and furnishings. The original owners said they built the guest house first, when they were just coming up here for a week or two at a time. They built the big place after they retired and moved here full-time, but it got too cold in the winter, and now they live in Arizona full-time."

"Yuck. I can't stand that place." Ryan, hand in hand with Erin, walked to the guest house in front of her. One of the many reasons she liked them—they remembered to not lurk behind her, even in her own house.

Ryan opened the front door but didn't go in. "Much better than it looked when we originally toured it last year." Erin closed the door.

"I'll show you the rest of the improvements after dinner if you want." Wiz backed away, letting them precede her to the outdoor kitchen.

"That would be great." Erin reclaimed Ryan's real hand. "You've done a lot. It was way too formal before."

Ryan bent around Erin. "Do you want me to grill?"

Another reason she liked Ryan—he stayed busy and away from her. "Sure. Thanks. Make sure you keep the wooden markers in the steaks though."

"My pleasure." He grinned. "You know, meat, fire, beer—that's all it takes to make a man happy."

"I wish that was true." After she came back from her last deployment, she'd tried everything she was capable of, but nothing worked with Jeff. She was too damaged to give her former husband the attention he needed. Her therapists all told her that was his problem, not hers, but failing was hard.

Ryan's smile turned upside down. "I'm sorry, Wiz."

She held up both hands. "No, no. Don't be sorry. I'm the one who broke the mood. I'm sorry."

"I should have thought about my words." He shrugged. "I was so happy to see you smile earlier. I've missed that." He worked the grill controls.

Wiz turned to the oven, which she'd preheated, and slid the flatbread and the par-cooked veggies inside. They should be done at the same time as the steaks. "Erin, there's a salad in the fridge with dressing if you'd like to pull that out."

"Sure." Once those tasks were done, she and Erin sat down, while Ryan stood at the grill, sipping his beer. "What have you been doing lately? Any more rescued ranchers?" Erin chuckled.

Wiz held back a shiver. "No, I've been mostly working. I have way too much work to do and more offers than I can possibly handle. I've had to turn a lot of people away."

"I guess that's a good problem to have, but it does put you in a bind as far as your company's reputation, doesn't it?"

"Yes. I'm not sure what to do. I want to keep working on specialty items only and not the basic programming people want from me. I'd like to turn some of my routine clients over to other companies."

"Maybe you should consider licensing some of your software, kind of like a franchise or a subcontract?" Ryan opened the grill, stepping away from the smoke and steam.

The meaty, charred scent of seared steak made her

mouth water. "I've thought about that, but then I'd get stuck with oversight, which means even less time for serious programming. Quality control isn't my favorite thing to do either."

"Hmm." Erin sipped a glass of water. "Maybe you'll just have to grow your company? Are there people you know from the Air Force you trust?"

Wiz let her nose wrinkle. "Maybe. I've kept in touch with some of my former co-workers, but most of them are either still in, or they work for one of the big companies, like Microsoft or Google. But I really don't want to be more than a one-person company. I don't want to be a boss. Even contracting other people makes me a boss."

"So, you need to find a business person to run that side, a manager you can trust. That's going to be tough." Erin tapped her bottle and stared into the distance. "Wish I knew someone with the right skills, but I don't."

Wiz nodded her head, glumly. They'd confirmed everything she'd already considered, but it was good to know she wasn't just being pessimistic.

"The steaks are done. We should let them rest a bit before digging in. Why'd you buy so many, anyway?" Ryan ripped foil from a roll.

"Oh, I forgot to tell you. We're taste-testing, so we need to cut each steak into pieces. That's why they have markers."

"Taste-testing steak?" Erin chuckled. "That's a new one on me."

"Yes. I've got a variety from different producers,

conventional, grass-fed, and organic. I got curious because Tom Borde told me was trying to get his dad to change ranching methods, but he didn't want to. I thought we'd do a comparison."

Ryan pulled a cutting board from her rack. "You want me to cut each steak into thirds?"

"You can have one-half of each steak, and Erin and I will each take a fourth." She looked at Erin to confirm, and she nodded. "You can take any leftovers home. Make sure you cut them in approximately the same way, and give us the same pieces from each steak. There's two more numbered markers for our servings."

Ryan waved his serving fork back and forth. "Trust you to bring science to a dinner party."

She nodded. He grinned, then turned to the steaks. Erin joined him at the counter. Wiz followed, pulling the flatbread and veggies out of the oven and placing them on the counter next the steaks. Erin tossed the salad and opened the wine. She poured a glass and turned to Wiz with raised brows.

Wiz looked at Erin's glass, full of deep red wine. She nodded, feeling safe enough to have one glass with food. It had been a very long time since she'd had alcohol of any kind. She rolled her shoulders to relieve the sudden tension. "I, uh, downloaded a taste-testing checklist. You can use it or not. I'm more curious about overall impressions rather than the details." She wasn't sure why she was doing it at all. She wasn't a cattle rancher, and she wasn't friends with the Bordes. Although, supposedly, there were health benefits to natural methods, and staying well was important.

She'd spent too much time with health professionals. She forced herself back to the present and gave herself permission to simply enjoy, rather than analyze. "Serve yourselves."

Erin and Ryan loaded plates and carried them to the dining table. Wiz followed, choosing a chair across from them. At the table, Erin tapped the checklist. "Wow. This is pretty elaborate. I think I'll stick to tenderness and general taste."

Wiz sat. "That's all I wanted, but when I found this, I thought it was interesting that people go to this much trouble."

Ryan and Erin smiled at each other, then grasped forks and knives. Wiz tried to cut an equal piece off of each steak, eat it slowly, considering the taste, and then eat a different food to clear her palate. She tried to forget she knew which steak was which. After they'd taken initial bites, she asked, "Which one do you like the best?"

Erin twisted her fork in her fingers. "They're all good but different. Any of them are good for dinner. Overall, I like number one the best. Number four is the most tender, and number three the tastiest but a little tougher than the others."

Ryan swallowed. "I liked number two best. I agree four is the tenderest, but they're all good." He grinned. "I think this is kind of lost on me. Steak is good, no matter which kind."

Wiz almost laughed. "And I agree with Erin. So, number one is grass-fed only, number two is a local cattle rancher's that's grass-fed, grain finished, number three is a certified organic farm, and number four is conventional but also local."

"That kind of makes sense from what I've heard. But they're all great. And I'm going to be way too full if I finish them." Erin took another bite.

"There's Deb's cupcakes for dessert."

Ryan groaned. "Later. I want to enjoy this now."

Neither she nor Erin could finish their portions. Erin told her about her latest vehicle project while Ryan kept eating. Wiz put the leftovers in containers and stuck them in the fridge. Erin refilled her wine glass and got Ryan another beer, then they sat near the fireplace. They took the couch, while she chose a chair at the end.

Erin sipped. "Since Tom brought up the steak, are you going to tell him the taste test results?"

"No." Wiz held back her shudder.

"Why not?" Ryan's brow wrinkled. "I think he'd be curious about a non-rancher's opinion."

She grimaced. "He might be, but I'm trying to discourage him. He keeps calling and emailing me, trying to get me to go riding or come to dinner or a half a dozen other things. I told him he was welcome for the rescue, but that doesn't seem to have satisfied him."

Erin and Ryan looked at each other, then turned back to her, Ryan scowling. "Do you want me to go have a talk with him? If he's bugging you, I'll be happy to put a stop to it." He clasped his hand and grasper together and stretched his arms out in front of his body.

Wiz slashed a hand through the air. No reason for Ryan to go all caveman; she could take care of herself. "No, no. He's not hostile, he's a good enough person, and his dad's ranch is well-respected. It's just..." She grimaced again. "He wants to be friends, and he's too scary to be friends with."

Erin's lips pursed like she'd eaten a lemon. "What makes him scary?"

"He's really big. And I think he..." She paused, not wanting to reveal her feelings. But she should; Erin and Ryan were safe. "He sees too much."

"Ah." Erin looked at the fireplace, then turned to Ryan. "Why don't you light the fire? If you don't mind, Wiz?"

"No, go ahead." Erin obviously wanted to talk to her, without Ryan listening.

Ryan got up slowly and gathered paper and kindling, crinkling the paper into balls. Erin scooted closer to Wiz and lowered her volume. "What makes you say that?"

She tensed but made herself relax. "He figured out right away that being behind me on the horse made me nervous. He asked a lot of personal questions but quit when I didn't answer. He also talked about the area and his ranch, rather than riding in silence, making me wonder what he was doing. And he told me what I was doing made his horse nervous." Although the animal wasn't drenched with sweat when they reached her house, and she had been.

Erin frowned. "So, he's a smart, friendly guy, who also happens to be really tall and muscular because he throws hay bales around. Is he good looking?"

"Yes. Here, look for yourself." Wiz pulled out her cell and brought up a society page.

Erin's eyes went wide. "Whoa. This guy isn't just a rancher. No rancher wears a suit like that."

"No. He used to be a fossil fuels analyst on Wall Street. The blonde is a model he dated for a couple of years. Here's a more recent picture." She pulled up the page with Tom and Sam.

Erin sat up straight. "Hey, Sam's been holding out on me." Her volume rose. "She didn't tell me she'd dated anybody this hot!"

Ryan returned, putting his hand out. "I gotta see that!"

Erin gave her phone to Ryan. His eyebrows rose. "Sam looks hot, and the dude, Tom, right? He is a pretty good-looking guy. They match."

Exactly. "Yeah, they do. So why is he bugging me? I don't do any of that stuff." Wiz pointed at her phone. The thought of all those strangers made her shudder.

Erin took her phone back from Ryan, frowned at it, then returned it to Wiz. "I don't know, but I'll find out. Sam needs to spill. I can't believe she didn't tell me and Deb about this guy."

With the fire going, Ryan sat at the far end of the couch. Erin scooted over, leaning up against him. He put his arm around her, and she slumped a bit to get under his arm. They were such a close couple. Wiz once believed that she had that kind of relationship, but she had been young and stupid.

Erin stared into the fire, then turned to Wiz. "You

know, maybe he's just trying to be neighborly. When you're way out in the middle of nowhere, sometimes you need to rely on each other. For example, have you thought about who's going to plow out your driveway this winter? And what you're going to do if you get, say, three feet of snow? It does happen sometimes."

"I've got a contract with a local company for cutting the grass in the horse-fenced area and for plowing in the winter. They were already contracted to plow the whole access road by the road association."

Erin put her hand on Ryan's thigh. "Good. But if we get three feet, the plow guys won't be out here for a few days. Are you ready for that?"

"Of course. I've got food for a year and a 10,000-gallon cistern with fire-fighting water that I can purify for drinking water, plus I've got a generator and wind and solar power. I also have a snow machine in the garage, along with a four-wheel drive all-terrain vehicle, the kind that sits two people beside each other. I can survive just fine for six months by myself."

They both stared at her, then laughed. Ryan shook his head. "Dang. You're prepared for Armageddon, aren't you?"

"Yes." Doing otherwise was silly.

"Maybe they're not so prepared. Maybe they'd need some help feeding livestock if their ranch hands couldn't get there. Would you be willing to help them or any of the other neighbors? And what about during a wildfire? Any of the neighbors might need some help. I wouldn't think you could just sit here and watch everybody else burn, right?" Erin arched her brows.

Shoot. Erin was right. She couldn't watch the horses and cows starve or burn, or their owners. But the thought of being around any of those big, strong, armed men was terrifying. She gripped the arm rests, trying to stop her trembling.

Erin pulled away from Ryan. "I'm sorry, I didn't mean to upset you."

Erin also saw too much. Wiz held up her hand, and Ryan pulled Erin back down.

She swallowed heavily and concentrated on her breathing, sitting with her discomfort rather than avoiding it like she'd prefer. She had to look at it the way Erin stated the problem, as neighbors helping neighbors in an emergency, not as individuals who might attack her. She'd done the research on all her neighbors, and they were good people. While she worked through her issues, Erin and Ryan stared at the fire and sipped their drinks. She was lucky to have such good friends.

She probably needed more, and the neighbors were the right people to start with, but she'd have to talk to her therapist about dealing with large, strong men. "You're right. If there was a fire or a disaster, I would want to help. But I might not be able to if I don't know what to do or who to call. And even worse, I might not be able to make myself do anything if I freeze up."

Erin leaned forward. "Are you in therapy?"

"On-line. I have sessions with a therapist, and I'm active in a survivor's forum."

Erin relaxed into Ryan's hold. "That's really good.

Better than I expected. I've had to bug Ryan to go, and he still 'forgets' on a regular basis unless I remember for him." She leveled a sardonic look at Ryan, who frowned at her. "But he's a guy, so it's expected." Ryan's expression soured, while Erin smirked. "Is your therapist telling you it's time to move forward?"

"Yes, she's been saying that for a while. That's one of the reasons I did the work on your place." Leaving her house had been so hard, and stopping for fuel was worse. Fortunately, she'd gotten beyond that stage, but she still felt pitifully unprepared for public interaction.

Erin smiled. "And thank you again for doing that. But maybe it's time to branch out just a little more. I'm sure you wouldn't be comfortable going out, but would you like to meet a couple of my good friends? You've already met Sam, but I don't think you've met Deb from the bakery. I could have them over to my house tomorrow night instead of us going out."

Wiz considered Erin's offer. Women would be easier, and she already trusted Sam to some extent. "Why don't you invite them here? I think I could handle that."

Erin and Ryan both grinned. "Excellent idea. We'll just do pizza. I'll bring all the stuff, you supply the place."

Wiz nodded. "Sure. I can get some more stuff if you want." Her back stiffened, but she made herself relax. Friends of friends were fine. Only one stranger, a woman. She could do that.

"Nah, we got it, Wiz." Ryan shook his head. "And speaking of Deb, didn't you say you had cupcakes?"

Erin snorted. "Of course you'd want those now."

Wiz got the cupcakes, putting them on the coffee table with some plates. She absentmindedly nibbled on one. Two more women wouldn't be a problem, but a big, tall, strong guy—no thanks. Well, baby steps, that's what her therapist said. She'd bring it up in their next session.

They chatted about Erin and Ryan's business and then on to more general subjects. After they left, Wiz cleaned up. Maybe she should stock some wine. She didn't know anything about it, but Erin evidently did. If she was going to have people over, she should be able to offer them common hospitality. Well, she could think about all that tomorrow. If she was hosting a party soon, she'd have to get more work done tonight.

Chapter 5

TOM

Tom growled at his computer. He and Dad had collapsed on the couch after a very long day of getting hay from the fields to the elk-proof enclosures. Good thing it was mostly tractor work because even six weeks after the accident, his ankle still wasn't 100%. At least he was off the crutches and out of the boot.

Dad let the magazine he was reading drop to his lap. "Now what?"

"Still no answer. She's determined to ignore me." He didn't understand why.

"Well, son, maybe you should honor her wishes. Clearly, she's said 'go away,' so I'm not sure why you're pushing so hard."

Tom rubbed his eyes and raked his hand through his hair. "I don't know either. I just can't seem to leave it alone."

Dad smiled, a small, knowing smile. "For the same reason neither of us can leave a horse without a decent home. You take one look into those big hurt eyes that want to trust again, and you melt. My guess, from what you've said, is that this girl looks the same way."

"Yeah, probably. Well, that and she is our neighbor. A full-time neighbor, not somebody who shows up for a week or two. We need to get to know her in case there's an emergency or something. And she's not from around here, so she might not fully understand the hazards."

Dad nodded. "It would be best, but if she doesn't want to, you can't force it. A woman isn't a horse, and this woman sounds pretty self-sufficient and smart."

"Yeah, I know." He might as well tell Dad the little he'd found out. "I heard from an IT guy I worked with back in NYC. Victory Cyber is considered one of the very best internet security companies in the US, but they're very selective. They work for very few people and only on particularly difficult projects. He also said nobody knows who the company owner is or anything about them and that they only communicate through email and chat programs. There's no face to face, ever, not even on video, so some people won't use them because they can't trust them. Could be Russian or Chinese or even some kid."

Dad pursed his lips. "You didn't tell this guy about our neighbor, did you? We don't want to reveal any secrets."

Tom didn't roll his eyes, but it was hard. He'd worked with a lot of sensitive data and situations. But Dad never had understood what he did. Or didn't want to understand. "No, I told him I'd run into the name doing some research for the ranch and was curious. I told him that some area ranchers had issues with modern-day rustlers and that we were trying to get ahead of the curve."

"Good. Wouldn't want to betray a trust, even if we

don't know that we are."

He sighed. He wasn't five. "No kidding. I was very cautious." She was wary enough; he didn't want to make it worse.

"Good." He picked up his magazine.

While he had Dad's attention, he should get his opinion. "There is one more route I could check, but I might do more harm than good."

"Oh?" His gray, bushy brows rose.

"Wiz told me that Erin at Coffee and Cars did the work on her van. I could ask her."

"Hmm. Don't know if that's a good idea or not. Although..." He stared at the far wall, then turned back to Tom. "You know I meet some of the guys there every week. Both Erin and Ryan are vets; sometimes Ryan joins us, if it's not too busy." He turned away.

Tom waited; he knew better than to interrupt his dad's decision-making process.

Dad nodded and looked at him. "Tell you what. Next week, I'll stick around after the meeting, and I'll ask Ryan. If Erin did the work recently, Ryan will know her too. And he'll ask Erin to talk to me if not. They were both Air Force; maybe they knew Wiz back then." Dad's eyes narrowed for a moment. "Actually, now that I think about it, they *have* to know her. I saw Erin's hotrod roll up our road last week. I knew that car looked familiar. It's not like we get cruisers risking our dirt road very often."

"The big silver one that scared the horses?"

Dad grinned. "Yeah, it's sweet. An Oldsmobile 442. She fired it up one day when I was leaving, and it sounds great. Ryan's a lucky guy."

"Oh?"

"Yeah. Erin Moore is a beauty." Dad chuckled. "I tried to set you up with her, but she didn't want anything to do with a man back then. She'd lost her husband in Afghanistan a couple of years before that. Guess it was still too soon."

"Huh. Surprising I haven't run into her. Marcus isn't that big a place."

"She's a small business owner just trying to make ends meet. I think she works a lot. She's not the type to go to the charity balls; she's a mechanic."

"We go, and we're ranchers." Tom frowned. He wasn't painting the town red every Friday night like a twenty-year-old, but he wasn't a recluse, either.

"Only one a year. The Youth Homes is a great charity."

"True." He went to more events, but Dad rarely did.

"And it's probably just as well." Dad shuddered. "Erin's mother is Sharlene Murphy. You know, from Marcus City Bank."

Tom jerked in surprise. "Yikes. Wouldn't want her for a mother-in-law." She was stone-cold, mean as a rattler, and one of the reasons Dad was so shy of debt. Plus, she'd tried to talk him into taking outside investors, something neither of them were the least bit interested in. She wasn't good at taking no for an answer, either.

"Yeah, but Ryan's handled her just fine." Dad grinned. "Figured she wasn't going to like him no matter what he did, so he made sure of it. Made a big scene at some fancy concert. One of the guys saw the whole thing. Right there in the lobby, Ryan kissed Erin for a good minute or so and then carried her out the door like they were in a movie. My buddy said Sharlene looked like she was going to blow the top of her head right off." Dad was laughing hard for a second-hand story.

Even not knowing Ryan, Tom could picture Sharlene Murphy's face and joined Dad's laughter. "That would have been worth seeing."

"A good part of the town did." He slapped his thigh. "I don't think she'll ever forgive them."

"That's probably smart on their part." He remembered a story from the last gala. "Sam Kerr told me Ms. Murphy was pushing Erin to hook up with Chaz Cust, and he's just a rotten apple. Always has been."

"So you do know Erin?"

"No, but she's Sam's friend. I'd just forgotten Sam knew her or that she'd told me that. I don't think she ever said Erin's last name or anything about her business, so I never put two and two together until you told me who her mother was." He shuddered.

Dad raised a brow. "I thought the two of you might get together. You looked like quite the pair."

Tom shook his head. "Sam is a nice person, but she's a town girl. She'd never be happy on a ranch. And I love the ranch. Besides, we didn't have any chemistry." Too bad, really. Sam was beautiful and kind. But they both had too much baggage.

"Ah, there's the real reason." Tom shrugged. Dad

sighed. "Anyway, I'll ask Ryan next time I see him, and we'll see." Dad wagged a finger. "He might not want to say anything about Wiz, and I won't push him."

"Thanks. I just hate to think of her in that house all by herself, especially if something was to happen. Bad stuff does sometimes."

"I'll ask."

Tom returned to his computer. Time to turn his brain off for a while and just surf. Stupid videos or memes; anything that let him forget a pair of pretty but sad gray eyes.

Later that week, Tom put bowls and spoons on the kitchen table, taking care not to drop them. His body ached and exhaustion made his hands tremble. But the rich, beefy scent filling the kitchen had his stomach grumbling. He'd recover soon enough.

"Thanks be for the invention of the slow cooker." Dad plopped into a chair.

What a long week. But they were ready for winter when it decided to hit. Whenever that was, it would probably be too soon. And too cold, and too snowy.

They'd invited the hands for dinner, but they were eager to get home or hit the bars. It was Friday night, after all. But that was fine; more beef stew for them.

Tom shoveled spoonfuls, slowing after the first bowl. The rolls Dad picked up from Deb's Bakery that morning were light, chewy, and perfect for stew. Filling both of their bowls, he grabbed beers from the fridge. They deserved a second and maybe a third later.

Dad popped the top on the local brew. "Knew I

shouldn't have taken the morning off. We could have been done an hour ago."

Tom scoffed. "No, we couldn't. We only have one tractor, and we had more than enough people. There was no reason for you to stay." Tom wasn't sure exactly what Dad's Friday routine was, but it was important. He got bad-tempered if he didn't get away at least once a week. Not that he'd admit it. Plus, he was getting pretty old for hard manual labor.

They ate in silence. Dad's spoon clinked in the bowl. "I talked to Ryan today."

Tom put his down, too. "Oh? And what did he have to say?"

"He knows Wiz from the Air Force, and she's a friend to both of them. He wanted to know why I was asking, and I explained that she's our neighbor, and that she'd rescued you, and that we'd both like to get to know her a little. He said he'd talk to Erin, but he wasn't willing to make any commitments." He played with his beer can. "He seemed very protective of Wiz. When I first asked, he was downright hostile. It wasn't until I told him that she'd rescued you that he calmed down, and he was still mighty cold about the whole thing."

Tom's stomach churned uneasily. "Shoot. I didn't want to get your friends upset at you. Sorry, Dad."

He flipped his hand, dismissing his concerns. "Don't worry about it. I told Ryan we were just tryin' to be neighborly and that if she ever needed anything, she should give us a shout. He was okay by the time I left."

"Good. I shouldn't have pushed. Sorry." Tom took a gulp of his beer. "Does kind of jive with everything we thought, though."

"Yeah, that it does." Dad shook his head.

They both picked up their spoons. His obsession had caused problems for his dad and hadn't helped him at all. He'd have to put up with the dreams of sad gray eyes until they faded. Eventually, they would; everything did.

They finished eating and moved to the living room. Tom put his foot up; the ankle was essentially healed, but it ached a bit tonight. His cell phone rang. The local number wasn't familiar but wasn't marked as potential spam. "Hi, this is Tom."

"Hi, Tom, this is Erin Moore. How are you?"

What a surprise. "Good, Erin. And you?"

"Just great, thanks. Hey, Ryan told me your dad was asking about Wiz today."

"Yes. I'm sorry if I stirred up any bad feelings. That wasn't my intention."

"No, it's okay. We're just very...cautious about our friends. So, why do you want to know?"

"First of all, I'd really like to say thank you for her rescue."

"She's more than aware of your gratitude," Erin snapped. "As a matter of fact, it seems to be annoying her a bit."

His heart thudded. It was one thing to suspect, another to be slapped in the face with the unpleasant fact he was making Wiz uncomfortable. "Oh. Sorry. I'll stop."

"You said first. What else?" Erin's voice softened a little but was still steely.

"Well, she's our neighbor, and she's got a big spread up there. If there's some emergency, we'd like to be able to help."

Erin chuckled. "I hate to tell you this, but it's far more likely that she'd be able to help you. You met her. Do you really think she hasn't considered every possible contingency?"

"She does seem a mite...careful. So, no, she's probably covered for just about anything and everything. Still, she's a neighbor."

She sighed. "If you really want to talk to her, maybe you should stop with the pretty excuses and tell me why. I asked Sam about you, and she said you're a good guy. That's the only reason we're having this conversation. Otherwise, you'd be getting a letter from lawyer Samantha Kerr telling you to cease and desist."

Tom closed his eyes and echoed her sigh. Opening up was hard. Opening up to a stranger, with his dad listening was almost impossible. But he had to, or forget the whole thing. "Sorry, you're right. You hold all the cards. Look, I don't really know why, but I just can't seem to forget her. She looked up at me once with those sad eyes, and I just can't get her out of my head. Guess I'll have to. Tell her I won't bug her anymore. She obviously needs to feel safe, and I'm making her feel less safe, so I'll quit. Tell her I'm sorry too, please."

"Hold on a minute. You said *sad* eyes. Did you mean sad or scared?"

"Sad. She was obviously worried about me being

behind her, and a little jumpy, but her eyes are sad. She reminds me of the horses we take in from abusers. I really hate that look." He stared at his foot, ignoring his dad's presence.

"You're a rescue ranch?"

"Not truly. Sometimes we foster horses for the local organizations, try to get them back to trusting again, enough that they can be safely handled. Doesn't always work." Sadly, not everything could be fixed. Including his obsession.

"No, sometimes you can't bring them back." She went silent, long enough that Tom looked to see if the connection dropped, but it hadn't. Erin said, "Let me see what I can do. Please stop contacting her; it really isn't helping. Don't expect anything for a while, if at all. She's...well, she's special."

She was special. "Yeah. Figured that out. Thanks, Erin. Please tell her I'm sorry to make her nervous. And if she does need help at some point, she can always call my dad, Pete. He might make her less nervous than I do. I think I sent her his number a while ago."

"Sure, Tom," she said, her voice soft. She followed with a more cheerful offer. "Hey, by the way, next time you're down on the highway, stop in at Coffee & Cars. I can't believe I've never met you. Marcus isn't that big of a place."

He laughed. "I said the same thing to my dad. I can't believe I've missed you or your big silver hotrod."

She chuckled. "Yeah, Smoky's hard to miss. He's a

real looker."

"Next time I'm in the area, I will stop in. Not sure when that will be, but I will. Thanks."

"No problem. Take care." The call disconnected.

Dad put down the newspaper. "Erin Moore?"

"Yeah." He wasn't sure how to feel about the discussion as a whole.

Dad nodded. "She's going to talk to Wiz?"

"So she said. Well, actually that's not exactly what she said. She said she'd see what she could do but to not expect anything soon, or at all. Guess I'll just have to get over it, whatever 'it' is." He shrugged. There wasn't any other choice.

"Sorry, son, sometimes that's the way it goes."

"Yeah." It didn't seem fair that letting go of a woman he'd met exactly once made him feel worse than Evon dumping him. He grimaced. In hindsight, he'd been lucky. Evon was shallow and not the brightest woman in the world. She hadn't shown her true colors until he brought up moving back to Montana. Maybe his connection with Wiz would turn out the same way; one interaction wasn't enough to get to know someone. He could be completely wrong about her. And his imagined connection could be just that—imagination.

Tom sighed and surfed channels. Maybe a good cowboy movie would take his mind off it. Or a bad cowboy movie. Yeah, that would be better. A spaghetti western where everybody loses. That would be about right.

Chapter 6

Wiz

Wiz sipped her delicious iced mocha; Ryan was an expert. It was almost too cold outside for iced drinks, but not quite. Erin shivered, making Wiz crack a smile. Happiness came a little easier these days. Having real friends made an enormous difference.

"I have some news for you." Erin wiped the counter.

"Oh?"

"Tom Borde agreed to stop bothering you."

"Oh." Relief warred with sadness and a little frustration. "Why am I feeling disappointed? That's what I wanted."

Erin raised her brows. "That's what you *said* you wanted. It may not be what you really wanted or need."

"Huh." Erin should be a therapist.

She wetted her cloth again. "If it's any consolation, he also apologized for making you nervous because he didn't intend to. He said he wasn't really sure why he was being so insistent, but something about your eyes," Erin pointed her elbow at Wiz, "your *sad* eyes—called to him. He suggested that if you needed something from them, you should call his dad, Pete."

"That was nice." More than she deserved when she did nothing but brush him off.

Erin moved to the next table. "Tom seems like a nice guy."

Ryan, cleaning the sinks, joined in. "I *know* his dad is a nice guy. Pete's one of the regulars here for the Friday veterans' meeting. He doesn't say a whole lot, but what he does say is smart or funny. He lost his wife to cancer a few years ago, which is really too bad. I guess she was a great lady. I never got to meet her."

Wiz nodded but wasn't sure what to say. She had the ranch phone number if by some weird chance she needed it.

"You know, I might have a solution to the neighbor problem." Erin turned to Ryan. "Why don't we have a little dinner party? It will be us, Wiz, Pete, and, hmmm, who else? Just one or two more."

"Deb. We already know Wiz loves Deb's cupcakes, right?" He flashed a grin.

Erin smiled sweetly at Ryan. "Good idea." She turned to Wiz. "What do you think? That means just one new person. Too much?"

"Noooo. I'm...not sure." She should tell Erin what she was thinking. She could be honest with both of them. "You know, I used to be almost fearless. Now, the thought of meeting two new people turns me into a big bowl of jello. I'm so tired of being worried and scared all the time. But I can't seem to break out of it either."

"Wiz, it's just going to take time." Erin shrugged. "Remember, you can leave at any time if it gets to be too much. None of us will be offended."

She had to take the next step soon or she wouldn't do it. "Okay. When?"

"Friday night? Ryan, check with Pete. I'll talk to Deb."

"What should I bring?"

Erin's smile turned into laughter. "Ooh. Didn't you say Tom was trying to talk his dad into going all natural?"

Ryan laughed. "You are so tricky, babe."

She hadn't gotten the joke yet. "Yes, and he said his dad didn't want to."

"You can bring the steaks. Get them from one of the natural grass-fed ranches we liked. You can tell Pete where they're from at the end."

Wiz laughed. Both Ryan and Erin stopped laughing and stared at her, which made her stop. Then they looked at each other, back at her, and laughed again. She joined them. It felt... good. For the first time in a long time, she felt something other than fear and uncertainty, and it was a huge relief.

On Friday night, Wiz arrived early with only two small concealed weapons and a knife. She knocked on the door.

Ryan answered. "Hey, Wiz. Come on in."

She stepped in and to the side when Ryan closed the door.

"Hey!" Erin waved from the kitchen. "We're eating on the patio. Thanks for dropping the steaks off earlier. They're ready for the grill. Got drinks out there, glasses and water, everything we need, I think. Go on out."

Circling the room, Wiz walked to the sliding glass door and out. Kindling and logs were ready in the grate, and the oven was off but still warm. The grill smoked; Ryan must be preheating it. A big tub with ice held beer and soda; condensation ran from a pitcher of water. Wiz poured a glass and sipped. The day had been warm but was cooling off; she wasn't sweating to death in her light hoodie.

A knock sounded from the front door, and Ryan answered, their voices too quiet for her to hear. Ryan led the man to the patio. An older man, with graying hair and deep wrinkles, a little taller than Ryan and unbowed by his years. He wore a pressed blue plaid cowboy shirt with pearl buttons tucked into dark blue jeans, with worn but shiny cowboy boots on his feet and a genial smile. A tough man, used to hard, physical labor, but she could easily subdue him if she had to, and by the lack of bulges around his waist and ankles, she was fairly certain he wasn't carrying a gun. The two men entered the patio, both of them staying near the door.

"Beer or soda?" Ryan pulled a local brew from the ice.

"Soda. I'm driving." Ryan handed him a can. "Thanks."

Ryan turned to her. "Wiz, this is Pete Borden. Pete, this is your neighbor up the road, Wiz."

"Nice to meet you, Wiz. Thanks for helping my boy." He nodded and cracked his can. "And Strawberry. That one is such a princess." He shook his head.

"My pleasure. It's good to meet you, too." Surprisingly, she wasn't lying. Pete didn't offer to shake her hand, nor did she get the feeling that he'd thought of her as a child, which was a refreshing change. So many older men took one look at her and assumed she was a little girl, rather than a capable woman.

Pete sipped and took a seat at the table. "Tom said you did real good with Strawberry on the trail. It's hard for an experienced rider to lead a nervy horse. If you ever want to learn more about them, just give me a call. We'll have you riding in no time."

"Thanks." She wasn't sure what else to say. How could it be so easy for him to offer a valuable service to a complete stranger? He wouldn't get anything out of the deal, except a lot of uncomfortable silence from her. But she used to be the same way.

Ryan came out with steaks, Erin and Deb followed, and the dinner party got started. Surprisingly, Wiz was able to relax and enjoy, and by the time she got home, her face ached a little around the mouth from smiling. She'd even laughed a few times. She couldn't remember the last time she'd had a meal with others and enjoyed it. Maybe in the chow hall during her last deployment. Maybe that's what drew the attacker's attention. She shivered. Maybe she shouldn't laugh. But Erin and Ryan's was safe. She could laugh there, and in her house, by herself. And she would. She was done letting that predator rule her life.

But she had work to do. She settled into her office chair with coffee and water, woke up her desktop computer, and got busy. She had to analyze the current security of a new potential client; a full day's job, at the least. She pulled up the client questionnaire and read.

Chapter 7

TOM

Tom poured a cup of coffee, yawning. The days were definitely getting shorter, and it was getting harder to get up early in the gloom. He'd get used to it soon, but it always took a week or two. Losing seven minutes of sunlight a day was brutal, and the snow was already falling but not sticking on the valley floor—yet. Next spring, they'd gain the sun back that quickly, and he'd be thrilled. Dad entered the kitchen, stretching, so Tom poured him a cup.

Dad got cereal, milk, and bowls out. When Mom was alive, she'd cook eggs and pancakes or something similar every morning, but with just the two of them, cereal was a lot easier and faster. Tom put energy bars in his pockets for the mid-morning munchies, and he ate some sort of protein on his way out the door. When he lived in the City, he'd stop for a super-smoothie every morning, but it definitely wasn't worth the effort at home. Especially after his initial attempt; Dad rolled on the floor laughing. He'd used too much kale and it tasted awful; he hadn't bothered since.

Dad smiled and hummed, sitting at the table. He poured milk and pushed it toward Tom.

Tom filled his bowl. "Dinner was good?"

"Yeah, it was great. I haven't laughed that much in a long time. It's nice to hang around a younger crowd every now and then." He sipped coffee.

"Younger crowd? I thought you said it was a veteran thing?"

He shrugged one shoulder. "It was, sort of. Ryan and Erin invited me, Deb, and Wiz to their house."

Tom almost spewed coffee. "Wiz was there?"

"Yep. Nice young lady. Wicked sense of humor though."

"Really?" He couldn't quite picture Wiz laughing.

"Oh, yeah." Dad chuckled. "When I complimented the steaks, she calmly informed me they were from Mannix. You know, those grass-fed folks you like so much."

Tom sprayed coffee across the table. He coughed until he thought his lungs would come up while Dad wacked his back and mopped the table. Once he finally stopped, he refilled his cup and refreshed his dad's. "Thanks for cleaning up my mess. Maybe I shouldn't drink anymore coffee until you finish telling me about last night."

Dad laughed. "Not much more to tell. We had a great time. They're all nice folks. Ryan has a great sense of humor, and Deb can be wicked."

"Glad you had a good time." His father had a better social life than he did; that was sad. Tom fiddled with his cup. He'd just ask. "What *did* you think of the steaks?"

Dad put down his spoon. "You know, they may be on to something there. A tiny bit tougher, but the taste was outstanding. Maybe we should do some research this winter."

Tom smiled. "Sure, Dad, we could do that. There's a couple of places to start, like the American Grass Fed Association." He spooned up cereal. Never mind he'd already done a lot of the research. Dad would have to ride the trail himself, but Tom could point the way. He ate until he couldn't stand the suspense. "What did you think about Wiz?"

"Nice girl. Quiet, for the most part. She does have a bit of a… haunted look about her sometimes." Dad frowned at the table.

"Hmm."

"Didn't seem very comfortable until about halfway through dinner. A little fidgety, but once she got to know everybody, she settled down."

Tom laughed. "Dad, you sound like you're describing one of the horses."

Dad chuckled. "Well, you compared her to a rescue horse, and I think you're right. She sat with her back to the fireplace outside, didn't say hardly anything, just watched, and then, when we sat at the dining table, she sat on the far side, where she could see everyone. Ryan offered to arm wrestle her for the spot, and that's when she started to calm down a bit. She laughed a good bit there toward the end, which seemed to surprise Erin and Ryan. Maybe she's getting over whatever happened to her. She said she'd been out of the military for a few years."

"I don't think she's over it, or she wouldn't be so worried about me."

Dad's mouth twisted, and he tapped the table. "I didn't say she was over it, I said *maybe* she's getting over it. Working on it. Gradually. Maybe you're just a bit much at this point. You're a big guy, in your prime, and you can be pretty intense and downright dogged. Just be patient."

Tom nodded and finished his cereal. The cows weren't gonna feed themselves, and they didn't care about his love life. Or lack thereof.

Later that week, he pushed his cart through the store. Grocery shopping might get him off the ranch, but it wasn't fun. When he'd lived in the city, he'd rarely shopped. Evon got the few things they needed at home. Neither of them cooked. Smoothies for breakfast, lunch out with co-workers, dinner was take-out or restaurants with friends on Friday and Saturday nights. Sometimes they'd have dinner at a friend's place on Sundays, but most of that was catered.

He was probably a lot healthier now. More physical labor, more fresh fruit and vegetables, less sodium. Still, meal planning and cooking was a hassle. Mom made it all look simple, but she'd grown up in a big family with ranch hands to feed; their family of five was easy, comparatively. He was just as grateful as Dad for the invention of the slow cooker and modern pressure cooker.

He got to the checkout and chatted with the clerk a bit, then loaded all the groceries up and drove back to the ranch. They'd have to hit Costco soon. Dad hated going to the "big city," but Tom loved Missoula's funky college town vibe. He laughed every time Dad called it a big city—it wasn't even close. He chuckled. Dad and Mom visited him in NYC once; Dad was shell-shocked and refused to return. Mom came back on her own, several times. He took her to all the restaurants she'd read about and to the latest theater productions, and she'd had a wonderful time.

He missed his morning coffee, the variety of ethnic restaurants, live theater, live music—those things existed on a smaller scale in Montana, but after a long day at the ranch, the last thing he wanted to do was go out. He attended the big events, remaining involved with the community, but it was hard staying awake and alert after a late night. He yawned.

The neon colors of the Coffee and Cars sign caught his attention. He'd seen it plenty of times before but hadn't stopped. Well, no time like the present. The groceries would be okay sitting in the car for a short time, and he could use a dose of caffeine. Erin had told him to drop in, too, so he put on his turn signal. As he entered the shop, the scent of deep, dark espresso woke him up immediately. He walked down the long dining area filled with wood chairs and tables, not seeing a soul. Well, it was Wednesday afternoon, which wasn't exactly prime time for coffee in the Bitterroot. The sign on the counter said "ring once for service, please," so he did.

The decor made him smile. Old service station signs from the 1920s through the 1970s covered the walls, along with the front end of a classic car. Near the counter, he recognized the work of a local photographer. He'd had a few of these same shots in his NYC condo.

The door behind the counter opened, admitting a young man with light brown hair pulled back from a slightly scarred, pale face. He was a little shorter than Tom, and a little leaner, but clearly in great shape. "What can I get you?" He turned his back, washing his hands.

"Espresso, double, please. Are you Ryan?"

"Yeah, that's me." He flicked the lever on a grinder, and the coffee scent grew.

He held out his hand, to the side of the espresso machine. "I'm Tom Borde."

Ryan's head jerked up, and his eyes narrowed into a glare. Tom held his gaze but kept his expression neutral. Ryan broke the stare-off to put the filter in the machine. "Cream? Sugar? Is this to-go or stay?"

"Black, and you tell me. Erin asked me to stop by, but if this is a bad time, or it's not going to do me any good, then I'll go." No point in pushing anything. He'd done too much of that already.

Ryan barked a laugh and handed him a to-go cup. Tom's heart sank. If Wiz's friends wrote him off, he'd get nowhere. Guess he wasn't so nonchalant about the outcome as he pretended. He paid for the drink, putting the change in the tip jar, picked up his cup, and turned to go.

Ryan said, "Come on, we'll cut through here to the garage."

What a surprise. Didn't think he'd even get to meet Erin, let alone anything else. Especially since Ryan hadn't shaken Tom's hand. But perhaps he hadn't even seen the offer.

Tom followed him back to the garage, and that's when he noticed Ryan's hand. Or the lack of a hand. Instead of a left hand, he had some sort of plastic gripper. It looked like one of those things they sold old people to get cans out of high cupboards.

At least Ryan had his back to him. He grimaced. It would have been nice if Dad had warned him, though. It probably happened while he was in the military; way too many kids came back damaged. They'd started with the best of intentions; living in NYC during 9/11, he'd been all for the war, but it wasn't long before he wondered if it was doing more harm than good.

On the far side of the garage, a coverall-clad person leaned into the engine compartment of an older model SUV. "Hey, babe," Ryan called. "Guess who came to visit?"

The coveralls straightened and turned. Tom just blinked for a few moments. *Wow.* Tall, redhead, gorgeous. She smiled. "You must be Tom. You look a lot like your dad." She offered her hand, then abruptly pulled back. "Oh, sorry, I'm all greasy. Never mind. I'm Erin Moore, and it's nice to meet you."

"It's nice to meet you too. Dad told me he'd tried to set us up a couple of years ago. Too bad that didn't work out." Tom smiled and winked. Ryan growled and slid behind Erin, wrapping an arm around her. Tom laughed. "Don't worry, I doubt I'd have a chance anyway."

"That's true. I'm a happily involved woman." Erin looked him up and down. "But if I had met you a couple of years ago, well, this might have been a different story." She laughed, turned in Ryan's arms, and whispered something in his ear. He laughed, too.

They were a lovely couple, and Tom was suddenly jealous. He wanted that.

Erin turned back. "I really like your dad; he's a great guy."

"Dad liked all of you, too. Said he hadn't laughed that much in a long time." He grinned. "Oh, and I owe you big time thanks for the steaks. I've been trying to talk him into trying them forever, but since we raise cattle, well..." Buy steak? Never.

They both laughed. "Yeah, bet that would be a hard sell. So why doesn't he want to go natural, so to speak?" Ryan asked.

"So to speak?"

"Sorry, Air Force flying phrase." Ryan waved.

There was a lot of that in his future, he'd bet. Or hoped, anyway. "Oh. Well, there's a lot of reasons, but number one is it's expensive. It costs more to raise cattle that way, so prices are higher and your market is smaller, and sometimes it takes a while to build up a reputation, so you're living on the edge for a few years with no guarantees. And for a guy like my dad, well, going back into debt is not only a no but a never. Especially if he'd have to talk to Erin's mom."

Ryan and Erin both shuddered. No love lost there. "Can't blame him there. I don't like being in debt to her either, and she's my mother."

"Won't take long, babe, and we'll be in the black." Ryan hugged her close. Erin smiled, but it seemed slightly pained.

"No offense intended." Tom held up his hands, palm out.

"None taken." She cleared her throat. "Are you still thinking about Wiz?"

Tom barked a laugh and scrubbed his hands through his hair. "Are you kidding me? I can't stop thinking about her. And I don't even know why. It's not like we had a deep conversation or really any conversation. I talked, she listened. Months ago, and I still can't forget."

"That's more than most people get. Wiz doesn't have a lot of tolerance for strangers." Ryan shrugged.

Her wariness had been clear; but at that point, he hadn't known if it was just him or everyone. "She rescued me, and she didn't leave me to make my own way down on an iffy horse. She must have a lot of compassion to overcome her dislike for strangers enough to do that."

"She told us it was extremely difficult for her to do that." Erin grimaced.

"She did?"

"Yeah. She came to see us right after she dropped you off at the hospital. Which surprised both of us. That was the first time she'd ever come in the shop during normal business hours." She smiled a little and raised her brows. "You must have made a real impression."

"Good or bad impression, that's the question." Still, his optimism rose. "Maybe there's still some hope then."

"Maybe." Erin's brows wrinkled and rose. "How willing are you to make a fool of yourself?"

He laughed, a little ruefully. "You must be kidding me. Aren't I doing that pretty effectively right now?"

Erin chuckled and shook her head. "Not really. It's sweet. But no, I was trying to think of a way to make you less physically threatening. You're a big guy and kind of... intense. I can see that already. But if we all do some sort of group activity that's inherently silly, well... maybe."

"Huh. Hadn't thought of that. I offered to teach her to ride. That way, she'd be up on a horse and well above me."

Ryan shook his head. "I don't think that would work. She wouldn't have enough control."

They all went silent. Tom couldn't think of anything but typical dating activities, and those clearly weren't going to work with Wiz.

Then Erin laughed. "Got it!"

Tom noticed Ryan was regarding her warily too.

"Oh?" Ryan arched his brows.

"Yeah! We'll have a sledding party!" She grinned.

"Sledding? Like snow sledding?" Tom hadn't sledded since he was a child.

"Yeah. Like when we were kids. It's fun, nobody's any better at it than anybody else, it doesn't take much equipment, and you can do it solo or in a group, and there's opportunities for friendly physical contact." Erin kept grinning.

"Hmm. We might have some old inner tubes around from floating the river—those will work on snow." Tom tried to think of a good spot; as a kid, they'd driven up the road, on the edge of the National Forest land. "Where were you thinking? We've got hills, but they're pretty far from our house." No snow there yet, either.

Erin shook her head. "No, Wiz could host. Her house is built into the side of the mountain, so we could make a run right above her house, and she's got that great patio for hot chocolate and stuff, with the fireplace. Another couple of weeks and she'll have plenty of snow."

Ryan turned to Erin. "Do you think she'll go for that? How big a group are you thinking about?"

She smiled at Ryan. "Oh, we'll ease her into it. She's hosted Deb and Sam with us, so if we do a small group first, with just us, and then add a few people the next time, then maybe by the third time we can get her to include the neighbors?"

Ryan tilted his head back and forth. "Might work. We can try. I think she's starting to be ready to move ahead, but I don't want to push too hard. You've never seen...well, never mind."

Tom's curiosity was killing him, but he couldn't ask. Although… "Look, guys, I know you don't want to tell me anything about what happened to her, but at the same time, it would help to know in general, just so I know what to avoid."

Erin and Ryan looked at each other with raised brows, and both shook their heads. Ryan's tone was harsh. "No. We're not going to tell you anything about it at this point. It's not our story to tell, it's hers. What I will tell you is this. Never initiate any kind of physical contact with Wiz. Even if she's falling, don't try and catch her. You could get hurt."

Shoot. Whatever had happened to Wiz, it must have been horrific. His heart sank, even as his eyebrows rose. "Got it. Not sure I'd be able to stop myself from trying to catch somebody who's falling, but I'll do my best."

"Yeah, the chivalry thing could get you killed in this case. Wiz is a mixed martial arts expert and not competition-style." Ryan shuddered. "I wouldn't want to try and take her, that's for sure."

Tom considered the man in front of him. Ryan was a fairly big guy, in good shape, even with just one arm, and Wiz was tiny.

"I need to get back to work on this thing." Erin patted the vehicle's fender. "It's a good plan, so just be patient, okay?"

"Sure. I can be patient." Tom shrugged. "I can give up. She's obviously been hurt enough. I'm not going to add to it. It will be painful for me, but it's obviously less than whatever she's gone through."

Erin nodded. "That's the best attitude you can have."

He raised both hands. He'd surrender to their best judgement. "Hey, what you're doing is more important for her sake, but I appreciate you even trying at all for me. Thanks."

"Sure. Stop in anytime." Erin picked up a wrench.

He spotted the exit, walked out the door, and climbed into his old truck. Maybe it would work out, or maybe it wouldn't, but at least Wiz had good friends. He sure hoped they could be at least friends, someday, because those sad gray eyes just didn't want to leave him. But he'd walk away if that's what it took.

Chapter 8

# Wiz

"You want me to do what?" Wiz looked at her phone. Maybe their connection was bad or she'd misheard.

Erin chuckled. "Host a sledding party. You know, sledding, hot chocolate, tea, coffee, maybe soup or chili, and bread? We'll bring the drinks, and I can bring a pot of chili. Doesn't that sound like fun? It would just be us, Deb, and Sam. And maybe a date if they've got somebody."

O-kay. She hadn't heard wrong. "Where are we sledding?"

"Oh, right above or below your house. Or behind the guest house. It's steep enough, isn't it?"

She had no idea. "I guess so. I've never tried. I don't think I have a sled other than the snowmachine."

"Even if it's not steep enough, we can stand around your fireplace and sip cocoa. That's fun in the winter."

"If you say so. I'm not sure I've ever actually gone sledding." Her childhood wasn't exactly fun.

"Really?"

"I grew up in Phoenix. Not a lot of opportunities for sledding. Later, I was stationed in Arkansas and New Mexico; they don't have a lot of snow, and Washington is rainy most of the winter. When it snowed, the network inevitably went down somewhere on McChord or Ft. Lewis. So, no. No sledding."

"Then you're in for a treat. We'll go sledding and then eat chili and watch the sunset. Then maybe we'll watch a movie inside. So, we'd start at fifteen-hundred or so on Sunday. What do you think?"

"Sure. Why not? I hope you have sleds because I don't." She'd get some extra exercise walking up the hill, anyway. Maybe she should pack a walkway with the snowmachine? Or with snowshoes?

"Yep. We've got some sleds. I love sledding. I can hardly wait to sled with Ryan."

"Oh?"

"Sure. Snuggling and tumbling in the cold is fun."

Something she wasn't likely to find out. Ever. Wiz shivered. "Okay, see you Sunday."

That Sunday, Wiz discovered Erin was right. Sledding was fun. Zoom down the hill, bumping and jumping, then tumble at the bottom, run up the hill, and do it all again. She waved at Deb and Sam, who stopped after a couple of runs, happier sitting by the fire sipping brandied hot apple cider. They waved back. She sat on the sled and zipped down the hill again, laughing and whooping, cold air whipping her cheeks.

Erin and Ryan slid together, Erin between Ryan's legs, his arms wrapped around her. They tumbled off about halfway down and kissed while the sled continued without them. Wiz caught the sled and pulled both of them up the hill. She could see the attraction in two-person sledding. What she couldn't see was Jeff, her ex, ever going sledding. Nope, just as well he was gone. She couldn't believe she'd married him in the first place; she'd been looking for stability and safety. Sadly, Jeff couldn't provide either; he was too selfish.

Oddly enough, the only person she could picture sledding with was Tom. Which was just weird. She'd spent all of three hours with the guy, months ago. And the mere idea of being that close to him was nerve-racking. He was too big, too forward, too… much. Still, she'd watched him work their horses using the spotting scope from her third-floor observation deck. He was patient but firm with the animals and seemed to have a dogged persistence for the other ranch chores. She'd watched him more than she was comfortable admitting. She wasn't obsessed, but her fascination seemed strange when she wasn't at all sure she could stand being around most men, especially Tom. She had to discuss her feelings with her therapist again. Her lack of openness wasn't a good sign.

While she mused, she'd reached the top, but suddenly, sledding didn't seem as much fun. She slid down and poured some cocoa. Erin made the real stuff and brought it in a thermos. It was so rich, it was like dessert in a cup. The smooth chocolate lifted her mood. Erin and Ryan made another run, then joined them, towing their sled.

"That was fun! You were right, Erin. I was missing out." Ryan put his arm around Erin.

"More fun with a snuggle bunny though." Deb

raised her glass.

"A snuggle bunny? Really?" Ryan frowned, then posed with his hands on his hips and chest thrust out. "What about me says 'bunny'?"

Deb rolled her eyes. "Oh, I'm sorry. Snuggle cheesecake? Snuggle Viking? Ooh, I know, snuggle stud."

Wiz laughed along with everyone except Ryan. He raised his chin. "Yes, that's a much better description."

"So, snuggle stud, when are you bringing friends? We want our own snuggle studs." Sam snickered.

Ryan's sputtering laughter stopped. "Actually, I've had a friend contact me recently. He's getting out, and he needs a place to live and a job. He's supposed to send Erin an application, but he's downrange right now, so he doesn't have access to his stuff."

"And is he likely to be a snuggle stud?" Deb giggled.

Ryan laughed, raising his hands. "Not gonna make that judgment call. You'll have to wait and see, if he follows through."

"Do I know him, Ryan?" Wiz was curious. She'd known everyone on her ex's crew at one point, but he and Ryan were on different crews.

"I don't think so, Wiz. He was a C-17 mechanic, but he hung out with a little older crowd than us. Actually, he didn't hang out a whole lot, period. He's a quiet guy. Did his job, kept his head down, went home."

"Okay. Just wondered." She missed some of the fun things they all used to do, like going to festivals and hiking.

Erin broke in. "There's chili and cornbread and coleslaw. Do you guys want to eat out here by the fire or go inside where it's warmer?"

"Oh, can we go inside? It's getting a little chilly. The other kind of chilly." Sam wrapped her arms around her waist, despite her fashionable wool sweater, down jacket, and knit hat ensemble.

Wiz pointed at the back door to the kitchen. "Sure. The food is actually inside. We can eat in the living room while we watch the movie or use the dining room table, whichever you want."

"Oh, chili and a movie. Let's do that." Deb rose from her seat at the fireplace.

"Sure." Ryan rounded up the sleds and stacked them in the corner of the patio. Wiz gathered mugs, everyone grabbed a remaining loose item, and they trooped inside. Wiz followed, but she stopped to look out over the valley.

The sun glowed red behind the purple mountains. Lights twinkled in the valley below. The Rocking B ranch was quiet, a warm yellow light shining from the house. Tom and Pete were probably having dinner, too. She wished she could invite them up, but she wasn't there yet.

#

Every other week, Erin, Ryan, and a couple of other people would come out for sledding, dinner, and a movie. The Sunday afternoon parties had become her favorite activity, even better than training with her martial arts coaches. Erin, Ryan, Sam, and Deb were regulars; Craig and his wife Amy from Ryan's previous job had joined them last week, bringing the party to seven. She'd been looking forward, nervously, to Sunday since the last one, because Pete and Tom were joining their regular group. Wiz paced across her foyer, watching her security cameras. Erin's truck rolled up the road, so she opened the gates and went outside to meet them.

"Hey, Wiz. Long time, no see." Ryan pulled a cooler from the back.

"Hi, Ryan, Erin."

"Hi!" Erin handed her two thermoses and pulled out a box.

Wiz led them to the patio. She'd made a pot of chicken chili, and Pete was bringing beef stew. Erin put a container in the fridge, probably dessert or a salad. Ryan walked the path around the outside of the house to the lower level. She'd stored the sleds on the patio below the deck.

"Wiz." Erin closed the refrigerator door. "Are you sure you're okay with this?" She raised both brows.

"Yes." Wiz nodded, but her head was bobbing a little too fast. "It's time. I need to move forward." She did, no matter how nervous it made her.

"Okay, but you let me know if you need some space, right?" Erin wagged a finger, then whipped it toward the house. "And if you need to just disappear for a while, you do that. I'll ride herd on the ranchers." She used an exaggerated drawl on the last sentence and pushed up an imaginary cowboy hat.

Wiz laughed. "I think I'll be all right, but thanks." She was so lucky to have great friends.

"No problem." Erin returned to the house.

Wiz checked the security cameras again. Nobody yet, but then Erin and Ryan came up a little early to help set up. She took a deep breath. It really was time to move forward. She'd gotten used to Erin and Ryan being around the house, to the point where she no longer needed to watch their every move. They felt like... family. Part of her. Deb and Sam were pretty close too, but they weren't quite so much family as just firmly in the "non-threat" category. Now the question was, could she stand to be around a couple of men she didn't really know at all? And big men, at that?

Stop freaking yourself out, Wiz. You know both of them. They weren't strangers. Not yet friends, either, but it was possible. She checked her tablet. A side-by-side off-road vehicle drove up the road. Wiz zoomed in—the Rocking B brand was on the side, with Pete in the passenger seat and Tom driving. Deb and Sam were right behind in Deb's old car; Sam had sworn she wasn't bringing her fancy BMW up the dirt road again. Wiz opened the gates and passed through the house to greet everyone. Butterflies tumbled in her stomach.

Everyone emerged at the same time; the group was a little overwhelming. Sam greeted Pete and then gave Tom a hug. Wiz watched from the top of the stairs into the house, a little envy adding to her churning emotions. Sam introduced both men to Deb, and they all shook hands. They returned to their vehicles, pulling out boxes and bowls.

Deb lifted a cake box. "You're my test tasters for a new flavor combination."

Sam followed her with a wine carrier and a bottle of vodka. "I brought the important part."

Pete held a crock pot. "Hey, Wiz, I brought some chili along with the beef stew. Figured you had a pretty big crowd, so you might need some additional food."

"You didn't have to, but thanks." Wiz tried to smile but couldn't quite manage it.

Tom stood two steps below Pete, carrying another crockpot on top of a case of beer. "Hi, Wiz. It's good to see you again." He met her eyes, and his low voice rumbled through her.

She shivered and turned away, pointing into the foyer. "Hi, Tom. How's the ankle?"

He walked inside. "Pretty much good as new. I did everything they told me to do, including all the physical therapy and exercises, so I've recovered." He stopped, looking around her living area. "Wow, this is really beautiful, both comfortable and pretty. Bet one of those western living magazines would love to profile this place."

Wiz grimaced. "The designer asked, but I said no. I don't want everyone to know what my house looks like. Besides, some of the art she wanted to add was too much for me. A lot of Native American art, but from the southwest, not here, which made no sense to me, and a bunch of stuffed heads." She shuddered. "I don't mind hunting for food, but trophy hunters make me mad."

He nodded. "I'll agree with that. Regardless, it looks really nice. Where should I put this?" Tom lifted the case a bit.

"Oh, sorry, keep going straight ahead and past the kitchen. We're out on the patio." Tom walked slowly, head turning. "I'll give you and Pete a tour if you want."

"Great." He continued to the patio and put the beer down on the countertop. "It's cold enough out, there's no reason to put it in the fridge right now." He pulled the crockpot off the case, placing it to the side.

Deb plugged it in. "Pour me a glass of that, Sam." Sam pulled stemless, acrylic wine glasses from the cupboard.

Tom grabbed two beers, offering one to Pete. "Dad, Wiz offered a tour."

Pete nodded and put the beer down without opening it. "That would be great, Wiz. This is a beautiful place."

Wiz nodded in return but still couldn't force a smile. "Thanks. Come on, we'll start from the top." She pointed at the back door, and they walked in. She took them to the third-floor observation deck; it was all screened windows, with outdoor furniture. Plus security shutters like the rest of the house, but they were discreetly mounted on the outside. The casual eye would also miss the rifle mounting points and the gun safe in the floor. She'd left her spotting scope out, turned toward the Sapphires, not the Rocking B.

"Beautiful and very secure. If you ever need someone to help you man the watchtower, just give me a call. I'll be right up." Tom lifted his arms, like he was peering through a rifle.

Wiz was a little surprised Tom had figured out the

real purpose behind the space. She'd expected that reaction from Pete. There was more to Tom than she knew.

"You can double that for me, Wiz. I'm a good shot with a rifle." Pete smiled.

"I bet you are, Pete. Scout-sniper during Vietnam, right?"

Pete's eyebrows rose. "I never said, did I?"

"No. Didn't have to." Wiz raised her brows to match him.

Tom turned toward Pete, a surprised look on his face. "You were? You said you were a personnel clerk and never left the base."

Pete shook his head once. "Not sayin' I wasn't."

"You know they've declassified just about everything during the Vietnam era, right?" Wiz asked. They had, but the military didn't exactly spread the word to the guys who'd fought those long, hard battles.

"Maybe. Nobody official ever told me so. Not that I know anything." Pete gave her a lopsided smile.

Wiz sniffed. She knew how to play that game. "Yeah, me either."

"Course not. Can we see the rest?" Pete walked to the door and down the stairs, Tom following.

Wiz unlocked the security door to the second floor with her phone. "This level has my office and bedroom." They entered the office, decorated similarly to the downstairs, with comfortable rugs on wood floors, an adjustable desk with a credenza behind it, and a small seating area. A vault door beyond that secured her servers and security and communications gear. She didn't unlock the bedroom door.

"Very comfortable working environment." Pete didn't try the locked doors. "Got enough room to hold a dance."

Tom strolled to her desk. "I assume you like the standing desk? I loved mine in the city."

"It's perfect for me." Changing positions kept her from stiffening up too much.

Pete turned back to the stairs, Tom following him. Wiz closed the door behind her. "Keep going, and I'll show you the basement." The gym, with mats, weights, and aerobics machines, took up the outer part of the daylight basement; the treadmill, bike, rowing machine, and stair machine faced the mountains. If she couldn't be hiking them, she could at least dream about it while she sweated. Behind her, another secure vault provided a gun safe, ammo room, and safe room with an escape tunnel, but she wouldn't show them that, either. She led them outside and up the hill.

"Son, now I'll take one of those beers." Pete sat next to Deb and Sam.

"Sure." Tom brought him over a beer. "Show me the hill where I will slide to my death, Wiz?"

She chuckled and pointed to where Erin and Ryan were poised at the top, ready to race. "Ready, set, go!" Ryan yelled, and they both launched themselves down the hill head first. Ryan was ahead until Erin yanked his ankle, sending him tumbling off. The motion threw Erin off a bit too, but she compensated and made it to the bottom still on the sled.

"Hey, you cheated!" Ryan ran down the hill.

Erin raised her arms in victory. "Hey, rubbing's racing."

Ryan wrapped his arms around her and whispered something in her ear. Erin laughed and kissed him, then pulled away and grabbed her sled. "Come on, we'll give it another try."

They headed up to the top of the hill. Wiz handed Tom a sled. "Here's yours. Is your dad coming up?"

Tom chuckled. "I don't think so. He said he liked his bones in one piece, but he'd be happy to watch us break ours." They started up the hill behind Erin and Ryan. "I do feel a little silly. I'm *way* beyond childhood."

"I felt that way at first, but it's just so much fun that you get over it quickly. At least I did."

"I guess there's hope yet."

They reached the top of the hill and watched Erin and Ryan race again. They were both so busy trying to knock each other off that they didn't even get halfway down before they crashed. Tom, Deb, and Sam all laughed, and even Wiz chuckled. Then the crash turned into a serious make-out session. "Get a room!" Deb pitched a snowball, falling well short. Eventually, they got back on their sleds and made it the rest of the way down.

Tom swept his arm, with a half-bow "Ladies first."

"Oh, no, you're the guest, go ahead."

"Thanks. Not so sure about this but..." Tom seated himself gingerly and brought his feet up. He was a big guy, so he flew down the slope. Wiz watched, and while he wasn't whooping and hollering, he did have a big smile on his face at the bottom. She slid down, the cold wind stinging her cheeks, and almost took Tom's legs out from under him, but he jumped out of the way.

"Hey, I made it down okay, so you try to make me fall now?"

"Sorry. Wasn't on purpose." Sleds were hard to steer.

He held up a hand. "I was kidding. These aren't exactly precision machines."

"Or machines at all. But it's great, isn't it?"

"Yeah, I have to admit, it's way more exciting than I thought it would be. Come on, let's go again!"

They went up and down the hill another half dozen times, Deb and Sam joining for a couple of runs before they decided on a break. They got drinks and joined Pete at the fire.

Tom sipped his beer. "Dad, you should give it a try. It's really fun. Way more entertaining than I thought it would be. Next time, we should bring Rusty up with us."

"Rusty?" Erin asked.

"Our Australian Shepherd. He'd love to chase the sleds down the hill." Tom laughed. "He'd probably try to herd them together."

"He'd bark the whole time, too."

"True." Tom turned toward Wiz. "But maybe you don't care for dogs?"

"Dogs are fine. I've thought about getting one."

"They're good company and can be very protective, depending on the breed. Aussies are herders, not as protective as some, and they need a lot of exercise and a job. They need useful work."

"I've thought about a Belgian Malinois. They use them in the military a lot. But they also take a lot of exercise." All those vicious teeth on her side was a comforting thought.

"They do tend to be a little hyper. Still, they are great dogs if you want to protect yourself and your property." Tom sipped.

Wiz nodded. Everyone else had wandered away, leaving her and Tom in the seating area. Being so close in the middle of a group was okay, but by themselves made her a little uncertain. She wasn't sure what to talk about. Or maybe she should get dinner ready? She wanted to stay but she wanted to run, too. Indecision was unusual and made her even more uneasy. She rose to sit on the chair's arm, where she could run easier.

Tom's bottle clinked on the side table. "Wiz, I wanted to apologize."

"For what?"

"For making you uncomfortable with the emails and phone messages." Tom looked away for a minute, then swallowed and looked back at her. Was he nervous? "Look, I am really grateful you got me down the trail safely, but that's not why I was bothering you. For some reason, I'm very attracted to you. I'm not sure why, since I can't pretend that I actually know you, other than you're obviously compassionate and brave, but I am. There's something about you that just calls out to me, and I'd like to get to know you much better, even if it's just as a friend." He swallowed again. "But... I also understand that you may not feel the same way and that whatever you went through when you were in the service seems to make it very difficult for you to be around people at all, let alone me." He sucked in a breath. "I really am sorry I upset you, and I won't do it again. If you can stand to just see me as a neighbor, that's fine. I just want you to know that I'm not going to press you in any way at all, but if you need something someday, please let Dad or me know, and we'll do our best."

Wiz wasn't at all sure what to say. Why would he be attracted to her, little miss nervous, armed to the teeth, scared of her own shadow? Certainly, some men found her pretty. But she didn't get a predatory feeling from him, nor did his attraction seem completely based on looks. If it was, he had some odd desires. She didn't get that from him, either. He seemed sincere, but she wasn't sure she could handle it.

"Shoot. I didn't mean to worry you more. I'm sorry. I'll go home." Tom pushed up from the couch.

"No. Wait."

He sat back down but scooted a little farther away from her, which helped.

She met his eyes. "I'm not sure what to tell you. I like your dad, and I think I like you just fine, but I don't really know either of you well enough to trust you. One of the reasons I agreed to hold the party was to get to know each other better in case the two of you need help someday." She couldn't keep meeting his gaze, so she looked at the fire, keeping him in her peripheral vision. She kept talking, even though it was hard to trust enough to do that little. "I don't trust people easily, and getting to know anyone is very difficult for me. Please stay, but just don't... loom over me. I know that's a ridiculous request because you're tall, and I'm short, but that's what I need. And I'm sorry, but I'm not sure I'll ever be ready to be in any kind of romantic relationship." She finished the last sentence in a rush, bounded to her feet, and ran into the kitchen. She needed space from all of them.

She skidded to stop in the kitchen, feeling like a childish idiot. Taking deep breaths, she picked up a spoon and stirred her chicken chili. May as well be useful if she was going to run away.

"Wiz?" Erin entered the kitchen. "Are you okay?"

"Yes. I'm sorry, I just needed to get away for a minute." She kept stirring.

"That's all right. It's your house. Did Tom upset you? We can tell him to go home."

She turned to Erin, shaking her head. "No, no. He should stay. I told him to stay. I just... needed a minute alone."

"Take all the time you need, Wiz. I'll go back to the sled hill." Erin spun on her toe.

"Erin, wait. I just...I got the minute I needed. I'm okay. It's just...hard, to feel again." She stared at the chili. "It was easy to be angry and get revenge, and then it was easy to hide and not feel anything at all. But I don't want to do that forever. I *can't* do that forever." She looked at Erin again. "I can't let them win that way. But it's hard."

Erin held out her hands, and Wiz grabbed them,

surprising herself. Erin squeezed gently and held on, but not hard. "It's okay. You're doing great. It is hard to trust someone after you've been betrayed. I think it's amazing you're doing this at all. I'm not sure I could, and I don't even know what you went through."

"Thanks. I want to be back to the person I was, but I don't think that's possible." That naïve little girl was gone, destroyed.

Erin smiled sadly. "Hey, we all change. Nobody stays the same."

"Yes, but I want to get better." Being scared was exhausting and lonely.

Erin squeezed her hands. "And you are. And you will! Look at you! You've got a bunch of people at your house. And now you're touching somebody else. You're making amazing progress, Wiz. Don't let anybody tell you otherwise, okay? Including yourself. Give yourself permission to go slow and be proud of how far you've come."

She squeezed Erin's hands back. "Okay. You're right. I just need to go at my own speed. I know that. It's just...hard." She wanted to run upstairs and hide in her bedroom, but she didn't.

"We'll be here. You can call me or Ryan at any time. Anytime at all, doesn't matter if it's zero three or fifteen hundred. Got it?"

"Thanks." Wiz swallowed. "I'm okay now. I think I can go back to everyone."

"Good." Erin smiled. "Stop in the bathroom and splash some water on your face first, though."

Wiz let go of Erin's hands and wiped her face,

surprised her cheeks were wet. She hadn't realized she was crying. She hadn't cried since she got out of the hospital. She nodded, and Erin left. Wiz went to the powder room behind the kitchen and looked in the mirror. Her eyes were a little red, and her nose was running too. She blew her nose, then did as Erin suggested and splashed some water on her face. Good thing she never wore any makeup. Not anymore.

She looked in the mirror again. She hardly ever looked at herself, other than to make sure she didn't have toothpaste on her chin. Jeff used to tell her she was beautiful, back when they were dating. She met some of the standards for beauty, like big eyes, a small nose, and a kind of pointy chin. She always thought she looked a little too much like an anime character, but there were lots of men who liked that look, Jeff among them. Well, until he found out she wasn't one dimensional, and she was smarter than he was. Way smarter. Cheating dumbass loser. But even though he'd been a terrible husband, his abandonment in her greatest time of need cut deep.

Even worse was the way his friends had rallied around not only Jeff, but every man who'd been downrange with her. They'd all been investigated, and most of them resented having to talk with officials because of "some dumb girl who got attacked." They should have never known who she was, but Jeff spilled the beans. He claimed it was an accident, but it didn't matter. They made her life miserable. But she'd gotten back at all of them, outing their cheating to their significant others, investigating their lives on her own, and turning over evidence of wrong-doing to civilian authorities or anonymous fraud lines, and posting pictures and video of their bad behavior on social media. She'd even found two who proudly claimed, on a dark web site, that they'd assaulted women. Those two she'd outed to their spouses and posted about them on social media. When they tried to cheat their former spouses by hiding their money overseas, she'd found it and transferred it all to the spouse after their divorces were final. She'd almost gotten caught on the second one.

In hindsight, her therapist had been right. Revenge hurt her worse than it hurt them. But it had been satisfying in the moment, and despite keeping her part in the revelations secret, it wasn't long before she had a reputation as an online white-knight of sorts. But in person was a different story.

She used to like being underestimated because of her looks. But no more; she wished she resembled Erin—tall and strong. No one would ever think she was a pushover. But Wiz wasn't weak, so she'd made sure no one could mess with her ever again. She was tough. And being tough meant she needed to learn how to live her life again. Really live, not just exist. In some ways, it would have been better if she'd been poor. Then she wouldn't have been able to hide. Maybe she'd have been forced to deal with her emotions sooner. But maybe she wouldn't have—she could have become just another statistic. That was all in the past. She had to deal with emotions and people.

So, buck up, Wiz. Get back out there and be the

person you want to be, not the person you are. Perception is reality. *You're tough but nice. Strong but compassionate. Smart. Pretty?* She shook her head. Not ready for that one yet. Ready to be someone's friend? Yes. She could be a friend, not just an acquaintance. *So, get out there!*

She left the powder room and returned to the patio. Erin, Ryan, and Tom were standing in a close group, deep in conversation on the far side of the patio. Ryan was glaring, Tom neutral, and Erin talking intently. She didn't need to get in the middle of that. She grabbed her water glass and sat near Pete. "Are you sure you don't want to try sledding? It's way more fun than you think."

He chuckled. "I'm sure it is, but I have old bones. I don't need to test them."

"You're not that old."

"Well, that's nice of you to say. But I am. And I test these old bones all too often already on the back of a horse, so there's no sense in pushing it." He smiled, then sobered and looked at her questioningly. "Speaking of pushing it, is my son pushing you? You left here pretty quick."

"No. Just the opposite. He was telling me he wouldn't push. And I appreciate that. It's just... hard... for me to talk about my feelings."

"If he does take things too far, and you need someone to tell him to back off, you let me know." He pointed at his chest.

"Thanks. But I think Ryan's taken on that role." She tilted her head toward the three of them. Erin was still talking.

"Yeah, he was in Tom's face as soon as you left." Pete laughed. "He's trying to pull off big brother, but he's younger than you are, right?"

"Yes, he is." She sighed. "But he was one of the only people I could rely on when I got home. He knows me better than anyone else. He's earned the right to play big brother all he wants."

"He's a good guy, if a bit of a hot-head. You could certainly do worse for found family. But I'm glad you came over to talk to me because I wanted to ask you something."

"Oh?"

"Yeah." He nodded, slowly. "If you'd be interested, I'd be happy to teach you to ride. Riding is a good skill to know out here, and some people say riding is therapeutic. I find horses soothing. Sure, the four-wheelers are easier and more efficient, but a horse, well, there's nothing better than riding a horse someplace to make you feel better. Something about controlling a beast that large helps me feel in control." He swallowed hard. "I know it's what kept me from going off the deep end when I got back. And my wife."

"I know they use horses a lot in therapy." She grimaced. "But I don't think I'd be comfortable having a bunch of people watch me." No way she could be in a class or with more than one or two people.

"Oh, no." He shook his head. "It would just be the two of us. The folks across the road, they're only here a few weeks a year. We watch their place for them, and in return, we can use it whenever they're not around.

They have a covered riding arena, so we can use that, just the two of us." Pete raised his brows with a small smile.

"You know, I'd actually like that a lot. I'd like to know more about horses anyway, and I can see where riding would be a useful skill to have. But I don't want to be a bother."

"You won't be. It's settled. We'll have lessons a couple times a week. You tell me what works best."

"I can work around your schedule. I do all my work remotely, at just about any hour of the day I'm awake."

Pete shook his head. "I'm an early riser, and I tend to go to bed pretty early. So, how about two or so in the afternoon on Tuesday and Saturday?"

"Great." Wiz pulled out her phone and added an appointment to her calendar. "There. It's on my calendar. I'll meet you at the arena?"

"At first, yes. Eventually, you'll have to come over and get your horse yourself, but for right now, I'll bring the right one over to you. Don't worry, I've taught lots of kids to ride."

Wiz huffed. "I'm not much of a kid anymore."

Pete just looked at her for a minute, brows raised. "You are to me, but I'm guessing twenty-nine."

She smiled. "You're closer than most. Thirty-four."

"I got almost forty on you, so to me you are a kid." He smirked.

"You don't look like a guy in his seventies." He didn't; not even close.

"Thanks, but I think I do. Well, my face does. Ranching keeps me in pretty good shape, and I didn't come home with any real injuries. I got lucky."

"Yeah? Just 'cause you don't have any physical injuries, it doesn't mean you weren't injured in other ways. They just didn't know about post-traumatic stress and traumatic brain injury back then. They're even looking at upgrading discharges from that era if it looks like the person acted out due to PTS."

"You mean if someone got a dishonorable discharge because they mouthed off or acted badly, they could get upgraded to honorable?" Pete sounded a little shocked.

"Depends on the circumstances, but yes, if it looks like it was due to an injury, they can."

He nodded, his lips pursed. "Huh. I'll have to tell a few of my buddies about that."

"You can apply online." She lifted her phone.

He snorted. "Not that popular with my set."

"You can get the paper form from other places too. Probably the vet center in Marcus. Or the Veteran's Administration medical centers."

"Good to know. Thanks, Wiz." He smiled.

"Sure. And thank you. I'm looking forward to Tuesday."

Pete nodded and got up, carrying his empty beer bottle. Ryan walked over, sitting at the far end of the couch. "Wiz, are you okay?"

"Didn't Erin tell you I was?" They all meant well, but the attention was getting a bit much.

"Yes, but I want to hear it from you." He scowled fiercely. "You left in an awfully big hurry."

She waved her hand, trying to brush both her

annoyance and Ryan away. "I'm fine. I'm trying to move ahead, and it's making me a little emotional."

He stared at her for a minute, then a big grin broke out. "You? Emotional? That's...awesome!"

Wiz had to chuckle. Her voice sounded a little rough. "It's really that surprising?"

"Yeah. It's been years. I was kind of giving up hope. Especially when you moved here, I thought it was to get even further away from people. But you haven't. I'm proud of you."

"Back at ya."

Ryan huffed. "Okay, come on. Let's do a couple more runs. Then we'll go eat?"

"Sure. Let's go." She was finally moving on, into the future. The ride might be rougher than her sledding hill, but forward was good.

Chapter 9
TOM

Tom sat back in his chair and put his feet up. A long day, but the steers were loaded and gone, and while the money wasn't in the bank yet, it would be tomorrow. Which would make Dad happy. And it made him happy because there were fewer heads to feed.

He checked his social media. His friends back in NYC were at some glitzy charity event. At least that's what the selfies implied. Nobody posted which charity was benefitting; to them, it was just an opportunity to be seen by, and see, all the right people. He wriggled his toes in his sheepskin slippers. He much preferred sitting at home with his feet up on Friday night rather than eating dry chicken while stuffed into a designer suit with tight, shiny shoes trying to look like he was having a good time. He missed some of his friends, though. And he occasionally missed the restaurants, theaters, and nightlife. But most of the time, he was happy with his quiet life.

Of course, he'd rather have a woman curled next to him on the couch. While he was dreaming, he'd rather sit next to Wiz on her couch. And if he really had his way, they wouldn't be sitting there long.

But she'd said she might not ever be ready for a romantic relationship. He wondered again exactly what happened to her. A sexual assault seemed likely. And, from what he understood, most sexual assaults during deployments were perpetrated by their fellow service members. Which was horrible. How could someone who had sworn themselves to service attack their brothers and sisters? It just didn't make any sense.

A window popped up on his laptop. "You should change your passwords from the default and make them harder to guess. Wiz."

He snorted a laugh. *Cute.* But she was right. He had no idea what program the chat window used. Maybe she could help. He typed, "You're right. You'll have to walk me through it."

"Sure. You play video games, right?"

"Yes. You?"

"Of course. HALO?"

Tom grinned. "Yes. I have to go upstairs."

"I'll wait."

Tom kept grinning and closed his laptop. Maybe he'd get to know her a little better through the game.

A few hours later, he was still smiling, but ruefully. He'd gotten to know her better, all right. The woman was cut throat. No holds barred, dirty tricks, the whole package, combined with a wicked sense of humor and a grasp of tactics and strategy that was downright amazing. He'd known she was intelligent but just how smart was a little disconcerting. Tom wasn't stupid, but she'd made him look like canned chipped beef next to a prime ribeye steak.

After they'd signed off the game, she'd walked him through how to properly secure his network and online life. And now he felt just plain stupid. Cyber security was her area of expertise, and a home network was child's play for her, but he was pretty sure it wouldn't take her very long at all to learn how to analyze economic sectors and do long-term forecasting. It would take him centuries to learn even the simplest home network security tasks.

He flopped back on his bed and stared up at the ceiling. He was fooling himself. She couldn't possibly be interested in him. He had some money but not nearly as much as she did, and while he wasn't stupid, he couldn't come close to her level of intelligence. He was just a cattle rancher; a cowboy with some fancy clothes. They had nothing in common. He snorted. He should just give up now.

Tom closed his eyes, and those sad gray eyes stared back. Even when she'd smiled and laughed, it seemed a little forced or an act. From Ryan and Erin's smiles, Wiz had made real progress, but Tom wasn't sure she saw it that way. And she still seemed sorrowful and rather...closed off, to him. Maybe that was what called to him. Maybe he wanted to take on the role of emotional savior, since he clearly couldn't help her with anything else. And that was a recipe for failure. She had to save herself. He could support her, but that might not be enough to build a real relationship.

Well, no matter what, he could be a friend. And if it never went further than friendship, that would be enough. Even virtual friendship was enough—he'd take whatever she could give.

Tom rolled to his feet. He'd done enough depressing introspection. Time to go to bed; the cows wouldn't feed themselves in the morning.

A week later, they were eating lunch after a long morning of hard work. Dad raised his spoon and nodded. "This is good. Where'd you learn to make this?"

"Found the recipe online. It is pretty good, isn't it?" Tom took another mouthful of delicious slow-cooker chicken and dumplings.

"Yeah, it is. Nice to have something other than beef sometimes."

"Blasphemy! I can't believe you said that!" They chuckled. "Maybe we can find someone to trade beef for pork or something. Different is good every now and then." Variety was the spice of life.

"I'll ask around. Trading is always better than buying, that's for sure."

They both ate; working in the cold took a lot of energy, and Tom was starving. Once he'd taken the edge off, his curiosity got the better of him. "Where have you been disappearing to in the afternoons?"

"I don't disappear every afternoon." He swallowed another spoonful.

"Didn't say you did. And if you don't want to tell me, that's your prerogative." He shrugged. "Tell me to mind my own business."

"I think you'll find out soon anyway, so I may as well just tell you." His face stretched in a wry smile.

"I've been teaching Wiz to ride."

Tom blinked, totally surprised. "You are?"

"Yup. Asked her if she wanted to learn, and she said yes." He smiled, a fond, proud smile. "But she isn't learning for herself. She wanted to learn so she could help us if we ever needed it."

Shocked surprise turned to hope, but it burned. "Even without the emotional trauma she's been through, I've got absolutely no hope. She's smart, pretty, knows how to think ahead and strategize, and she's giving and compassionate. I'm totally outclassed."

Dad laughed. "Oh, don't give up yet, son. She asks about you occasionally. And..." he gave him a mock glare, "it seems you've been holding out on me too. You've been playing video games online with her?"

"Yeah." His shoulders slumped. "And she's so far ahead of me on that it's surprising she agrees to play with me at all."

He chuckled. "She told me you saved her a couple of times."

"But she only needed help because she was running a totally innovative, out-of-the-box offensive, so I did defense. The woman is brilliant."

"I think she's played a lot more than you have." Dad frowned slightly.

"That's true, but still, she comes up with stuff I'd never dream of. She's legendary in a lot of the online forums. And when she signs on, almost everyone wants to be a part of her team. Doesn't matter what we're playing." Tom scowled. "The ones who don't are constantly pushing her, harassing her, trying to find out who she really is. Ticks me off, but there's nothing I can do about it. Either way, I'm tilting at windmills."

"Like I said, don't give up yet." Dad waggled his eyebrows. "I have a plan."

"Of course you do. Everybody's got a plan except me." He used to be the one with the plan, but since moving back home, the few plans he made fell apart.

"You'll just have to be patient." He sniffed.

"That I can do. One advantage of getting a little older, you do manage to get a little wiser. Or dead. And I'm not dead yet."

"Not even mostly dead." Dad used a terrible British accent.

Tom groaned and cleaned up the remnants of dinner. They had to go over the ranch's finances tonight, which probably meant he wouldn't get to play online. But maybe if they got started right away... Games with Wiz were the highlight of the day. A highlight he didn't want to miss.

Late that night, he logged off with a goodnight to Wiz, but she didn't answer. She'd been unusually determined, well, more like downright vicious against one of their opponents. Must be somebody she knew already, someone who'd attacked her in the game before. He'd never seen her that aggressive. He'd hung on as long as he could, but he had to get some sleep, or he'd fall off the tractor tomorrow. And staying alive in the real world was way more important than a video game. He hoped she remembered that too, but he wasn't too sure she would. But she'd just about killed off the character when he logged off, so maybe she would be off soon too.

He got up to brush his teeth, surprised at the time. Way too late. Tomorrow would be a bear. Sleep deprivation was easier at twenty, that was for sure. Pushing forty? He snorted at his own idiocy. Impossible. He yawned and turned out the lights. He hoped Wiz was okay. And if she wasn't, that she'd call him. But that wasn't horribly likely.

A phone was ringing. His phone. Tom picked up his cell, blinking at the time—3:13 am? Before dawn calls were usually bad news. "Hello?"

"Tom?" Wiz sounded plaintive.

"Yeah. Are you okay?"

"Yes. I just...I wanted to apologize for not saying goodnight to you. I was too wrapped up in the pursuit."

"That's okay. I figured as much. Who was that guy, anyway?" Tom yawned, then reconsidered. "Sorry, if you want to tell me. You don't have to." But there was something else going on—she wouldn't interrupt his sleep just to apologize. He sat up, hoping he'd wake up a little.

"No, I know. Thanks. But...that's my ex's character."

"Your ex? As in ex-husband?"

"Yes."

Anger roared through him, shockingly hot. He stood up to pace but controlled his impulse. She didn't need a jealous rant, especially when he wasn't entitled to such a thing at all. "I'm sorry. Tell me?" He deliberately softened his voice; he didn't want his crappy knee-jerk emotions impacting her.

"Marrying him was a mistake. A big one. He divorced me, so I made sure he didn't get anything he didn't earn. I hired the best lawyer in the state to make sure he couldn't claim alimony or anything else later because I *knew* I'd be successful." Anger and determination coursed through her voice.

"Good for you. Guy must be an idiot not to know what he had." He wanted to suggest a video call, but she was sharing, and he didn't want her to stop.

She chuckled. "You must be still asleep to say something like that."

"No." He yawned. "Well, yes. But I'd have said that anyway. Because it's true. I don't know how anyone could be around you for any length of time and not feel lucky." Maybe voice-only was good for both of them; he might not have said that to her face.

Silence rang on the line. Tom glanced at his phone—the call was still connected.

"That's nice of you to say."

He huffed. "I'm not being nice. I'm being truthful. You're smart, talented, brilliant, brave, and you have a huge heart. What's not to like?"

She snorted. "Oh, all my issues? Just maybe?"

Tom scoffed. "He was a dumbass. Marriage is for better or worse, sickness and health. If he didn't believe that, he had no business being married."

"I thought so, but he made it pretty hard to believe after a while. None of our vows meant anything to him."

"You mean he cheated on you?" Truly an idiot. Tom

couldn't imagine inflicting more hurt on Wiz. Or cheating, period. Even if he'd been stupid enough to marry Evon, he'd never cheat—it was the worst sort of betrayal.

"Yeah. He did." She almost whispered.

She'd better not be blaming herself. "Like I said, a dumbass. Anyone dumb enough to not see what a wonderful person you are doesn't deserve you. You deserve much, much better."

Wiz sighed. "We were too young."

"If it was just that, you wouldn't be so pissed off at him. Just for the record, he deserves your anger."

"Maybe. No, you're right. I'd put up with so much from him. Every time I came back or he came back from a deployment, I forgave him. But after this last one, well, he couldn't do the same."

No way she'd cheated on him; she was as loyal as they came. "I truly doubt you needed forgiveness."

"I did, but not in the same way. Or for the same reason."

She thought being sexually assaulted was equivalent to cheating? No way. Maybe her ex said it was. Dirtbag. Fury ripped through him like a wildfire, and Tom's fingers ached from the grip he had on his phone and comforter, but he kept his tone soft. "You don't have to tell me."

"I don't think I can. Not yet. Maybe not ever."

"I can guess that you told him, and he couldn't handle it, and he just left, right?" His free hand strangled the covers.

"Yes. He left me to deal with it by myself, after

everything I'd done for him and put up with from him. I still can't believe how selfish he was or how much I still hate him for abandoning me like that. Just when I needed him the most." A sniffle, then she sobbed.

Helplessness ripped away his anger. If only he was with her. He could hold her, or her hands, or offer some other form of comfort. Although, considering her skittishness, physical expression might not be welcome. Words weren't his best tool, but it was all he had, so he'd have to do his best. "He's not worth your tears. He's a fool and an idiot. And it may not have felt like it then, but you're better off without him. He's a loser. I don't understand how anyone could ever abandon you, never mind during a crisis. The guy is slime."

She sniffled. "Sorry. Wait a sec." She blew her nose. He smiled; maybe he said the right thing after all, or she recovered on her own. That seemed more likely. Wiz was smart. "Sorry. I don't do that usually."

"No. Don't be sorry. I'm happy to listen. I wish I could do more." His free hand extended across his bed, reaching for her, so far away. He wanted to hold her, to comfort her, so badly his chest ached.

"Thanks."

"Of course. Anytime." He couldn't hold her, so he'd get her focused on the positive—her success. "Did you kill him off?" It was a rhetorical question—he had no doubt she'd triumphed.

She laughed. "Yeah. I got him. He's going to have to rebuild from level one. Hah! Take that, you jerk!"

He joined her laughter, thrilled not at her words,

but at the joy in her voice, crowing victory. "I wish I'd seen it. I should have stayed online."

"No, no, you were smart. It took me longer than I thought it would, and it's really late. Oh. Oh no. I'm so sorry, I didn't realize how late it is. Or early."

He chuckled. "Don't worry about it. I'm happy to talk to you whenever." That was absolutely true.

"Yes, but you have a job to do; you have to be alert. I don't want you to get hurt because you're listening to me whine."

"You're not whining. And you needed somebody to talk to. That's me. And we have ranch hands for a reason. I help with the work, but I don't necessarily have to, unless someone's sick. You can call me any time. Really."

"Thanks. I feel better."

"Good. Wiz, none of this was your fault. None of it." He'd have to say those words until she believed them.

"I, uh, should let you get some sleep."

He'd pushed too hard. "If you're all talked out."

"I am. Thanks."

"You're welcome, anytime."

"Okay," she whispered. The call clicked off.

Tom slid down in his bed, smiling.

She'd called him.

Chapter 10

Hah. Got him. In more ways than one. Wiz did a celebratory war dance. And she'd talked about her ex and her emotions to someone other than her therapist. A man. A physically large male she didn't truly know or trust. But she had faith in him, or she wouldn't have called. She hadn't called her other friends, not even Ryan or Erin.

She closed out her games and did her nightly security rounds. Returning to her master suite, she locked all the doors, double-checked the security system, and got ready for bed. By the time she washed her face, she was exhausted. Too many emotions in too short a time.

And yet, she kind of wanted more.

She'd called Tom and told him things she'd only told her therapists. She'd almost blurted out the whole story. And she'd wished he was present, holding her, hugging her. Which was horribly unfair. She wanted a hug when she cried, but not at any other time. She shivered at the thought of male arms around her body. The dream of Tom holding her was better than the reality.

Tom couldn't be that different from her ex. He was a

man, after all. He wouldn't put up with her issues for very long. He'd get tired of it and leave. They all did. She couldn't rely on him. Sure, he knew she had problems and claimed she could call anytime. But he didn't know what he was getting into, not fully. And she highly doubted he'd be satisfied with a platonic relationship forever. She shuddered.

Wiz checked the pistols on the nightstands and the others stashed around the room. She climbed into bed and curled around her pillow, leaving the light covers loose. She couldn't stand anything holding her down. But the bed felt empty. Usually, she was beyond relieved to sleep alone. No one else to worry about, no one else's needs to put ahead of her own, over and over. No reason to wake up in a cold sweat because she'd dreamed that the hands on her body belonged to a stranger. Even when her ex had been supportive, she couldn't sleep next to him; she'd wake up screaming at a single touch. It hadn't been long before he'd demanded she "get over it." She'd tried, so hard, but once he touched her, she recoiled, and he got angry.

He'd always been selfish, and he'd gotten worse after she didn't recover immediately. In an unusually harsh condemnation, even her doctor said the guy wasn't worth any tears. But would she ever be different? Time healed wounds. But emotional wounds were hard. They couldn't be fixed with stitches. She was getting better; all the support helped, along with therapy. Pete, Ryan, and Erin, even Sam and Deb, they all helped. And Tom.

But she couldn't believe they'd stay. Everyone gave

up eventually.

It didn't matter. She had too much to do tomorrow—she needed sleep. She recalled her last lesson with Pete, riding bareback. The movement of the horse was soothing, the warmth comforting, and controlling such a large animal was satisfying. She drifted off with a smile.

The next afternoon, Wiz brought the horse to a halt in front of Pete, using her body properly, not the reins. Dust glimmered in the bright winter sun shining through the open door of the arena, the smell of horse and dung rising but not unpleasant.

Pete tipped his hat back. "You're doing good. I think it's time to move outside."

"Really? On the snow and ice?" That seemed unnecessarily risky, especially when she'd only ridden under controlled circumstances. Even when Pete had put out obstacles, or waved something to make Brownie shy, they could only go so far because of the arena walls. Brownie was a well-trained, steady, older horse, but Wiz had landed on the dirt a couple of times. She hadn't hit her head yet, but Pete's insistence on a riding helmet had proven wise. It would be doubly so on ice.

He shook his head. "We'll stay off the road. It's too icy. But we can ride around one of the pastures where the cows and feeding have packed the snow or pushed it away. These are stock horses; they're used to being around cows in the winter."

"Okay. When?"

"No time like the present." Pete untied his horse

and mounted. She'd never look that natural. Of course, Pete's legs were much longer than hers; she had to use a mounting block or a fence rail. He turned his horse back toward her. Rusty bounded up from his spot near to the arena gate, tail wagging. "And how would you feel about Tom joining us?"

She jolted, and the horse jumped, but she quickly got him under control.

"Sorry, I didn't mean to startle you." His frown reflected his unease.

"That's okay. It shouldn't have." A horse reflected every emotion and movement; the rider had to control both.

"Sure it should have. It's a big step. I should have asked when you were off the horse." Pete shrugged. "If it's too soon, that's fine, but I know he's riding Strawberry this afternoon. Trying to teach the horse some manners." He snorted.

"Oh. So this wasn't planned?"

Pete's smile turned sly. "Well, it was by me, but no, Tom had no idea."

She smiled. He was tricky. Somehow, her twice a week riding lessons had turned into three or four days each week, claiming she needed an intense course in horse psychology first, then horse care, and only after that, riding. Grooming and cleaning tack was soothing but not terribly difficult, so they talked a lot; she'd told him more about her past than anybody else. He'd opened up about his past, too—a mutual venting-slash-healing society. But she wasn't sure if she was ready to add Tom. She hadn't seen him since her late-night confession. The horse sidled under her, and she controlled both of them again.

Pete's mouth twisted. "Nah, it's too soon."

"No, it's okay." She didn't have to talk. She'd be concentrating on riding. "Call him."

"Okay." Pete pulled his phone. "Hey, you still got Strawberry saddled? Good. Why don't you come across the road? Wiz is ready for her first ride out of the arena. Uh huh. Yep. Good." He slid the phone back into his coat pocket. "He'll be here in a few." Pete held up a finger. "Now, the only thing different about riding out there is staying alert. You can't drift off into a trance. You have to be looking for things that will injure or startle a horse. Big holes in the path, downed trees, deer running, dogs that don't know horses, and people. Or a branch or tumbleweed. Or a plastic shopping bag—those things are the worst. Any little thing can startle a horse. Or nothing. You have to be ready for that, or you end up walking." Pete chuckled. "Or not walking, if you're dumb enough to ride in city boots." He raised his voice.

Tom stopped Strawberry near the arena gate. "Thanks, Dad. Appreciate you reminding me. Again." Tom's low voice rumbled with self-depreciating amusement. He looked so natural sitting on a horse. Big, confident, with an easy smile and his eyes slightly wrinkled from the sun. Unlike Pete, he wore a fleece beanie, not a cowboy hat, but a similar tan jacket and jeans. He sidled his horse next to the gate and opened it.

On her horse, she could meet his gaze. Almost an

equal in physical power, it gave her the confidence to face him. Although her late-night phone call still made embarrassment burn through her. Good thing her skin was dark and the cold already pinked her cheeks.

"Sure, son. Anytime." Pete winked at Wiz, then turned his horse and walked across the paddock. Rusty ran ahead, nose to the ground, turning back to Pete every fifty feet.

Wiz lifted the reins and squeezed her thighs, and Brownie plodded ahead, following. Tom rode up beside her on Strawberry. From her sidling and shifting, she wasn't very happy. Tom didn't seem to have any trouble controlling her or keeping his seat. Brownie ignored the fractious mare. Wiz wanted to watch Tom but paid attention to her horse and the path.

They rode in silence for a while, along the pasture fence, crunching through the snow. Strawberry eventually settled down, seemingly resigned to her fate. Wiz relaxed into the slow walk, enjoying the sun on her face, the brisk breeze, and the crisp scent of snow.

"You look pretty good up there for a newbie." Tom patted Strawberry's neck.

"Thanks. Your dad is an excellent teacher."

"He's had lots of practice. Taught me, my brother and sister, their kids when they come out, the neighbor kids, just about anybody. I think it's one of his favorite things to do."

"Lucky me." She was extremely fortunate to have so much help.

Pete circled back, bringing his horse on Brownie's other side. "You're not too cold, are you? I know you didn't plan for the outside."

"No, I'm fine. It's a nice day, and the sun is warm." She always wore gloves, and the arena was often colder than outside, since the sun was too weak in the winter to heat it.

"Oh, so I'm not the only one who wasn't told about this outing?" Tom chuckled.

"Nope." Pete smiled. "I didn't plan it, but I figured you needed to get Strawberry there out with other horses, and Wiz was ready."

Tom raised his brows. "Uh huh. Pull the other one, Dad."

Pete grinned. "It wasn't planned until you told me you were going to ride Strawberry. She does need the work, or we'll never get rid of her."

"You're going to get rid of her?" Wiz was shocked; she didn't think Pete would ditch a horse.

Pete slashed his hand through the air. "Oh, not that way." He frowned. "You should know I'd never do that."

Wiz swallowed hard. She knew better. "Sorry."

Pete kept talking. "We'll find a kid who needs a horse for 4H or show. Strawberry needs some manners first, though, and she'll never be a good beginner horse. But she's perfect for somebody who has progressed and is serious about riding, someone who wants to work with horses. She'll teach the right person some good lessons about control. Probably a girl, with the coloring. No boy is going to want a pretty palomino."

"Maybe. Might find the right boy." Tom shrugged.

Pete snorted. "Not who will admit it around here. Still too backwards sometimes."

"Maybe, maybe not. Anyway, we'll have to talk to the folks who work with kids."

"Yep."

They rode in silence again, turning to cross the back end of the field. Strawberry tried to shy at the fence, but Tom wasn't having any of it.

Pete pulled his hat down. "The family I got her from, well, the girl had gotten her to show in the ring, and they'd bought her just for looks. They didn't know anything about horses. So, she's been spoiled and lazy because she really couldn't be ridden safely. Then the family had to move, and they couldn't find anyone to buy her, so I ended up with her. But she's too nervy to be a good cow horse." Pete chuckled. "By the time we get done, she'll be grateful to be ridden by some kid half of Tom's weight."

They turned back toward the arena. A small herd of deer looked up as they approached and leapt over the fence, bounding away. Rusty chased them for a hundred yards, then ran back. Brownie just snorted, and even Strawberry stopped only momentarily.

"Now, you see what Tom did there? He saw the deer and knew Strawberry would try to shy, so he tightened up a bit to let her know ahead of time that she wasn't going to get away with it." Pete nodded firmly. "Proactive. That's how you have to ride."

They neared the arena. Pete pointed. "Wiz, did you leave anything in there?"

"No." She hadn't brought anything except what she wore.

"Good, let's ride over to our place."

"Okay." They'd always walked the horses back to the barn.

Pete led the way, opening the gates, and Tom closed them behind her. Having him back there, out of sight, didn't bother her because he had to pay attention to his horse and work the gates. The ice on the driveways and road was a little nerve-racking, but Wiz remained calm, conveying confidence to Brownie, and she walked across without any issues.

They trod past the ranch house and dismounted in front of the big red horse barn. Pete tied his horse next to Brownie, but Tom used the hitching post on the other side of the barn door. She pulled Brownie's tack, put it in the tack room, and curried the horse, checking his hooves and legs for any rocks, cuts, or bruises.

Tom led Strawberry to Brownie's far side. "He's okay?"

"Seems to be." Being on the ground, looking up at Tom, was a little unnerving, but having Brownie's bulk between them helped.

"Good. I got him." Tom unwrapped both lead ropes from the hitch and led all three horses away to the corral, where he opened the gate and led them inside. Tom unhooked the leads but kept walking to the other side of the corral, checking on the water trough.

Pete leaned against the hitching post. "How do you think that went?"

Wiz smiled. "Pretty good. It was fun. Thanks." She'd

been getting bored, going in circles. Outside was much better.

Pete smiled back. "Good. Now, from here on out, I'd like you to come over here, and we'll get the horses and tack them up together. Then we'll ride, either to the arena or somewhere else. Sound okay?" Before she could say anything, he continued, "Don't worry. Just like usual, the ranch hands will be gone for the day. It will just be me and maybe Tom. If someone else is here, just go back home or into our house."

She thought about his proposal. She'd never been inside his house. "Okay. I guess I can do that."

"Now, do you want to come in for some hot chocolate, or have you had enough?" Pete raised his brows.

She bit her lip, trying to decide. A strange place with two big men. She held back a shudder; she could trust both of them. "I'll come. Thanks." She swallowed. "I might not stay."

"No problem. Whatever makes you comfortable." He turned toward the ranch house. "Watch your step— it's a little icy."

She followed Pete inside, Rusty charging ahead. They stepped into a too-small entryway; coats and hats hung on both sides, with boots on the floor below. And a shotgun and a couple of rifles on a rack above the coats. The shotgun was a Remington 870, and the rifles looked like a .22 and 30-06, which made sense for a rancher. She wondered if they were loaded. Probably.

"You can leave your boots on. In the spring, we'll be taking them off, but right now is fine, especially with

Rusty tracking dirt in. You can give me your coat." Pete hung hers over his.

He opened the door and led her into the kitchen. An open door at the end led to a living room with a couch and two recliners. In the kitchen, pale wood cabinets hung above worn Formica countertops with a big stainless steel sink in the middle. Ruffled floral curtains were pulled back from a window above the sink looking out to the driveway. A worn, dark wood dining table with six chairs sat below a bigger window overlooking the barn. A rich beefy scent made her mouth water and a crockpot bubbled on the counter.

"Have a seat if you want, and I'll put some water on. It's just instant, but it's still good." He filled an old-fashioned kettle. "Unless you'd rather have coffee?"

"No, hot chocolate is perfect." She sat at the far end of the table, where she could see the whole kitchen and both doors. Her leg jittered, betraying her nerves at being in a strange house with the bare minimum of weapons, but she'd quickly learned that riding with a pistol strapped to your thigh was not comfortable. She'd downsized to a concealed carry 9mm in a holster at the small of her back and a single knife in a boot sheath.

Pete pulled coffee mugs from a cabinet. "If you'd like to see the rest of the house, you can look around, or I can get Tom to show you when he comes in. Bathroom right around the corner if you need it."

"That's okay. I'm all right here." She knew there was a front door out of the living room, but the upstairs would have bedrooms, and she didn't want to be anywhere near those.

Pete nodded and scooped powdered chocolate. "I've kept you a little longer than I normally would. Do you need to check anything? You can use Tom's computer, if you want."

"That's okay. I don't have anything scheduled." Like usual, she'd stay up late tonight. And she had her phone if she had to get something done.

"Good. Because I don't know his password."

"I do." At her urging, he'd changed most of his passwords but gave her access to his home network, so she could secure it. She should check on Pete's accounts, too.

Pete chuckled and shook his head. "Of course you do."

She'd ease into the idea; in her experience, many older men and women didn't understand the necessity for cyber security. "He told you that I helped him secure your ranch network, right?" A door opening in the entryway signaled Tom's return.

"Yep, he told me. And made me set passwords on everything, which is a hassle, but I get the idea." He turned and leaned against the counter. "Never thought the day would come when I'd have to worry about that way out here."

"You probably don't have to, most of the time. But it's a good habit, and it makes you a harder target. Just like having a dog makes you a harder target physically than the people down the street who don't have one."

The door opened, and even knowing it was Tom, she got up, ready to run or fight. Tom closed the door behind him and blew on his hands. "Brr. The wind picked up a bit."

"Good timing, chocolate's done." Pete picked up two mugs, setting one down in front of her, then he sat down on the opposite side of the table. Tom got his and sat next to his dad. They were both careful to leave her a clear path to the door, so she sat and sipped her cocoa.

Pete put his cup down. "I know it's cold and snowy, but I'm planning for the summer. Wiz, every year, we take a least one trip into the backcountry. And it's been a couple of years, but we used to go out during hunting season too. You're more than welcome to join us, if you can take a week off." Pete raised his cup to her, then took a sip.

"Really? You think I'll be good enough?"

Pete and Tom both laughed, glancing at each other. Pete waved his hand over the table. "We take newbies out, like the grandkids. You'll be more than good enough. You'll be helpful."

"There will be other people too?" She'd have to know who they were and check them all.

Pete shrugged. "Maybe. It depends on everybody's schedule. Last year, Marie and her family didn't make it out here at all, and Alex and his family couldn't come for a whole trip. Alex's kids are a little young for a big trip anyway. They're all pretty busy with their own lives."

Tom put his cup down. "Marie and her husband live in Seattle. They've got two teenagers, and Alex and his family are in LA. They'd love to come out here more, but it's hard when you've got a family and two careers to manage."

She'd so often wondered what it would be like to have family, people who truly loved her.

Pete must have read her mind because he asked, "Do you have brothers or sisters, Wiz?"

"Not that I know of. I was raised by my grandma until she passed away when I was five, then I was in the foster system. My mother is in prison for selling drugs. I don't have anything to do with her. I have no idea who my father is. I went in the Air Force as soon as I could to get out of the system." So many families she'd lived with who only saw dollar signs. At least she hadn't been abused, only emotionally neglected. Which was why she'd married her ex.

"I'm sorry. That sucks." Tom's eyes looked a little bright, and he swallowed hard.

"Well, you've got us. You're a part of our family." Pete jabbed a finger at her. Tom nodded, with a smile. Pete gave her a sly grin. She'd learned that smile meant he was up to something; usually something that he thought would be good for her. "Since you're family, why don't you join us for dinner? It's in the crockpot there, and there's plenty."

Wiz chuckled. "You really are a tricky one. If I didn't know better, I'd think you'd been talking to my therapist."

Tom's brows rose. "You have one?"

She'd be insulted by his surprise, but she knew how weird she was. "Yeah. We talk online at least once a week."

"Good. Too many people don't."

"I have no intention of becoming a statistic." She'd been too intent on revenge and anger to give into depression early on, and by time she had started feeling depressed, she'd already started therapy. She'd been fortunate to find a great team of therapists, too.

"Living well is the best revenge." Pete raised his cup to her.

"Oh, other types of revenge are pretty good." She clenched her cup, the anger that was never far away raging through her.

"Tom, why don't you heat some rolls? They're in the freezer." Pete tilted his head toward the door. Tom nodded, stood, and rooted in the bottom of the ancient refrigerator/freezer, the rustle of frozen plastic loud. "Be careful with the revenge. All too often, the anger hurts you worse than the other guy." Pete spoke softly.

She leaned forward to hear him, but the words fanned the fire of her anger. "That's easy to say but hard to live. I know who at least some of the bad guys are, and I'm not their only victim. And I'm not the only one who got ignored by their chain of command. If I hadn't acted, or my friends hadn't, nothing would have happened. There would have been nothing, absolutely nothing, keeping it from happening again and again." Her hands ached around her mug, longing to form around a rifle. They deserved to die, not the petty revenge she'd enacted.

"But they've gotten their comeuppance, right? And the system has changed?"

"Some. Not anywhere close to what they deserved.

And the system has changed, but not nearly enough. So-called leaders in the military continue to ignore the issue." She sneered. "They think it only happens to women and the weak, so they don't care."

"They're wrong. You know that. And some of them do care. I heard that the number of people reporting sexual assault has risen from one in ten to one in four. That's good progress."

"It should be one to one. And it shouldn't happen at all!"

Pete held up his hand. "No, you're right, it shouldn't happen at all, and if it does, the system ought to punish the criminals immediately and harshly. But it is changing, and it's changing for the better. Just like racial integration during my time, it will happen, if slower than we want, and there will be issues and problems because people are humans. And there's always some who feel they're entitled to more. It's not good, but it's true."

"Yes. It's true. But that doesn't mean it's okay."

Pete shook his head. "Didn't say it was. We have to keep pushing." He gave her a warning look. "But inside the system, not as some sort of vigilante justice. That kind of thing will hurt you worse because, in the end, it makes you just as bad as the bad guy. And it makes you feel worse than that guy ever will. You can't change him."

"Maybe. I felt pretty good about a lot of things I did." Wiz read her emotions, like the therapists taught. "Matter of fact, I don't regret any of it. But... I'm not going to continue to go after them. That's one of the reasons I moved. I had to get away from the military and the constant barrage of bad news." She put her cup down with a thump. "But if any of them come after me, they're going to end up dead. And I won't lose a minute of sleep over it."

Pete's lips clamped for a moment. "You may think that, but killing someone...that's forever. Even in self-defense, it's not something you can do without consequences. I still have nightmares." He looked away.

Wiz opened her mouth, but Tom set bowls of beef stew in front of her and Pete. Her stomach rumbled.

"We'll discuss this again, count on it." He thumped the table with his forefinger. "But it will be later. I'm starving." Pete chuckled and picked up his spoon.

Tom returned with another bowl and a basket of rolls. "Water?"

Pete nodded. "That would be good, thanks. Wiz?"

"Yes, please. I can get it." She breathed in and out steadily, letting her rumbling tummy take over from the anger.

"Nope, I'm already up." Tom brought glasses for the three of them, then he sat down. They both bowed their heads, evidently in a silent prayer of thanksgiving.

She did the same. She wasn't religious, but thankfulness was a good trait to cultivate. She spooned up stew. "Wow, this is really good."

"Yep, we're masters of the crockpot. We cook everything in that thing." Pete jabbed his thumb over his shoulder.

"Winter, summer, doesn't matter. It's always good to come in off a long day of working to a hot meal."

"But I still miss Elise's cooking." Pete sighed.

"Yeah, Mom was an awesome cook. And her menu was a good bit bigger than ours."

"Fried chicken, chicken-fried steak, homemade bread, lasagna, mmm." Both men looked wistful.

"I can make lasagna. It's not hard." Wiz took another spoonful.

"Really? You cook?" Tom seemed surprised.

Staying healthy was important, so she had to cook. And she didn't go to restaurants, and delivery wasn't available so far from town, so if she wanted a particular dish, she made it. "Not a lot, but there's some things I know. Lasagna's one of them. And pizza. I use Erin's recipe. I eat a lot of salads."

Tom pushed the basket to her. "The rolls are Deb's. They're almost as good as Mom's."

"Pretty near." Pete took a bite of his.

She'd received so much from them already, a dinner was nothing. "I'll make lasagna next week. I can bring it down and put it in the oven while we ride."

"We'll give you ground beef. We have lots and never enough recipes to use it all in. Rusty there, he never eats dog food, just beef." Rusty's tail thumped on the floor and Pete grinned.

She scraped the bowl, eating the last bite. But the room closed in, and sweat rolled down her back. Wiz jumped up, her chair scraping across the worn linoleum. "Okay. I should get going, I have work today."

"Sure, Wiz." Pete smiled fondly at her. "And since you're family, you can just come on in anytime. The door is never locked unless we're gone for a few days. Don't even knock."

She'd never be able to say the same. "Thanks. And thanks for dinner."

"Sure. Come by anytime." Pete raised his glass.

She took her dishes to the sink and almost turned to leave, but she couldn't, even with both men sitting at the table with their backs to her. She walked sideways to the door, opened it, and put on her coat. At the exterior door, she surveyed, but no people were evident. Closing the door behind her, she trotted down the steps and strode up the road toward her house, turning to look at the road behind her until she reached the outer gate.

Entering the gates and her front door, she contrasted her show-ready secure house and the Borde home. And that was the difference. They had a home, while she had a house. She sighed and plodded upstairs to work.

Chapter 11

TOM

"Well, that went well." Dad nodded, obviously proud of himself.

He should be. "Way better than I expected. She actually seemed fairly relaxed." Tom rinsed dishes and put them in the dishwasher.

"Yes, and even though I offered, she didn't search the entire house, just looked around the kitchen carefully and sat down. Didn't even ask if the long guns were loaded."

Tom snorted. "I'm sure she assumed they were."

"First rule of firearms, always assume they're loaded. And I'm sure she knows ranchers have to deal with things that require weapons." His mouth twisted for a moment. "I'll be sure to tell her we'll both be carrying in the backcountry."

"She knows. I had a rifle that day she found me." And she'd promptly confiscated it, rather than unloading it and replacing it in the holster.

They settled in the living room. Their place was awfully shabby next to Wiz's, but it was comfortable.

"You know, I told her that riding was good therapy, and I think she's coming to agree with that." Dad nodded thoughtfully as he gazed into nothing.

Tom agreed, too. "I imagine it helps that we're at eye level on a horse. She asked me not to loom over her, which is kind of hard to do when I'm six four and she's all of, what, five two maybe?"

Dad squinted at him. "Maybe a little taller, but not by much. She is a tiny thing but very strong."

"Ryan said she did some sort of martial arts. And the gym in her basement is certainly not there to hold clothes and gather dust." One more thing he missed — his gym in the city.

"I wonder how she does martial arts all by herself?" Dad asked.

Good question. "Video? There were punching bags and stuff down there. Maybe she's got an instructor who works online with her, like her therapist."

Dad's brows raised. "I'm just glad she's talking to a professional."

"Yeah, I'm kind of surprised. But she's a smart woman. She'd know she couldn't do it all on her own."

Dad nodded but didn't say anything else.

Tom waited, but obviously, Dad wasn't going to bring it up, but he really wanted to know. "Was Wiz right? You were a scout-sniper?"

Dad sighed. "I asked around, and I guess they have declassified a good bit of stuff. Shoot, A Troop got a Presidential Unit citation in 2009 for a rescue mission they did back in 1970. And more guys just decided to talk, and the heck with the system. After all, they did us no favors. From the very top on down." Dad glanced at him. "So I guess I can talk about it. Don't usually like to."

Tom just nodded. He wouldn't force the issue.

He slapped his palms on his thighs. "Well, you're an adult, guess you deserve to know. I started out a plain old infantry grunt, but I was a real good shot, from hunting. So they gave me some special training. I wasn't a true sniper like Carlos Hathcock or anything. And then there was a typical Army screw-up; I was assigned to the 1st Squadron, 11th Armored Cavalry, the Blackhorse, and we operated out in Cambodia a lot. We weren't supposed to be there, but there we were. As a sniper, I really shouldn't have been assigned to Armored Cav, but my commander at least had a clue as to how to employ me properly. We got in some bad situations, and I killed a lot of people." Dad held up a hand, to stop the protest Tom wasn't going to make. "Sure, they were gonna kill us if we didn't kill them, but it's not easy. It's even harder to live with in the long run."

Tom couldn't imagine. He'd shot animals but never came close to a person. "Maybe *you* should talk to somebody. The Veterans Administration's got good programs now, you know. Not like the old days."

"So Wiz tells me. Nah, the Vietnam vet's group I belong to, we talk about this stuff now. Used to be we'd all just bull through it, especially since we weren't exactly appreciated when we got home. Glad the guys and gals coming home now get some respect."

"Still, a professional could help."

"I'll talk to my doc next time I go."

"Sure, Dad." He probably wouldn't, but Tom couldn't push any harder. "Thanks for telling me a little about it. I really didn't want to be one of those people who found a trunk years later with all the patches and medals and not have a clue how you got them all or what you did."

He shook his head. "Don't have a trunk anymore. Got a few patches. The medals are all in the shadow box in the hall."

"Someday you'll have to tell me what they were for, and don't give me a bunch of crap about 'perfect attendance' and 'penmanship."

Dad snorted. "Sure. Maybe I'll even write it down. Sometimes that's easier than talking."

"That would be good. You can borrow my tablet; you can hand-write on it. If you like it, I'll get you one for Christmas."

Dad frowned. "Hey, what are we doing for Christmas anyway? Got to make sure we take care of Wiz."

Tom grimaced. "Oh, boy. What do you get for the girl who doesn't need anything and can buy anything she wants?"

"Don't think she'd care about traditional presents. I was thinking more about Christmas itself. I figure we'll go to the vigil Mass like usual, have brunch the next day. We can invite her down for that, even if she's not interested in church."

"She might not be able to handle being in a church. Too many people, strange place, all that." He didn't know if she was religious; he longed to know more about her thoughts and feelings.

"True. Well, we can ask, anyway." Dad shrugged.

"Sure. Worst she can do is say no. I wonder if Erin and Ryan have anything planned?"

"You thinking a big group of people without other family?" He raised a brow.

"Yep. I can't imagine Erin is going to spend any time with her mother." Dad echoed his shudder. "Sam's family is here, but I think they get on her nerves after a while, and Deb's the same. Might be others. How about Christmas dinner or maybe day after, so they can get away from the comfort and joy for a bit?" Tom chuckled.

"Maybe we ask Wiz to host. Her place is a lot better for something like that."

Tom pointed at Dad. "You ask. She'll do it for you."

"You don't think she'd do that for you?"

He shrugged one shoulder. "Maybe she would, but I think it would be better if you asked."

"Sure, I'll ask her next time we go ridin'. Now, what are we gonna get her?" Dad's quizzical look made him laugh.

"I have no earthly idea, but we'll think of something." Tom prayed for divine intervention because that's what it would take.

"Yup, we'll think of something."

On Christmas Eve, Tom's hands flexed on the steering wheel and his dress shirt dampened. Nerves were bad because, just like a horse, Wiz was likely to pick it up and echo it back, and she was surely nervous enough already. As her gates opened, he let the Volvo roll through. He pulled under the portico and got out of the car. Wiz walked out the front door.

"Hello, Tom." She nodded. She wore a long, dark trench coat but no hat. And while her hair was still in a braid, she'd actually left it down and a little loose, rather than snugged tight against her head so no one could grab it.

He'd love to undo that braid and run his fingers through her thick, heavy hair. *Come on, idiot, get it together. Treat her like the little sister she isn't.* "Merry Christmas. Are you ready?"

"Yes." She walked to the back door of the car, which he opened for her. As she got in, black clothing flashed, but the pants and boots looked more fashionable than functional. Surprising. She exchanged greetings with Dad.

He got back in the driver's seat, and drove up the long drive, the gates opening and closing behind him. "I still can't believe you can do all that on your phone. What if your battery goes dead?"

"There's a panel by each gate. That's what I use when I'm on foot."

"And what if the power goes out?" Dad turned slightly toward her.

"Didn't I show you the battery banks and generator?"

"No, or if you did, I was too overwhelmed to remember them."

"Oh, I have solar and wind power and an automatic backup generator."

"Of course you do. The solar's on the roof?"

"Yes, south side of the second and third floor. They supply most of my electric needs in the summer. I have to supplement from the grid in the winter. I could design a system for your place if you'd like."

Dad laughed. "Oh, maybe sometime in the future. When I have to replace the roof."

"Sure, Pete. Just let me know. Although, we'd have to have someone check and make sure your house could support the load."

Dad scoffed. "Oh, that wouldn't be a problem. You should see the beams they used back then. Tom can take you down to the cellar next time you're over."

"We could put the system on the barn instead. That way you wouldn't have solar panels all over your house."

Tom nodded. "Good idea. Although I'm not sure the barn is oriented for that." The roof was placed to provide the least resistance to the constant winds.

"Not ideally, but it could be done. We could also mount them on the ground."

Dad shook his head. "I don't think that would be a good idea. Too many animals to crash into them. Or use them as scratching posts."

"Excellent point."

Tom drove, content listening to his dad and Wiz argue about the merits of solar and wind power. Her mere presence made him happy. Which was different from every other relationship he'd ever had. He wanted more—a full relationship. But his needs and desires simply weren't important next to her comfort and happiness. A year ago, he'd have never believed he'd be living in an old-fashioned romantic movie relationship, all glances and mild flirting. But he was happy, if hoping for more someday.

He pulled into the back lot of the church, parking so they could leave easily. Knowing it would be a little crowded, they'd come early, so they could get seats in the very back, where Wiz would feel safer. They got out of the car, Wiz not waiting for him to open the door, and sauntered to the front of the church. Wiz walked between the two of them but about a half step behind, her head turning from side to side, inspecting the beautiful but aging Queen Anne-Cape Cod style church, the pastoral center next door, and the others joining them. Tom opened the front door for her and she entered, immediately turning left to the old choir loft door. She must have checked the church out online. No one was supposed to use the loft—it was a fire trap—but he doubted anyone would confront them. Even though there wasn't a second exit from the loft, in an emergency, they were all in good enough shape to escape using the columns holding it up or going through a window to the outside.

Tom smiled and gestured for Dad to go ahead. Wiz would feel better with his dad at her back. But she stopped and motioned Tom to go first, then stepped in behind him, leaving Dad to follow.

They climbed the narrow circular stair and walked to the back row of the four small pews in the choir loft, where the three of them took up the entire pew on the left side. There was a matching set of short pews on the other side of a narrow isle. Wiz inspected the ornate gold and white interior, decorated in red, green, and more gold. Tom did too, but probably not for the same reasons.

"The decorations are beautiful," Dad murmured. "They always do such a great job. Of course, it's gilding the lily. They really knew how to build back in the 1880s."

"Yes, they did. And I'm sure the music will be spectacular as usual." Tom smiled.

"Really?" Wiz asked.

"Oh, yes." Dad nodded. "We have a lot of talent in this little town. The choir is very good, and they've been practicing for months."

The musicians crowded onto benches at the front. Craig—Ryan's former coworker—popped around the corner. Wiz jumped, then relaxed. Craig walked toward them.

"Merry Christmas, Craig." Dad offered his hand. "Your wife's singing in the choir?"

Craig nodded. "She sure is. Merry Christmas, all. I see you've taken my favorite place." He winked.

"Merry Christmas. You watch my six, I'll watch yours," Wiz said.

"Deal. I'll sit for now, but I'll probably end up standing. It's always crowded." He sat.

The pews below filled, and the choir started singing. As usual, it was very good.

During a short break between songs, Craig leaned over and whispered to Wiz, who shook her head then giggled. Tom shared a startled glance with his dad, then they both grinned. That little giggle was a huge Christmas present.

People trickled in, and they pulled off coats, warm

air rising from the crowd. Wiz wore a surprisingly
snug fuzzy sweater in swirls and shades of gray with
black slacks. Tom forced his gaze from her, but he
wouldn't be forgetting her beautifully athletic form
any time soon. She always wore baggy clothes covering
every inch of skin.

The opening song announcement startled Tom, but
he stood with the rest. He didn't have a great voice, but
he could stay on key, so he sang along with Dad. Wiz
joined in on the second verse. She was on pitch, with a
high, slightly breathy soprano. Surprising, since her
speaking voice was fairly low. He exchanged smiling
glances with Dad.

He let the familiar cadences of the Catholic Mass
wash over him. Luckily, no one else had joined them in
the loft, so Wiz and Craig seemed comfortable. During
the final song, Tom was surprised again at Wiz's pretty
voice. He was almost shocked when she leaned against
his arm; the first physical contact they'd had since she'd
wrapped his ankle. He was sure the whole
congregation could hear the smile in his voice as he
sang *Joy to the World* because his heart sang too, his
whole body warmed by the small touch.

They waited until almost everyone left, then trod
down the stairs, offering greetings to the few
parishioners they saw. Tom and Dad bracketed Wiz as
they returned to his car. He opened the doors, and Wiz
went for the back seat. She'd made real progress, but
not enough that Dad could sit behind her. Well, baby
steps.

As they cruised through the silent streets of Marcus,

Dad turned toward her. "What did you think?"

"It is a very pretty church, and the choir is very good. Craig was right, though. You've got an awful lot of aerobics for church."

Tom and his dad both laughed at the old joke. "It's true, there's a lot of up and down. But it's all got roots, so it's not going away anytime soon. Besides, that way your rear doesn't go numb on those hard wood seats."

"That's a good point. But it didn't last as long as some religious services I've been to."

"Are you a member of any particular religion?" Tom glanced in the rear-view mirror.

"No. I've been to several different Protestant services, and I used to go semi-regularly when I was deployed because I figured praying was a better use of my down time than most other things."

"Good point. There's few atheists in foxholes." Dad grimaced.

Tom drove in silence, enjoying the bright stars above and watching for wildlife crossing the dark highways. But he was curious. "You've got an awfully pretty voice, but I thought you'd be an alto because your speaking voice is low."

She didn't answer, and Tom thought he'd made a major blunder. He glanced in the mirror several times, but she was looking out the window. After he'd given up on a response, she said, "That's nice of you to say, but I've been told I sound like a badly-played piccolo. And my speaking voice is low because I learned to speak this way. Men take me more seriously."

Tom's scowl matched Dad's. "Whoever told you

that is wrong. You have a beautiful voice. I was going to suggest you join the choir if you can stand being up front. They can always use more voices, especially high ones." Dad grinned. "A lot of the people around here are older, and sometimes those high voices get a little shrill later in life."

Tom couldn't hold back. "I'm guessing it was that idiot you were married to. What a bunch of rubbish." Tearing anyone down was bad, but doing that to your partner was cruel.

"Yes," Wiz whispered.

"He was wrong. Dead wrong. I may not have a great voice, but I know when someone's on key, and I've been to concerts by some of the greatest singers in the world. Your voice isn't going to get you to the Met, but it's very pretty. Reminds me of Alison Krause a bit." He looked in the rear-view mirror again; she was wiping her eyes. "I'm sorry. I didn't mean to upset you." He should learn to keep his mouth shut.

Wiz shook her head. "You didn't. I just... well, it's nice to hear."

"That guy was such an ass." Worse, but Tom wasn't going to drop to that guy's level.

She snort-laughed. "Yeah, I guess he really was, wasn't he?"

"Must have been. I can't imagine cutting anyone down like that. Or ever letting you go." Tom growled.

"Double for me. You're better off with us." Dad put a hand on his arm and shook his head once. Tom nodded in acknowledgment of Dad's warning. He was pushing too hard. She wasn't ready for that kind of relationship.

She smiled, but it seemed tremulous. "Yeah, I think I am. Thanks."

"Oh, no." Dad shook his head. "Thank you. It's nice to have another family member around, rather than just us grumpy guys."

Tom chuckled. "Especially if you can get some work out of them, huh, Dad?"

"Work? All I'm doing is riding."

Tom snorted. "He's sucking you in with the riding. Soon, you'll be exercising all the horses, and then he'll have you out moving cattle, and the next thing you know, you'll be feeding them and working like a dog."

She laughed. "I don't mind helping once I know what I'm doing, but I do have my own job to do if I'm going to pay the bills."

Dad mock scowled. "Don't pay any attention to Tom. He has no idea what he's talking about. I'm only teaching you to ride so you can ride. That's it."

"Uh huh. I figured there had to be a catch someplace." She giggled and Tom grinned. Twice in one night, that was a great Christmas present. He pulled into her driveway, through the gates, and up to the portico.

Wiz leaned forward. "Do you want to come in?"

"Oh, no." Dad shook his head. "It's late, and we're not used to staying up. Come on down about ten or so for brunch."

"Okay. Thanks. I'll see you then." She leaned between the seats and brushed a kiss across Dad's cheek. Tom smiled. Then she turned and kissed him, too. "Merry Christmas." She ran to her door.

Tom was so surprised, he couldn't move. Her lips were soft against his cheek; the feathery brush of butterfly wings, precious and rare. He blinked, forcing back tears, and looked at Dad. Dad looked equally shocked, then grinned at Tom. "Merry Christmas, Wiz," Dad called.

He swallowed hard, put the car in gear and drove, his heart pounding in his chest and his eyes trying to spring a leak.

Dad cleared his throat. "Best Christmas present ever, huh, son?"

"Yeah, Dad. Best Christmas present ever." Tom rubbed his burning heart and thanked God for that, while hoping for more.

Chapter 12

Wiz

Wiz woke, picked up her cell phone, and blinked. *Zero-nine?* She never slept that late or that long. She'd better move—she had brunch with Tom and Pete at ten. She smiled and stretched. She'd anticipated a lot of anxiety last night at church, but instead, she'd felt slightly wary but mostly safe and protected. Scoping out the building and surroundings before the event had helped, and Craig's presence did too. She wasn't the only one carrying a concealed weapon in a house of worship—she'd seen the slight bulge at the back of Craig's leather jacket. But mostly, it was Tom and Pete's presence. Which was strange because she was fairly certain neither of them had been armed. But she still felt safer with them.

Her cheeks heated, then burned. She'd kissed them. It had seemed like the right thing to do on Christmas, after church, but what if they expected more? Or if Tom assumed it would be okay for him to kiss her? She was being ridiculous. Neither of them would do anything to make her uncomfortable.

Wiz threw the covers back. They were both good people who happened to be male. Not men looking for power or sex. Well, at least not at her expense. Tom had looked at her, especially her sweater. But only a quick glance, then he looked away. He hadn't tried to do anything, not even a hand on her back on their way out the door. Of course, they were in church.

She swallowed and bit her lip. She kind of wanted to know what his hand would feel like on her back, or holding hers. But he'd never make the first move. She'd have to initiate any physical contact, and she wasn't sure she could. Maybe not ever.

She'd wasted too much time. She rose, showered, dressed, and made a cup of coffee. She wore the same pants and boots from last night, pairing them with a dark burgundy cashmere sweater. She added a simple gold necklace and some diamond studs, then braided her hair back loosely. It felt odd not to put it all the way up so no one could grab it. She'd cut it short, but regularly allowing a stranger with a weapon at her back was out of the question.

Downstairs, she put on her coat, hat, and gloves and grabbed Tom and Pete's presents. Outside, she slipped her micro spikes over her nice boots and walked. The mini crampons were a wise choice; the road was icy, and the packages were big and awkward. When she reached the ranch house, she pulled off the spikes and let herself in the door, petting Rusty. The smoky goodness of bacon made her mouth water.

"Merry Christmas!" Pete stood in front of the stove. "Have a seat. Do you want some coffee?"

"Merry Christmas. Coffee would be good, thank you. Where can I put these?" She held up the brightly wrapped packages.

"Oh, under the tree in the living room. Tom is still upstairs; he should be down soon."

"Okay." She placed her gifts under the tree, then returned to the kitchen. Pete put a platter of bacon on the table. She circled to her normal spot in the corner where Pete had already left a cup of coffee for her. She sat and sipped.

Tom entered the kitchen. *Wow.* He'd looked good in his designer suit last night, but today he was... sexy. Dark designer jeans, tight across his muscular thighs, and a thin knit sweater in a warm chocolate that matched his eyes and clung to his broad shoulders and chest.

"Merry Christmas. You look beautiful." Tom smiled.

She blinked up at him, startled. She did? He was the beautiful one. "Merry Christmas." She took another sip of coffee to hide her hot cheeks.

He grinned, then turned to the counter, pouring a cup of coffee. Pete placed more dishes on the table, then they both sat. Smiling, Pete nodded to Tom, then her. "It's too bad the rest of the family couldn't make it, but I'm glad you're here. Seems more like Christmas when there's more than just the two of us."

Tom nodded like a bobblehead.

Warmth rising through her chest, Wiz was still amazed they'd included her, the weirdo. She'd never had family who cared as much as these two men. "It's nice to spend it with someone in person. Thanks for having me."

Pete snorted. "No need to thank us. You're family. You don't need an invitation, either. Now, let's say thanks and eat."

They all bowed their heads. Wiz said a short prayer of thanks, but it was thanks for the men across from her, not for the food. Pete pulled a plate off the stack and stuck a spatula into a casserole dish. He handed her the food.

Toasted bread and cinnamon wafted to her. "Pete, this smells delicious. What is it?"

He served another piece to Tom. "Stuffed French toast. You make it the night before, letting it soak in the fridge, then bake it in the morning. Serve yourself some bacon too."

She took a bite and moaned. Soft, maple egg-custard bread with a vanilla-cinnamon-sugar crust and creamy sweet cheese. "Wow, this is so good. You'll have to give me the recipe."

"Sure."

They ate. Wiz didn't need to talk; she was content to enjoy the food and the company. Plus, she was hungry.

Tom cleared his throat. "We'll let the roast cook here, then we'll take it up to your place to finish it off at high temperature, so you'll want to bring your oven to its highest setting around three or so. That way, it will be preheated before we get there, and we'll roast it for thirty minutes, then let it rest for another twenty. That way, we'll be able to eat right around four, which is what you told everybody, right?"

"Perfect." She took another bite. "This is so good."

"Yep, you outdid yourself this year, Dad."

She ate slowly, enjoying every bite because otherwise, she'd eat too much. They weren't talking, but the silence was comfortable. When she looked up from her plate, one or both of them were usually smiling at her. She'd return the gesture, but the men's smiles were definitely different. Pete's was warm and friendly, and a little proud, like she really was a part of the family. Tom's was also warm and friendly, and there was some pride, but the warmth was different. She glanced over her coffee cup, trying to figure out the difference.

Well, for one, Pete kept his eyes on her face, and Tom... didn't. His eyes wandered lower occasionally. Even when he gazed at her face, it was hotter somehow. As she watched, he looked back at her again and smiled, then dropped his gaze down her body and smiled again. And, instead of scaring her, it made her feel warm and...she couldn't quite put a finger on it. She looked down, ate another bite, and looked up again. He was focused on her mouth. *Oooh.* He wanted her? *Oh. Too much.* She shivered and scraped her chair back. She couldn't handle that; maybe she should go.

Clothing rustled and a muffled smack followed. "Ow. What'd you do that for?" Tom glared at Pete.

Pete frowned. "You're pushing. Go get me some coffee, son."

"Sure. Give me a moment in the bathroom, first." Tom left the kitchen, a door closing a moment later.

Pete tapped the table, drawing her attention. "If he makes you uncomfortable, just kick him. Like a cow when Rusty nips."

She snickered. "Okay. But you don't have to intervene. I'm an adult, and I should handle my emotions on my own."

"You're not on your own." Pete huffed. "And it's not just your emotions involved. Tom's a driven kind of guy, so occasionally, we have to remind him that his enthusiasm isn't shared and tell him to back off. I'm happy to tell him; the dad part of my job never ends."

She swallowed. She'd never had a real father, so she didn't know. And in her experience, telling a man "no" did very little. Other men saying no wasn't much more effective.

Pete pursed his lips and tapped the table again. "Wiz, you've come a long way. But you've got to ride your own trail. Tom is extremely patient, and he has more self-control than 99% of men out there, but sometimes, you'll have to remind him it's your pace that's important, not his." He grinned. "A swift kick to the keister will do nicely." He sobered. "But I promise you, all it takes is words. You just have to say them."

Wiz forced a smile. Words never worked. "Okay, Pete. I'll do that. But I'm telling him you said to kick him."

"Won't have to tell him. He's smart enough to figure that out on his own."

Tom came back in the kitchen and picked up the coffee pot, pouring some into his dad's cup, then asked her with lifted eyebrows. She nodded, and he filled hers, then his.

Pete leaned his chair back. "Brunch was pretty good, wasn't it?"

Tom smirked. "Now you're just fishing for compliments. You know it was."

He deserved the compliments and more. "It was awesome. Really."

"Good. Let's take our coffee into the living room?" He stood, pulling the last piece of bacon off the plate, tossing it to Rusty. "Merry Christmas, Rusty."

Happy chomping filled the kitchen for maybe two seconds, then he bounded to the living room. Pete sauntered to the Christmas tree in the corner and grabbed a small oblong package first, unwrapping it, cutting the plastic off, and tossing it to Rusty, lying on his bed. "That ought to keep him busy for a while longer than a strip of bacon." Rusty gnawed on the foot-long bone immediately.

Then Pete handed her and Tom packages. Hers was a rather large, flat, square box, and Tom's was very small, both wrapped in a Christmas plaid.

"Thank you, Pete." After carefully unwrapping the box, she pulled it open. Dark brown leather was nestled in tissue paper. She lifted a cowboy-style belt and holster, embossed with a beautiful pattern of flowers and leaves winding around the cartridge loops and continuing down the holster. "Oh, it's beautiful. Thank you, Pete." It was the best gift she'd ever gotten, and she had to blink back tears.

"Well, we couldn't have a real cowgirl out with us wearing all that tactical black stuff, now could we? That holster is sized for a standard .45 ACP, and we can add another one on the other side if you want. You don't have any wheel guns, do you?"

Wiz swallowed back the incipient tears. "No. I've never owned a revolver. This is absolutely gorgeous.

Thank you!" She smiled him.

Pete grinned. "You'll have to wear it for a while so the leather softens and conforms to you. I guessed on the size. Does it fit?"

She bounced up and out of the chair and wrapped it around her waist. Pete stuck his thumbs in his belt. "The folks who made it said it should fit down on your hips, and the belt is shaped to fit a woman, rather than flat like a man's."

She buckled it to rest on her hip bones, like a backpack. "It's perfect. And it's pretty comfortable already. I won't have to wear it in much." She rubbed the leather; soft but tough.

"You can attach other things, like a knife or bear spray, too. And Cathy wasn't happy, but I made her put a plain, dull bronze buckle on it, because I just couldn't see you wearing a lot of bling."

No, never anything shiny. "It really is perfect. Thanks, Pete." She crossed to stand in front of him and rising on her toes, kissed his cheek. Then she ran back to the chair. Pete's cheeks were red, and he turned away to sit.

Tom got up next, telling his dad thanks on his way. She didn't know what he'd gotten. Tom brought her a small square box wrapped in bright red, about twice as big as a jewelry box, and gave a flat package to his dad.

"Thank you, Tom." She unwrapped the present and took the lid off the box. Inside was a doll-size black cowboy hat. She pulled it out. "I don't think it will fit."

Tom laughed. "It's a stand-in. Like Dad said, we can't have you out on the trail without proper gear. But you can't pick out the right hat without trying it on. So, I made arrangements with a custom hat maker we know down in Darby, and we'll go down there for a private fitting session, just you, me, Dad, and the owner. You can pick black if you want, but it tends to get hot and dusty on the trail."

She blinked at him, stunned that he'd go to that much trouble. "Thank you, Tom. That's really, really nice of you."

He smiled. "Figured you'd like it a lot better than jewelry you hardly ever wear."

She grinned at him and Pete. "Thank you, both of you. These are the nicest, most thoughtful gifts I've ever gotten."

"You're welcome." Tom shrugged. "I'm just happy I thought of something good."

Pete guffawed. "Thank you, son. I think." Tom chuckled. Pete held up his present so she could see it. It was a book, titled, *Raising Beef the Natural Way*.

Wiz joined their laughter, then she got up. She had to swallow again and wipe her hands on her pants. She wasn't sure exactly how Pete would take her gift. "I guess it's my turn." She pulled the long thin box out first and handed it to Pete. "Now, before you open it, tell me again what the serial number of your sniper rifle was."

"582283." Pete fired the number.

She smiled, and Tom laughed. "You still remember that, Dad?"

Pete barked a laugh. "Are you kidding? I'll never forget. It was drilled into my brain. Winchester Model

70. One of the guys going home handed it to me. Told me it saved his life and now it would save mine. He was right; that rifle saved me dozens of times." He shook his head. "The first sniper rifles issued in Vietnam were terrible, so the new sniper-scouts bought their own from the BX in Japan. Then they'd give them to the guy taking their place. I think the last guy brought it home during the fall of Saigon, but I lost track of most of those guys a long time ago." He tore off the wrapping paper and lifted the plain cardboard box in his hands. "Heavy." He opened the box and slid his hands gently under the stock and barrel, pulling the rifle out of the molded cardboard. The rifle was a little beat-up, but Wiz had an expert go over it and make sure it still operated to military specifications.

Pete examined the rifle and grinned. "You got me a pre-64 Model 70? Just like I shot in the war. Hot diggity dog. Man, I loved that rifle."

"Check the serial number, Pete."

He pulled the rifle close and mouthed the numbers. "Holy Mother of God," he whispered. "How did you find this, Wiz? This is *my* rifle." He looked at her, mouth open, eyes wide.

She smiled, eyes a little watery again, raised her phone, and snapped a picture. His eyes shone, but tears hadn't fallen—yet. "It's amazing what you can find on the internet, Pete. I got on some gun boards, and some Vietnam Vet boards, and put the question out there. A couple of guys helped me track it down; they'd done it before. As you said, the last guy using the weapon in Vietnam brought it back with him after the fall of Saigon, and since it was privately owned and not Army property, he got to keep it. He passed away a few years ago, and his widow sold the gun. It went through several owners and then a private collector. The collector didn't want to sell it until I told him I was buying it for one of the original scout-snipers. Then, he said he'd sell it to me as long as I sent him a picture of you with the rifle when I gave it to you. I told him you had to agree." She held up her phone. "You don't mind, do you?" Pete shook his head, still staring at the rifle. She scrolled through her email, attached the picture, and sent it off to the collector and to Tom. That should make them both happy. Her heart burned, and her entire body warmed with joy. She hadn't been this happy since the incident. Maybe never.

Pete ran his hands over the rifle and examined it minutely, checking the serial number over and over. She glanced at Tom; he wore a huge smile. He turned to her, the smile still on his face, but it had softened and changed. He mouthed "thank you" and blinked. She smiled and nodded, then turned back to Pete, sniffling. She wiped her eyes with her hands. "And Pete?"

Pete looked up at her, disbelief riding his expression. "Yeah?"

"The collector said he'd love to have a picture of you with the rifle back in 'Nam, too, if you have one. I found one a guy in your unit had taken, but it's pretty grainy and faded. He'd arrived in country just before you shipped out, so he figured you didn't even know him."

"I'll have to look. Not too sure I've got one. They didn't encourage pictures, especially with us operating illegally in Cambodia." He stared at the rifle, practically caressing it, then worked the bolt to check the chamber. He looked up at her, blinking rapidly, and swallowed hard. "Wiz, next to my kids and grandkids, this is the most remarkable present anybody's ever gotten me. Thank you."

"You're welcome, Pete. It was fun to find, and I've just emailed you a list of the guys I worked with to find it, so you can connect with them yourself." The pride and joy would carry her through a lot of dark nights.

He wiped his eyes with his hands. Tom handed them tissues and took one himself. Not many guys, especially tough cowboys, would show that kind of emotion, and she had two. She was so, so fortunate. But she couldn't take much more. She blew her nose and returned to the tree, getting Tom's gift. She brought it to him. "This one's not quite so exciting or personal, but I think you'll like it."

Tom smiled. "I'm sure I will." Then he unwrapped the present and laughed. He held it up so his dad could see it. Pete looked at it with a wrinkled brow.

"It's the latest Play Station." He grinned. "Guess Wiz got tired of me using the 'it's my equipment' excuse for my poor performance." He waggled his brows. Pete chortled.

Wiz grinned. "It's got a year of premium service with it too."

"Thanks, Wiz. This is a great gift." Tom grinned back. "I doubt it will help against you, but maybe when we team up."

"You're welcome." She stood. "I have a couple of things to finish up at the house. You can come whenever you're ready."

Tom started to get up, then sat back down. "We'll be up in a bit. Dad will come up first, and I'll be up after I feed the cows. It will be a bit early, but that's okay."

Pete laughed. "I'm sure the cows won't mind. I'll bring the roast up with me." He lifted the rifle. "And Wiz? Thanks again. This is such a wonderful gift."

"You're welcome, Pete. It really was my pleasure." She trotted from the room, carrying her little hat in the box and wearing the cowboy belt, threw on her coat, and got out the door. She managed to get her spikes on and reach the road before she couldn't hold back. She bawled.

It was her best Christmas, ever.

Chapter 13
TOM

Dad was still examining the rifle in disbelief. He'd be jealous, except Wiz probably got more from the gift than Dad. He was envious of their shared connection—without a military background, such a gift wouldn't even cross his mind. But again, Wiz needed Dad, especially since she didn't have any other family. Tom gathered the coffee cups and cleaned up, smiling. And occasionally brushing away a tear. Such an amazing gift; not the piece of wood and metal, but the physical sign of a life-changing experience, both good and bad, along with all the work she did to find it. And the gift cemented a new relationship between the two of them.

Dad had adopted Wiz—she was family, and her love was the most important gift for both of them. She didn't have to do anything or earn their devotion. She might not quite understand or believe it yet, but they'd keep telling her, through words and deeds. He couldn't understand how anyone could throw away Wiz's love. He'd give almost anything to have her love as more than a family member. His hands clenched on the sponge. It took every bit of his willpower to say "thank you" rather than "I love you." Which was an incredible gift by itself. He hadn't even held her hand, but he was head over heels in love with the woman. Ridiculous and wonderful, sad and a little scary, all at the same time.

He had to go slow. He wasn't twenty or even thirty anymore, so he had *some* patience to go with his determination. They'd get there. He had to have faith. And if they didn't get to a romantic relationship, he was still lucky to know her and be family for her, even if it wasn't exactly the kind of family connection he wanted. If he was stuck as a big brother, well, that's what he'd do. He wouldn't let her down.

But her soft sweaters combined with her big heart made the friend-zone a difficult place to be.

Dad joined him in the kitchen, cradling the rifle like a baby. "Can you believe this? I'm holding the thing in my hand, and I have to keep looking at the serial number to make sure this isn't some sort of strange dream. Wonder if it still shoots like it used to?"

"Why don't you take it out back and give it a try?" Tom grinned. Wiz didn't realize how happy her gift made him, too.

Dad's expression held longing and uncertainty. "Not sure it's safe after all these years."

"I'm sure Wiz thought of that, but let me check." Tom fired off a quick text and got an immediate answer. "You're good to go. Says she had it checked by an expert. He said if you want to fire it a lot, you should get a fiberglass stock, but it's fine for occasional use as it is."

"Great. I'll be right back." Dad rushed out the door, Rusty on his heels. Tom finished cleaning up. A shot blasted the quiet, followed by the neigh of horses. Another rang a minute later and then a few more.

Dad tromped back in with a big grin on his face. "Works great. Action is actually a little smoother, probably all the use over the years, and it's just as accurate as back in the day." He shook his head, slowly. "Still can't believe it."

"I can't either. Never thought of it and didn't know it was possible. Of course, I'm sure you talk to Wiz about your military career more than with me." Tom didn't speak the right language, and he regretted it. But Dad had actively discouraged him from joining the military. And with everything both of them had experienced, he'd been right.

Dad frowned. "Well, sure, but it's not for me. I'm trying to get her to talk. But a lot of what she did is very technical, or classified, and it's pretty much all beyond me."

"It wasn't intended as an accusation. I don't know anything about that stuff because I didn't do it, so I don't even know where to start. And guns are just tools to me, not friends."

Dad laughed. "Yeah, when your weapon saves your life, it definitely becomes more than just a tool. And if you'd asked me yesterday, I wouldn't have thought this would mean so much." He looked down at the rifle again. "I mean, to a civilian, this probably seems gruesome, keeping something that you killed with. And not just keeping it but being so emotionally tied to it. But it's not the lives it saved and took, or even the gun itself, although that means a lot." He looked at

Tom, blinking hard. "It's the fact that that little girl went to so much time and effort to find it for me. I can't imagine what I could ever do to come close to that."

Tom snorted. "Are you kidding me? Hello, riding lessons? Dinner? Family? You've become the father she never had. There's no question about it." He laughed. "I have no doubt that she thinks the same thing, that this could never come close to repaying you for the time and effort you've put in."

Dad sniffed. "Like I need repayment. Pshaw. That girl needs dependable people in her life, and I'm not doing a whole lot with mine, so why not?"

"Oh, you do plenty. But it is a real joy to see her come out of her shell. I think back to that first day when she rescued me, and she's an entirely different person."

"I think she is. I wish we could have met her before all the bad stuff happened. I suspect she wouldn't have gotten so scared and isolated had we been there from the start." Dad sighed and shook his head.

"Oh, no doubt there either. If I'd known her from the start, well... this would be an entirely different life. I can't imagine abandoning her like that ass she was married to did."

"She was married?" Dad frowned. "She didn't tell me that. Although, now that I think about it, she kind of implied it. I just didn't put it all together."

Good, because Tom didn't want to betray her trust. He didn't see it that way, but she might if she hadn't already said something to Dad. "Yeah. She told me over the phone one night. We were in a role-playing game, the kind where you build up a character as you play, sometimes for years. Anyway, she'd gone after this one character viciously. No holds barred, every trick in the book, and she cleaned his clock. I signed off before she'd finished because it was really late, and she called to apologize for not saying goodnight, of all things." He looked up at the ceiling for a moment, still amazed. "Anyway, she told me that character was her ex-husband's. After she came back, and she needed him, he just left, had divorce papers served on her." Tom shook out his clenched fists. "He'd better not show up in person, ever, or I'll clean his clock."

Dad sighed heavily. "Makes you wonder, doesn't it? But just like I told her, you got to be careful about revenge. It usually bites back."

"If he ever shows in person, it will be about protection, not revenge. And I'm okay with her on-line revenge. It's just a game, after all. It will cost him time and money, but he can rebuild his character. I thought it was pretty appropriate, actually. He had to know she was there and stayed anyway."

Dad grimaced. "Maybe. I'm going to clean this beauty and put her in the safe, then we can head up."

Tom grinned. Wasn't very often Dad forgot the chores. "You can head up. I'll feed the cows."

Dad jolted, then chuckled. "Thanks, son." He slapped Tom on the shoulder and left for the garage, where they kept the gun cleaning supplies, humming as he went. Tom grinned. It was a very, very merry Christmas so far.

After dinner, Tom sank into the comfortable mission-style couch at the far edge of the living room. Ryan and Craig played a video game, fortunately with headsets, while Amy and his dad watched. Wiz, Deb, Sam, and Erin stayed at the table, commiserating with Deb about her family's noisy, kids-filled celebration, but they seemed a little envious too. Which he understood; he was pushing forty with no real prospects in sight. Well, he had her in sight, but whether or not it was a real prospect? Too soon to tell.

He took another sip of wine. Wiz had outdone herself on this selection. Sam had declared it "love in a bottle," and she was right. The pinot noir was smooth, dark, and delicious. The entire meal had been wonderful and the company better.

Wiz broke away from the others, sitting in the chair next to his seat on the couch. "You look happy."

"I am. This has been the best Christmas we've had for a very long time, and that's all due to you." He raised his glass. "Thank you."

She blushed and clamped her lips together for a moment, looking at her feet. "It's the best one I've had for a long time too. No, the best one ever." A tiny smile lit her face.

"How did you think of the rifle, anyway?" He didn't want to embarrass her too much or start her down the road of denial, and he really wanted to know.

She looked up at him, happiness still quietly blazing. "Oh, I've known a lot of Marines. Memorizing the serial numbers on their rifles is practically beat into

them in basic training. They memorize all their
weapons. The Army isn't quite so insistent on it, but I
figured with your dad's additional training, he'd know.
So, I asked him one day, and sure enough, he spouted
it right off. And not just his sniper rifle but the M-16
he'd had before that, and the one he had in basic. It got
to be kind of a joke. He'd tell me the serial number on
his rifle, and I'd tell him the IP address of some server."

Tom chuckled. "Neither of which would tell me
anything."

She shrugged. "It's definitely a military thing.
Never know when the computers and comm will go
down, so you memorize what you can. And the grunts
pile their guns together in a pyramid when they go to
chow, so they have to be able to tell them apart, and
the only way to do that is by serial number."

"I guess that makes sense. They would all look
alike."

"The Winchester doesn't look like an M-16, but
there were lots of scout-snipers too. Anyway, to these
guys, their guns are kind of like, hmmm, cops with
their K9s. Leaving them behind is unthinkable; they're
precious and cherished. So, I was trying to find a
Model 70 of the right era, and when I did the research,
I realized that there were quite a few guys out there
who had theirs from Vietnam. A lot of them were guys
who had bought their own, when the scout-sniper
school had just started and the military didn't have the
right weapons. So, I did just what I told you—I asked
the question on a couple of boards, and we found it. I
had a lot of help. The Vietnam vets are pretty excited

about doing stuff like this; it makes their day when it works. Still, it was a minor miracle."

Tom smiled and shook his head. "Oh, I think it qualifies as a major miracle, myself, one that required the intervention of an angel." He pointed at her.

She looked at her feet again. "I'm no angel. A long way from one, as a matter of fact." Her tone was mournful.

"I beg to differ. I think you're angelic in every possible way. If you don't agree, at least remember that even the fallen angels were forgiven when they repented. Not that I think you've fallen in any way, shape, or form or need repentance. Regardless of angelic status, forgiving yourself is the hardest part." Nothing was coming out right; hopefully, she understood what he meant.

She frowned skeptically. "When did you start spouting the same stuff as your dad?"

Tom chuckled. "Honey, the apple doesn't fall far from the tree. Don't you think I've heard all this before? And we did just go to Christmas service, remember? I can't help but pick up some of that."

Wiz laughed, softly. Sam, Deb, and Erin joined them. "What are you laughing about?" Erin asked.

"Oh, Tom is comparing me to an angel. Which is ridiculous." Wiz smirked.

"I don't know about that. I can totally see you in white with a pair of wings." Sam squinted. "No, not pure white. With your coloring, it would look terrible. A nice ivory would be lovely." She nodded sharply. "Yup, wings it is."

Tom agreed but didn't want to put Wiz on the spot. "I was talking about her actions, not what she looks like." He grinned. But maybe her self-esteem could use another boost. "But you're absolutely right. She'd look marvelous in a pair of wings. And she's tiny enough, I could pick her up and perch her on the top of the tree there, no problem." He didn't have long to wonder how she'd react to his teasing. She hauled back a fist and socked him in the arm, hard. "Dang, woman, that hurt!" Tom rubbed his arm.

"Serves you right."

"I have no doubt about your ability to defend yourself without a weapon in sight." Tom rotated his shoulder, flexing his arm. "That's going to hurt tomorrow when I'm feeding the cows."

"Then maybe you'll remember not to belittle the mighty Wiz!" Deb raised her arms high.

Wiz jumped to her feet in a Superman pose. "That's right. I'm a superhero, not a useless tree-sitting angel."

Tom smirked. "I was thinking more of the angels who smite evil-doers with fire and the sword, but superhero it is."

"Oh, well, that's different. If it's a smiting angel, Wiz is definitely one." Ryan swung an imaginary sword.

"Who won?" Erin asked.

Craig poked his chest with a thumb. "I did. Of course. Pilot here, not one of you mortal beings. Me and Wiz can go hang in the clouds together, far away from you dirt huggers."

"Yeah? Well, let me know how that works out for

you, trying to sleep on clouds, while I'm curled up on the comfy couch in front of the fire." Amy raised her brows. "Not that your head will fit through the front door anymore."

Tom smiled at the circle of people surrounding him. Wiz had built herself a great family, and he was really lucky to be a part of it. Now, if he could just manage to play a little bigger part in that family, it would be perfect. He joined the rest, teasing Craig.

Within an hour, the party wound down. Erin, Ryan, and Deb left first, so they'd be up for the after Christmas coffee-and-treats rush. Dad left with Deb, saying he was exhausted, which was probably true. Extreme emotions were tiring, even when they were happy. Amy, Craig, and Sam were next. Tom rose, pulling Sam's coat from the entryway and helping her into it while Craig got Amy's.

"You're taking what's left of the roast back with you." Wiz pointed at him.

"Why don't you keep it for sandwiches, Wiz?"

She shook her head. "Because it would take me a month to eat it all."

Amy picked up her bowl. "Wiz, sorry to interrupt, but we need to get going. Got a dog to feed. Thanks again for having us."

"You're welcome. I'm glad you could come."

Sam waved. "Bye, Wiz, thanks!"

Wiz closed the door behind them. She turned away, crooking her finger over her shoulder.

He followed her into the kitchen, grinning. She trusted him enough to have him at her back—real progress. She picked up their platter, covered in foil, and she pushed it into his hands.

He took it. Dad would never forgive him if he dropped his grandmother's platter. "All right, I guess I don't have a choice. Did you keep some for yourself?"

She nodded. "Yes, I did. And I gave some to everyone else. So, you get the rest. The two of you probably eat four times what I do. And you brought it."

He had to give in gracefully, not that he had any choice. He carried it to the front entry and handed it back to Wiz so he could get his coat and hat on. Gripping the antique firmly, he left Wiz's house, turning back after he dropped one step. He was still taller than she was but wasn't looming, he hoped. "Thanks for having us. It was fun, and you definitely made this the best Christmas Dad and I have had for a long time."

"Like I said, Tom, this is the very best Christmas I've ever had. If anyone owes thanks, it's me." Wiz put her hand over his, holding the roast, rose on her toes, and brushed a kiss across his lips. She twirled and sprinted into the house, the door closing behind her. He stared at the door until his fingertips tingled from the cold. He turned and put the roast on the passenger seat of their side-by-side ATV. He put it in drive and laughed, loud and hard, then grinned the whole way home. There was hope—he'd gotten a real kiss.

Tom didn't stop grinning until he fell asleep. And maybe not then.

Chapter 14

Not bothering to read it, Wiz saved her ex-husband's email in the harassment folder she shared with her lawyer and blocked Jeff's new email address. She'd already blocked his phone number. Take, take, take, that's all he did. She'd had more than enough. If he truly believed he deserved some additional consideration, he could talk to her lawyer. He'd quickly find out he deserved less than nothing, legally and morally. But she was successful, so he kept bothering her. But she didn't have to fight him personally—she paid her lawyer to do that for her.

She closed the laptop and ran down the stairs to the kitchen to finish her last-minute preparations. Tom and Pete were coming up for lasagna, bread sticks, and a green salad. She opened the last "love in a bottle" pinot noir left from the Christmas party, then set the kitchen table and added a wreath of pine branches and candles. Normally, she wouldn't bother with decorations, but she'd gathered the branches earlier, and the candles were left over from Christmas, so why not use them?

Decorating couldn't keep her from trying to figure out how her ex found out about her business. She certainly didn't tell him, Ryan didn't tell him, she hadn't kept in touch with anyone else, and she'd been careful to keep her name separate from her company, using a professional business management service. There was no way Jeff had the money to bribe them.

Perhaps it was a fluke. Her business wasn't a top-secret military operation; not if she wanted new customers. Maybe a mutual acquaintance told Jeff she was moving to Montana. While the house was owned by a holding company, if someone dug into the records hard enough, they'd find her. Plus, she hadn't been exactly quiet once she arrived. Well, not as quiet as she was in Washington anyway. Still, it was puzzling. None of her old friends would tell Jeff anything. Her enemies didn't know she'd moved or started a business.

But it didn't matter. She'd ignore the idiot, and the three of them would have a good time during dinner, and she could forget all about Jeff. She had people who cared about her, and she cared about them—a found family and they were so much better. She was on the edge of true happiness, and her selfish ex couldn't take that away. She wouldn't let him.

Later that evening, Pete sat back, patting his stomach. "Well, I gotta say that you really know how to make lasagna. Delicious."

Tom nodded. "Very, very good. Of course, this was a huge mistake on your part because now we'll expect you to cook on a regular basis. You're stuck." He grinned.

She smiled. "That's okay. You've been feeding me

and taking me riding. I don't mind cooking. But I don't have a big or fancy repertoire. I can make lasagna, pizza, a few other pasta dishes, and I can grill stuff. That's about it."

Tom chuckled "I can promise we'll be up here all the time in the summer. That patio grill you've got is irresistible. Especially to a man. You know, fire and meat." He shrugged. "Who needs green stuff?"

She chuckled with them, then sobered. She wasn't sure how they'd take her offer. "Since you'll be up here a lot more, I thought I should give you codes for the gates and front door. That way, you don't have to call or text me, you can just let yourselves in." Pete and Tom stared at her with raised brows, then they looked at each other and back at her. "You look so shocked."

"Because we are." Pete frowned. "Are you sure you're okay with this? I wouldn't want to do something that makes you feel unsafe." Tom nodded.

"I offered. It's not like you asked." She shrugged. "Besides, it's limited access. You can get in the gates, and the front and back doors, and the main level of the house. And the program notifies me when you use your code, so I won't be surprised."

"As long as you feel safe, that would be very convenient." Tom smiled gently.

"I'll program it into your smart phone, Tom." She held out her hand. "Pete, since you won't get a smart phone, you'll have to put the code in manually, but I'm sure that won't matter to you. Let's make yours, hmmm, your Blackhorse M-16 serial number, maybe? Or some other number you know well, at least eight digits." She picked up her phone, pulled up the house security and the profile she'd called "Pete," then handed him her phone. "Here, enter it, hit the tab, and repeat it."

Pete did, then she brought up Tom's profile and handed him her phone. "At least eight numbers. Don't use anything that someone can easily find out about you, like your phone number or current address."

"How about parts of old phone numbers?"

"Perfect."

He entered everything and handed her phone back to her, along with his, unlocked. She downloaded the app and entered her credentials and his profile, then handed the phone back to Tom. "It's pretty simple. You pull up the icon labeled Wiz, put in your code, and then there's three buttons, with the current status of the gates or doors, and you just press to unlock or lock." She tapped on Tom's phone, demonstrating. "If there's something wrong, but you still need to get inside, like if someone's got a gun to your head, put in your code but add a double star to the end. The gates and doors will open, but I'll be notified there's a problem. And if you need to send out an emergency call, without it being secret, just enter 999. That sends an alarm to my monitoring company, and they roll the sheriff, fire, and ambulance."

"Double star?" Pete asked.

"Oh, sorry. Just press the asterisk key on the entry pad twice after you enter your code. It looks just like a phone."

"Got it."

"Isn't three nines the equivalent of 911 overseas?" Tom asked.

She nodded. "In many countries, yes. And the double star is a duress code. If I'm not here, and someone wants my stuff bad enough to hold a gun on you, let them have it." She shrugged. "But it's not likely. It's more likely someone will be after me specifically. Someone who's been caught because of my software."

Tom leaned forward, brow wrinkling with concern. "People are threatening you?"

Wiz shook her head. "Not actively, but you know me. I'm paranoid. I keep myself separate from my company, but it's not perfect." She held up her phone. "Plus, somehow my ex got my email and my actual phone number, not the public number I put on my cards, and if he got that, well, he probably knows where I live now."

Tom scowled. "Maybe you should show us a picture of the guy, in case he shows up. Not that we'd tell anybody anything about you, but..."

Tom had a determined, intent expression, like he would protect her. Which was nice, although she was probably better at protecting herself. She scrolled through her pictures and pulled the last Jeff picture she had. "This is from, let's see, four years ago. He probably has longer hair now, I heard he got out of the military." She handed her phone to Tom, and he held it so Pete could see it too.

Pete pulled the phone closer. "Pretty good-looking guy. How big is he?"

Wiz snickered. "He's skinny and only five-seven. He wears boots a lot, so he looks taller."

Tom and Pete both snorted. "Unless he's got stilts, he's just a short stuff to me. And we'll just tip him over." Tom poked his pointer finger to the side once.

She giggled. When had she become a giggler? "Anyway, there are a couple of other emergency protocols you should know about. If the triple nine gets put in, and it's summer season, and/or two or more of the fire sensors on the horse fence go off, sprinklers start automatically in the horse fence area and on the roof."

"Really?" Pete asked. "That's a great feature. How long can you keep that going?"

"I've got a ten-thousand-gallon firefighting cistern buried in the hillside above the house, with a dedicated well. So, for a long time. But the well is pretty low yield, so there are moisture sensors in the grass. When it's saturated, those turn off."

"Did you know that won't necessarily put out a fire?" Tom asked.

"It won't?"

Pete shook his head. "Not if the fuels are dry. I've seen a wildfire burn across a swamp with standing water. It's important to keep the grass short, just for that reason. We can bring some cows or horses up every now and then to mow yours down."

"Sure. You can use my pasture as part of your natural beef raising. I haven't used any chemicals." She aimed a sly smile at Pete. Tom burst out laughing, and Pete scowled.

Pete raised his brows. "I can see Tom's got you convinced. I'll probably lose this 2-v-1 argument, but I'm going to make you work for it. And to make that harder, I'm going home. Tom, feel free to stay if Wiz will let you. But you get to walk." Pete rose and walked to the front door.

"I think I can manage a short stroll down the hill, old man," Tom called, then chuckled.

"Not if you're wearing those city boots again, boy!" Pete yelled, the front door closing behind him.

They both laughed. Wiz finally got herself under control, then met Tom's gaze and laughed again. It felt so good to be happy and express it without worrying someone might see and use it against her. The reminder made her shiver, so she stood and gathered the plates. Tom gathered the glasses, and they brought them to the kitchen. He stayed at least an arm's length away, probably so he didn't loom over her, just as she had requested. Maybe it was time to tell him she felt safe enough that he didn't have to be quite so careful. He was okay. More than okay.

She wrapped the leftover lasagna, and her phone chimed. She looked at the notification and scowled.

"What is it?" Tom put glasses in the dishwasher.

"My stupid ex won't stop emailing me. I keep deleting his emails and blocking him, but he won't get the clue."

"What does he want?" Plates clinked.

"I don't know and don't care. Probably money." The refrigerator blew cold air on her, and she put the lasagna inside.

Tom chuckled. "Why don't you open this one? Let's look."

She didn't know why Tom wanted to see it, but she shrugged and opened it. She didn't have anything to hide regarding Jeff. "Let's see, oh baby I miss you, blah, blah, blah, want you back, blah, made a mistake, blah..." She shuddered and put the phone down. "Yuck. I can't read anymore."

Tom grinned. "Ah, but you don't have to. Let's give him something to think about, shall we?"

She gazed up at him, a little warily. "What did you have in mind?"

His grin turned into a smirk. "We'll send him selfie. I'll move behind you, just to the side a bit. You smile, nice and pretty, a little up toward me, and I'll scowl, straight into the camera. Then you can send it off with a nice, short message, like 'too little, too late' or 'go away, little boy.' Don't you think that would work?" He waggled his eyebrows.

"Oh, that's evil." She grinned up at him. "Perfect. Let's do that."

His brows rose. "You'll be okay with me behind you?"

She nodded. "Yeah. You're not surprising me, so it should be fine."

"Good." He stepped toward her, looking beyond her, then turning. "Oh, wait. Let's do this in front of your Christmas tree."

"Great idea. Yes, let's." She grabbed his hand, ignoring his jump, and towed him to the tree. "Yep, right here." She twirled on her toe. Tom stepped behind her, sliding one hand down her arm to her waist and putting his other on her shoulder, touching her gently, not grabbing. Still, she shivered a little as she put the camera in selfie mode.

"Are you sure you're okay with this?"

Tom's voice rumbled along her back, creating another shiver. But it was a good, anticipatory shiver, not a shudder. "Yes, it's okay. I'm all right. Ready?"

"Oh, yeah."

"Say cheese!" She aimed the camera, turning to look up at him, and clicked the shutter. She brought the phone closer. She'd managed to cut Tom's head off. "I'm not sure we can get both of us in a selfie. You're too tall, and I'm too short."

"Here, my arms are longer, let me try." He took her phone and aimed it, then clicked. He'd gotten both of them.

Wiz smiled. "Oh, the menacing stare is very convincing. Let's try one where we're both looking at each other and see which one would make him madder." She handed the phone back to him and turned toward him again.

He held out the phone. "Ready? Say cherish." He smiled down at her. The camera clicked, but she wasn't paying any attention to it. No, she kept looking at him, and he gazed down at her. He finally broke their stare and handed the phone back to her. Then he swallowed, hard, and met her eyes again. "Wiz?"

"Yes?" She couldn't get a deep breath, and warmth rose in her body.

"I'd really like to kiss you. Do you think that would

be too much? It's okay if it's too soon." A tiny smile lifted the corners of his lips.

It was her turn to swallow hard. "I think... I think I'd like that." She could barely whisper.

Leaving one hand lightly on her shoulder, he brought his other hand up to her cheek. He brushed his thumb over her lips and up her cheekbone, barely touching the side of her head with his fingertips. Then he lowered his head to hers and kissed her gently, just barely meeting her lips.

His lips were firm but soft. His touch firmed, deepening the kiss slightly without pushing, keeping his lips closed. He kept his fingertips on her cheek and the other hand on her shoulder, feathering his fingers in a caress but not moving to other parts of her body. He was being so careful with her, and she felt precious and safe.

She slid her arms around his neck. He kissed a little harder, then pulled away. Still holding her, he blinked, a tiny smile rising. "You are so sweet." He cupped one side of her face, lightly. "I just can't understand how anyone could ever hurt you." He kissed her again, and it was just as wonderful.

All she could think of was "more." She opened her mouth a little, and he copied her, kissing her a little harder but still not pushing. *Oh.* He was following her lead, not taking anything she wasn't willing to offer.

So, she gave. She pressed a little harder and swept her tongue just under his upper lip. He groaned, and his fingers tightened, and his tongue teased her mouth.

She rose on her tiptoes, firming her grip, cupping

the back of his neck.

He pulled his lips away. "Would a hug be all right?"

She nodded and stepped into him, wrapping her arms around his waist. He put his arms around her upper back and rested his cheek against the top of her head. His voice rolled through her. "That was... that was amazing, love. And I really, really don't want to stop, but I have to, or you won't have time to think." He loosened his arms, but she tightened hers and pressed into him a little harder. He hugged her firmly. She wasn't scared but felt treasured and special. It had been so long since a man's touch   brought her joy. They stood there, wrapped around each other, for a long time. Finally, he broke the silence. "Will you tell me what you're thinking?"

She nodded against his chest, but she was having trouble getting the words out around the lump in her throat. She might burst into tears, and that would give him the wrong idea entirely. She blinked and swallowed.

He chuckled, the sound rumbling through her chest. He loosened his arms again and said, "How about we go sit down on the couch, and I'll tell you what I'm thinking. Then you can tell me when and if you're ready."

She stepped out of his embrace and shivered, slightly chilled away from his warmth. He walked with her to the couch, wrapping his arm around her shoulder. Before he sat, he handed her phone back and tugged her down, pulling her under his arm so she was nestled up against his side, with her head on his chest.

"Is this okay?"

His body was warm and firm and his arm solid over her shoulders, but not confining or constricting. "Yes."

"First, I'll never push you for anything you don't want to give. If you want to be just friends, we'll do that. If we can kiss and cuddle on the couch, I'll be ecstatic. Never, ever think that you owe me anything. Your friendship is vital, and I never want to lose it. I understand that your feelings might change from day to day. Tomorrow, you might not want me to hug or kiss you, and that's fine." He clasped her a little tighter, then shrugged. "But you have to tell me. I'm a man, and I'm not the most enlightened person on the planet. I might not pick up on something subtle. Words are best. Please."

Wiz nodded. "Okay, but you have to do the same. I don't always pick up on signals either. Tell me what you want or need, even if you think it will make me uncomfortable."

Tom released her slightly, bent, and gazed into her eyes, with a small smile. "Deal. Now, if someday we go further physically, you still don't owe me anything. Even if you made me the luckiest guy on the planet someday, you could change your mind the next day, or in the next minute, and that's absolutely your choice. I won't take that decision from you. I'm certain you experienced some sort of horrible trauma. I know you might not ever tell me what happened to you, and that's okay too. I'd be honored if you confided in me, but I understand if you don't. It's your life, your mind, your body. You have all the control." He pulled his arm away and shifted to face her. "Do you believe me?" He held out his hands, palms up, to her.

She mirrored him and put her hands in his. "Yes. At least in my head. But it may take a while before I can really internalize it. Same with trusting you. I do trust you, but..."

He smiled gently. "Just tell me. I don't want to play games with you. That's the second thing. I already know that I love you, and I want to spend the rest of my life with you. But again, this is going to go at your speed, not mine. We might not ever get there. Just be my friend." He squeezed her hands carefully.

Astonishment swept over her like a tsunami. Wiz wasn't sure what to say. "You love me? You don't even know my name!" He couldn't possibly love her. They'd only known each other for a few short months. But... she trusted him and Pete more than anyone else, even more that Ryan and Erin.

Tom laughed and squeezed her hands. "Like I care. Names are just a label. You're who you are. You've labeled yourself, rather than sticking with the label somebody else gave you. It suits you." He smiled and shrugged. "Besides, I didn't fall in love with your name or the way you look, although you're beautiful. I fell in love with who you are inside, your heart." He pointed at her chest, at her heart, then ran the back of his fingers just under her clavicle, with her hand still gripped in his. Wiz's heart, already beating hard, sped to double-time, and her face and chest warmed. "I fell in love with your compassion and bravery and intelligence. Everything else is unimportant."

She squeezed her eyes shut for a few moments, then opened them. He was still there, still holding her hands. "You can't be for real. I don't get stuff like this. I..." He was too good to be true. No one loved her, not really. Not when the chips fell. And they always did.

He shook his head slowly, smiling ever so slightly. "Love, you deserve way more than me. I'm just a rancher with fancy boots. I'm nobody important or particularly smart or special in any way. I'm pretty sure that I'm way older than you are too. You're way more than I'll ever be, and I'm proud to call you friend. That's enough. But if you think there's even a tiny chance you could love me someday, I'll be the happiest man on earth."

Her face heated and her heart throbbed. His grip on her hands was the only thing that kept her from running, even though she didn't want to leave him. Not ever. "I... I don't know what to say, except that you are smart and special and all those things you said you weren't. I'm not." She'd practically wailed the words like a child.

He squeezed and released her hands. "It's okay. I know I'm pushing too hard, and it's an emotional overload. But I want to get it all out in front of you, so you can think about it. Then you can decide how you really feel and not just react. Okay?"

She nodded, but she couldn't force any words out. She missed the feel of her hands on his but couldn't reach for him, either.

He swallowed hard, and his smile faded a little. "Third, if you don't return my feelings, can't even be friends with me, I want you to know that won't change the relationship between you and my dad. I'll always love you and want you, but if you can only be my sister, even my estranged sister, well, then that's what it is, and I'll suck it up." He gave her a rueful look. "You'll have to put up with my puppy love looks, but don't let that keep you away from your family. Because we are your family, first. I'd like to have a different family relationship with you, but if you don't, then we won't. I'll deal. Got it?"

That dried her tears. "You are important to me. I don't know if I can ever give you what you deserve, but you'll always be my friend." She put her hands over her aching heart.

His smile saddened. "I don't deserve anything, not even friendship. If you want to give it to me, I'll be honored to accept. But full trust will take time. Maybe talk to your doctor?" He shrugged. "I'm more than happy to talk to her too, if she thinks it would be helpful."

Wiz placed her hands on top of his. Tom's smile grew happier and sweeter, and he enclosed her fingers in his gently. "Now, can you tell me a little bit more about your feelings? Or should I go home?"

She wanted to go back to cuddling, and some kissing, and stay in their quiet little bubble. Because it might break tomorrow. But no matter what he said, she owed him some information. "Look, I want more. I treasure your friendship, and the hugs and kisses were wonderful." She couldn't help her smile or the heat rising from her chest to her head again. Good thing she had naturally darker skin or she'd be blazing like a brake light. But she had to warn him. She was dangerous in more ways than one. "I want more of that. But if we have a full relationship, I could still have a flashback or a stress reaction. I will talk to my doc, but a year from now, you might try something new, or wake me abruptly, and boom, I'm stuck in my head, and you're knocked out cold." She bit her lip, chills running down her spine. She'd never considered all the consequences of being a self-defense expert. "Or seriously injured or even dead. A physical relationship between us could be dangerous for you."

She tried to pull away, but Tom gripped her hands a little tighter. "Oh, sorry." He released her fingers, but she shook her head and left her hands in his, and he clasped them firmly. "That might be, but it doesn't change the way I feel about you. I knew from day one that I had next to no chance with you, but I'd rather take the chance than live with the regret." He chuckled. "Besides, I'm forty-two. I've had a great life. What I'm clumsily trying to say is, I don't care. I love you, and I'm willing to take my chances. The potential loss is nothing next to the gain."

Her forehead ached because she'd raised her eyebrows too high. "Tom, I'm not sure what to say." Warmth lit her from within, but experience had taught her to watch for the fall; higher hopes meant a mightier crash.

He shrugged. "That's okay. I don't have any expectations." He smiled, his eyes crinkling. "Even if it never happens again, that kiss is something I'll remember the rest of my life."

She smiled. "I can safely say I'd like to kiss you again."

He grinned and tightened his grip. "That's more than I hoped for." His brows rose. "Now?"

"Okay." She let go of his hands and cupped her hands around his face. His beard was a little rough on her palms, but his lips were soft against her thumbs. *Ah!* His tongue caressed the top of her thumb. Ooh. She leaned over, putting her lips against his, gentle and soft. He put his hands on the outsides of her knees and slowly moved them up the outside of her thighs to her waist, pulling her closer. Passion swept through her, rising with his hands. She deepened the kiss, but their position was awkward. He pulled back, and she let him go, not sure what he was thinking.

He ran his hand down her hair. "Someday, I'd love to see this down. It's so pretty and soft." She reached up to unbraid it, but he put out his hand. "Oh, no, love, not tonight. I'm having enough trouble with control. If I had this to stroke, well, we might not stop. You should probably talk to your doctor, first."

She shook her head, more than a little embarrassed. "I'd be willing to bet that stopping is not something you've had to do a lot of, not since high school." The man dated models—she wasn't sure what he could possibly see in her.

He smirked. "Make that after college, and you'd be right. Took me a while to get my full growth." A giggle jolted from her. He tugged her braid. "I love hearing that little giggle. It's so out of character for you. And yet, it fits you perfectly." He gave her a wicked little grin. "I'll be trying to make you do it more." She couldn't help giggling again; he was adorable. He gave her a quick kiss, enough that she wanted more. Which surprised her enough that she rolled off the couch. He sprawled across the cushions like he didn't have a care in the world. And down there, he didn't seem scary or threatening or have a negative association. No, he looked sexy.

She took a step back and another. If they went too much further, things wouldn't go so well. She cleared her throat. "You look so harmless there, but I know better. You're dangerous."

He smiled. "Oh, but not next to you. I told you I wouldn't push, and here I am, having to use every bit of my vaunted self-control not to reach up and pull you back. You're the dangerous one. Besides, you can kick my ass. You're doubly dangerous."

Wiz sat on the coffee table, and he put his hand over her knee, leaning toward her. She wanted to melt into his arms and stay there forever, but that wasn't smart. "Maybe we should call it a night before we both regret it."

His smile softened. "Oh, I could never regret anything I did with you, but let's not test that theory. You said go, so I shall go." He stood and reached down to her. Taking his hand was oddly difficult. It was a polite gesture he'd held back from making before. Could she accept even symbolic help?

She bit her lip and put her hand in his. His closed around hers, and his small smile grew into a grin.

"You, Wiz." He paused, his thumb running over her knuckles. "You've made me so happy tonight. I think this is the happiest I've been since I graduated from college. Maybe ever." And he brought her hand up to his lips and kissed it. It was a trite gesture, but not from him, not with what they'd just shared. He chuckled. "And I think we should retake that picture. Yes, I think this one will be more effective."

She frowned up at him. "Why?"

"Because right now, you look like a woman who's been thoroughly kissed." He ran his hand along her face. "If I had known we'd be doing this, I would have shaved before coming up."

Heat blazed across her cheeks, but it wasn't completely caused by his beard abrading her skin. It would probably sting when she washed her face, but she kind of enjoyed the feeling. "Sure, let's do that. We'll put a nail in his coffin."

They stood together in front of the tree, and Tom put an arm around her waist, pulling her back into his body. "Okay?"

Wiz grinned. "More than okay." She handed him her phone and kept gazing up at him. The click of the camera startled her.

"One more."

She kept her eyes on him, and he scowled at the camera. He handed the phone back to her, wrapping both arms around her and resting his chin on the top of her head. She felt so safe in his arms. She pulled up the pictures and flipped between them. "Which do you think?"

"Oh, the one where we're looking at each other. The one where I'm glaring is too obviously aimed at him. We don't want him to think this is about him in any way."

She recovered his last email from the garbage, hit reply, and attached the picture. She changed the subject line to read, "No." In the body of the email, she typed, "I have a real man in my life now. Don't contact me again." Tom laughed, the sound rumbling through her body. She hit send and put the email back in the trash.

"Will you send those two of us looking at each other to me, please?"

She did. His hands slid across her waist, and he stepped back, retrieving his coat and gloves. They both walked out the front door, and after he took a step down, he turned back. He was still taller than she was, but not overwhelmingly so. She put her arms around his neck and kissed him; he returned it enthusiastically. She pulled back and took a deep breath. Her heart ached with joy. "Tom?"

"Yes, love?"

"Thank you. This is the best day I've had in a very long time. And I can't imagine I deserve all this care, but I appreciate it."

He smiled. "You deserve way more. This is nothing."

Her heart pounded, but she wasn't sure if it was terror or thrill or both. "And Tom?"

He tilted his head and raised a brow.

"My name is Victoria May Meadows. But I like Wiz

better."

She twirled and ran inside. Revealing her name was so risky, but she trusted him. She collapsed against the door. She panted, trying not to think, then turned to peer out the peephole. He was still standing there, a sweet smile on his lips. He waved, turned, and walked away. But she knew he'd be back.

Chapter 15

TOM

Tom relaxed into the old recliner, pulling his tablet onto his lap. The background picture of Wiz smiling up at him in front of her Christmas tree warmed his body and heart. Wiz brought him so much happiness; he only wished she could feel less conflicted about him.

Over the long winter months, she'd gradually shared more about her life, both before the Air Force and while she was in, but she hadn't been able to tell him everything about her last deployment. Small pieces emerged occasionally when she was comfortable or when her therapist asked her to share. Unfortunately, the more she told him, the angrier he got about her ordeal, but he had to remain calm because his anger increased her anxiety. He definitely understood exactly why she'd sought revenge, even though he knew it wasn't helpful in the long run. But she'd earned it.

Wiz had also told him more than enough about her slimeball ex-husband, an opportunistic narcissist. With therapy, she realized why she'd accepted his terrible behavior and increasing emotional abuse. She'd been all alone, in an unfamiliar environment, and then a good-looking guy started paying attention to her, and it felt like love and safety. Same reason lots of people got married right after high school and college, and they often regretted it later. Unfortunately for Wiz, her ex wasn't stupid and had carefully played on her fears and insecurities, escalating his behavior. Then, when she needed someone to lean on, he'd coldly abandoned her. Since she'd recovered, he evidently believed he could reuse his old playbook, but Wiz was too smart to fall for that.

At the creak of plastic, Tom relaxed his death grip on his poor table and stretched out his fingers. Whenever he recalled the little she'd shared about her last deployment, rage roared through him. Not only that she'd been assaulted, but at the criminal behavior of her so-called superiors, trying to cover up the crime and blame the survivor, and their failure to bring anyone to justice. They hadn't even protected what little evidence had been gathered. So many in her chain of command had failed Wiz. There were probably many other victims, too; ignored and belittled because the fragile egos of their so-called leaders couldn't handle the truth—they were weak incompetents.

For the perpetrator, sexual assault wasn't about sex, it was about power. But Tom didn't understand how overpowering a tiny female could make anyone feel strong. Especially in the military, where strength was prized, oaths to protect and defend were supposed to mean everything, and attacks should be against the enemy. Only slimeball criminals reveled in such evil.

Back then, she'd been vulnerable, both emotionally and physically. But no more. She'd made herself into a weapon. A week ago, he'd been there during her virtual training with her sensei, an elderly, tough as nails man. When Wiz introduced Tom, the man grinned. Tom had ended up flat on the mat twenty times in a row. Back, front, side, it didn't matter; Wiz had him down in seconds. At the end of the session, her sensei cautioned Wiz that Tom obviously knew nothing about martial arts. But the look of triumph on Wiz's face made the bruises feel like nothing. He'd been stiff for a week, but it was worth it.

"What are you smiling at, Tom?"

"The usual." He tilted the tablet toward Dad.

Dad smiled at the tablet, then grinned at Tom. "Wiz beat you up recently?"

Tom barked a laugh. "No. She's taught me a few moves, but she's strong, fast, and very flexible. It's like a mouse and an elephant. I might get lucky and step on her, but that would be the only way for me to win."

Dad chuckled. He thought it was hilarious that his tiny, hopefully future daughter-in-law could take down his big, tall son. "Is everything ready for the big family invasion?"

"Yup." Tom nodded. He was looking forward to the visit—their kids were growing so fast. They were lucky the across-the-road neighbors let them use their house because hosting eight more people was way beyond their capacity. "I had the cleaning service in, and I checked everything. The fridge and pantry are stocked with most of the stuff they asked for, beds are made, towels are out, there's soap and toiletries in the bathrooms. It might be a little crowded with both families in one house now that the kids are getting older, but it's not like it will be forever. They should be able to handle a week."

"It's bigger than our house by a long shot." Dad's head tilted. "Hmm. Maybe we could use Wiz's guest house, and then one of them could stay at our house, if it gets too cramped. Did you give her the details about their visit?"

"I told her Marie and Alex and their families were coming for Easter and spring break, but I don't think she realizes what that means. I'm sure she's not really ready for it. I'm not sure I'm ready." Tom was uneasy, to say the least. "It's been almost a year since we've seen them, and that's a long time for kids. They'll have changed a lot."

"Yep." Dad nodded. "Wish they could get out here more often, but that's the way it is. Not enough good paying jobs here. I previously asked Wiz to help me with the kids if they came out, and she agreed. It will be interesting to see how she reacts."

"And how *they* react." Tom sighed. "Quite frankly, I'm more worried about that. Not the kids, the adults. Marie, in particular, is likely to be a little judgmental, and I don't know how tolerant Wiz will be. We may not see much of her." Every second they were apart was too long for him. Trading Marie for Wiz wasn't a good deal. He loved his sister, but her entitled attitude got old.

"We'll talk to them tonight." Dad's mouth twisted for a moment. "They'll all be getting in pretty late, so I don't think she'll meet them now. I'm assuming you're telling them you're going to marry her, right?"

"Yes. Or at least that I hope to, and that she's dealing with stuff she suffered while she was in the service, and the rules. We'll probably have to warn Marie's kids as well, but Alex's are small enough that they shouldn't be an issue." He grinned. "I'm sure none of them have gotten any quieter."

Dad laughed. "No, probably not. That's okay, laughter is good for the soul." He sobered. "But I don't think you'll have to worry about Marie too much. She'll just be happy you found somebody."

Tom wasn't so sure. "She didn't like Evon, and she didn't keep it a secret."

Dad huffed. "Evon was pretty but kind of selfish and shallow. I didn't like her much either, but it wasn't my decision, so I didn't say anything."

Tom snorted. "In the end, it wasn't my decision either, but I'm happy it worked out this way now." They'd have both been miserable. And divorced.

"Wiz is a better match for you." He chuckled. "And me."

Tom nodded, agreeing. Wiz was a big step up, probably too big. One of these days, she'd figure out she could do better. He could only hope his love and devotion were enough. He swept the picture away; he had work to do. He answered emails and updated the books, then surfed the internet.

"Which Easter Mass should we go to? Sunday morning?" Dad interrupted his time wasting.

"Sure." Tom shrugged. "I don't think Wiz will go. Too many new people, and not enough flexibility with a big group. She offered to get brunch ready at the neighbors' and hide Easter eggs for the kids if we give her a key."

"Oh, that's sweet of her."

"She suggested it. I certainly didn't ask or even hint. She's got eggs filled and baskets ready for all the kids with different colored eggs for each age range."

Dad frowned. "What makes Wiz think the older kids will go for an egg hunt? Last time they were out here, they were getting to the 'too cool to play' stage."

"Wiz said she'd obtained the right incentives. She knows a lot of important tech people, so I think she's got some really unusual stuff, like new video games."

"Huh."

Tom's phone buzzed with a text. "Marie's just turning onto the highway now. Shall we go over?"

"Sure, let's go."

With Rusty on their heels, they crossed the road, opened the driveway gates and the front door. Dad toured the house, but he didn't ask any questions or make any comments after he returned. An engine rumbled, gravel crunched, doors slammed, and feet ran.

"Grandpa, Grandpa, Grandpa!" Yvonne and Peter threw themselves at Dad, then him. He happily hugged both of them, pulling them off their feet. After he set them down, they tore into the house.

Marie, who'd walked sedately to them, hugged him, then pulled away, nodding. "You look good. Have you been working out?"

"A little." When Wiz exercised, he did too. "Bucking

hay gives you pretty good muscles."

"Yes, you're a real cowboy now, instead of a stock broker." She smirked. "It's good to see you."

"Good to see you too. The kids have gotten so big!" Tom grinned, enjoying the rare happy exchange.

"They do that. You should find out someday." She wagged a finger. "Soon, big brother."

"Yeah, yeah. We'll see." He smiled.

"You won't see anything as long as you keep yourself stuck on this ranch. You need to get out there." Marie swept her arms out dramatically.

"Not true. Not true at all." He grinned wider.

She pierced him with her stare. "Oh, really? You found a cowgirl?"

Tom laughed. "I'm not entirely sure I'd call her a cowgirl, although she has learned to ride and herd a bit. You'll meet her tomorrow."

Marie glared and opened her mouth, but she was drowned out.

"Grandpa, Grandpa, Grandpa!" Two smaller whirlwinds ran in, followed by their parents. Another round of hugs and exclamations, and the noise level quadrupled. Tom decided it was a very good thing Wiz hadn't joined them because she'd have been gone already.

They assigned rooms, had drinks, and Alex's kids were put to bed. They gathered in the living room, and the adults shared stories about the last year. Yvonne and Peter played on their phones. The moment Tom had been both anticipating and dreading came.

Marie narrowed her eyes and stabbed a finger at

him. "So, Tom, tell us about your girl."

"You have a girlfriend?" Alex smiled. "About time."

Tom sighed. "Yes, I have a girlfriend. She's our neighbor up the hill. You'll meet her tomorrow. But we need to tell you a few things first."

Dad interrupted. "First thing you need to know is she's family. She doesn't have anyone, so I've essentially adopted her. She's a sweet kid, but she had some real bad stuff happen to her while she was in the service. So, she's a little jumpy." He shrugged. "Kind of like a rescue horse. Tom will give you the rundown, but if you scare her off, I will be very angry at you. Clear?" Dad stared at each of them in turn.

They all nodded in agreement, but Tom didn't miss the wary glances they threw at each other. "Like Dad said, Wiz went through—"

"Wiz? Her name is Wiz?" Marie broke in. "Really?" Her brow wrinkled and her nose scrunched.

Tom frowned. Marie lived for drama, creating it when there wasn't any. "Really. It's not her legal name, but it's the one she prefers to be called, and you will use it because she won't answer to anything else." Tom gritted his teeth. He'd warned Dad—Marie was a pain. "Did you not listen to Dad? Treat her nicely, or you can just go home now. Got it?"

"Sorry." She rolled her eyes ostentatiously. "Geez, lighten up."

"You wouldn't complain if you knew what she's been through. And no, I'm not telling you the details, just that it was horrible, and she needs and deserves care. We have rules." He paused, glaring at Marie, but for once she shut up and seemed to listen. "Don't ask her what happened, don't try to hug her, don't touch her, not even a handshake. Try not to loom over her, which is tough because she's tiny, and we're all tall. Don't be surprised when she always keeps a wall at her back, and please don't gang up on her. And never, ever, ever surprise her. Don't ever sneak up on her, or you could end up dead."

"Dead? I'm *not* going to endanger my kids for your girlfriend." Alex reared back in his seat.

Tom shook his head, raising his hands to calm him. "She'll be fine with the little kids. It's adults she's got issues with. And no, I wasn't kidding. She's got some killer martial arts moves. She put me on the mat like twenty times in a row." He rotated his sore shoulders.

"You? Awesome." Alex grinned for a second, then frowned. "You sure my kids will be okay?"

"Yes. And in case you're not taking me seriously, Yvonne and Peter," their heads snapped up from their phones, "if you piss her off, you won't get to play on her systems, which are the best you've ever seen. She knows people, so she's got beta test stuff that none of your friends will have. So, please, all of you, just be nice to her and don't scare her. Please. I'm asking her to marry me when she's ready, so don't ruin this for me. And if you do, well, I'd rather be with her than you, and that's the choice I'll make. Clear?"

He looked at each of them. Marie, Scott, Alex, and Tara frowned at him, mostly skeptical. Yvonne played with her phone, while Peter bounced in place. "Uncle Tom?"

"Yes, Peter?"

"Can we call her Aunt Wiz?"

He snort-laughed, surprised. "Uh, you should ask her."

"Okay. What's she got?"

He laughed. Of course that's what Peter cared about. "You'll have to wait and see. As you've already figured out, there's no wi-fi over here, but there is at our house. I wrote the passwords on the fridge, but it won't be very strong here. Come on over anytime. The door is always open."

"You have wi-fi now? Since when?" Peter's face was a study in incredulous amazement.

"Since Wiz."

"Cool." Peter ran to the kitchen.

"Is she, like, handicapped?" Yvonne asked.

"She doesn't have any physical injuries, no. We do have a friend, who you might meet, who lost his left forearm in Afghanistan. And I'd expect you to be nice to him too."

"Duh." She joined Peter in the kitchen.

"I hope you know what you're doing." Marie shook her head.

"We do. Just to be clear, she's got way more money than we do, so don't think she's some sort of gold digger." Dad frowned.

"Dad..."

"She had horrible things happen to her while she was in service to our country. You know, one of the people protecting us and our cushy way of life? So, at the very least, you can give her the respect she deserves. Understood?" Dad rose from his chair.

They all nodded, but Tom suspected he wouldn't see as much of his family as he'd like. Because if Wiz went home, he was going with her. He'd try one more time to make it clear. "Marie, I meant it. You scare her off, I'll be going with her."

Marie held up both hands with an offended look. "I got it the first time. Don't worry, big brother, we'll be nice."

That would be the day. "I would appreciate it."

Dad walked toward the front door. "I don't know about you guys, but I'm tired. We'll see you in the morning. Just come on over when you want. We don't have anything formal planned for tomorrow. The kitchen's got food, so you can do breakfast here or over at the house, it's up to you."

They made another round of hugs, then left. The cold night air cooled Tom's temper but not his concerns. At his bedroom door, he turned to Dad. "Maybe I'll just go hide with Wiz. They didn't come to see me anyway."

Dad clapped him on the shoulder. "Give it a chance. It will work out."

"Sure." He got ready for bed. Marie might think he was kidding, but if she forced his hand, Tom would pick Wiz over her every time. She deserved it and so did he.

Chapter 16

 **Wiz**

Four days after the arrival, Wiz stood where the mudroom entered the kitchen of the neighbor's house. The Borde clan was large, loud, and boisterous, even the littlest, but it was joyful noise. Every one of them was happy. Well, except his sister, Marie. She was always complaining about something. If Wiz was around, Marie showed up, making little barbs and passive-aggressive comments. She didn't know if Marie was nasty to all of Tom's girlfriends or it was just her, but she was feeling a little persecuted. And she'd had enough of that in her life. She'd kept the peace so far, but she'd had enough.

Tom was deep in conversation with his brother Alex. He was friendly and polite, could hold an intelligent conversation, and never pushed her for personal information. His wife Tara was equally pleasant, and their kids were cute and well-behaved. Marie's husband, Scott, was the invisible man. He hardly said anything but "yes, dear," and Wiz had yet to hear a no from him. Their daughter Yvonne was rather self-absorbed and vain, and while that was expected at fourteen, she might become a mean girl if she didn't get a better role model. She was also smart, clever, and pretty; she'd probably turn into a true beauty as she aged. Peter was an intelligent and obedient kid, quick to offer help. She wasn't sure how he'd survived so far, but his sweet nature wouldn't last with those two as parents.

Marie's eagle eyes swept the room, so Wiz slid back into the mudroom. Marie seemed to have a sixth sense for finding Wiz, and she didn't want to endure another confrontation. Wiz had done her best to be polite, but she'd done enough. The sun was going down; she'd just leave. Maybe tomorrow would be better.

"Wiz, there you are! Why don't you come join us?" Marie's voice was cheerfully malicious.

She spun. *Caught.* "It's late, and I have work to do. I was just going to tell Tom goodnight, but you can pass it on for me, if you don't mind, please?" Wiz kept reverting to her old tactics—placating people. Overcoming childhood habits was hard, but it probably made her seem like an easier target for a bully like Marie.

"You sure do work a lot. We've hardly seen you." Marie stalked closer.

Wiz took a step back. Two more and her back would be against the door. She stretched to her full height and stared in Marie's eyes. "My company has a reputation to protect, and that means me working. I'm sure you can understand."

"Oh, of course." She grabbed Wiz's arm.

Wiz twisted out of her hold. "Marie, I've asked you not to touch me before, and I'm asking again now."

She rolled her eyes and huffed. "Geez, lighten up.

I'm just trying to be friendly."

Wiz was done. "No, you're not. You're deliberately doing everything Tom told you not to do." She brought her hands up. "Touch me again and you'll be on the floor."

"Well, I never." Marie huffed in an over-the-top offended voice.

Wiz kept her voice low but cut off her words, trying to emphasize them and get through Marie's head. "Never what? Listen? Care about others? Stop picking at people? I've tried to be polite to you, but you just won't stop."

Marie glared, putting her hands on her hips and leaning forward. "Fine. You're using my dad and brother. You're one of those people who do nothing but take, and you're not good enough for my brother. You're a freaky, whiny little girl who won't grow up and join the real world."

Wiz didn't return Marie's glare, but she didn't drop her hands either. "Oh, really? And just what do you know about the real world? Have you even been out of the country? And I don't mean a Caribbean cruise or a quick trip to Canada. I mean to a third world country where they hate Americans." The so-called real world wasn't fun; Marie had no idea what it was like outside her protective bubble.

She sniffed. "No, why would I? And that has nothing to do with you being a clingy little weirdo who thinks she deserves special treatment. You've done nothing to earn anything from anyone in this family."

"Really, Marie?" Tom put a hand on Marie's

shoulder and spun her around, dragging her into the middle of the kitchen. "How would you know? And who made you the one who decides that for the rest of us? Exactly how are we being used? Wiz hasn't asked us for anything. I've had enough of this. Do you think I've missed how you've been treating Wiz? Who do you think you are?" Tom pushed Marie back against the countertop, then put his hands on his hips and loomed over her, just as Marie had done to Wiz. Red flags highlighted his sharp cheekbones and the muscles in his jaw jumped.

Wiz stepped forward to the edge of the back entryway, but she was trembling. Too many people, too many emotions. She clamped her hands to the doorway, just so she wouldn't run.

"Yes, Marie, I think I'd like an answer to that as well." Pete's drawl was exaggerated. "We both asked you to have a little consideration for someone who matters to us; some basic manners. And you can't even be polite. I'm ashamed of you and your behavior, and I'm grateful your mother isn't here to see how you've broken the golden rule. Or do you still remember that at all?" Pete leaned across the doorway into the kitchen, keeping the rest of the family out, but they crowded close. With the open plan, they could see and hear everything in the kitchen anyway. Wiz appreciated Pete's attempt to keep the confrontation quiet, but it was futile.

"You're being taken in by this woman." She jabbed a blood red nail in Wiz's direction. "You don't really know who she is or what she wants, and she just bats her eyes and you both come running!" Marie threw her arms in the air.

Tom leaned away, avoiding her claws, then returned to loom over Marie. "What is wrong with you? I've had enough of this. I've given you money, time after time. I've never said one word about your husband or how you raise your kids. How about *you* grow up and join the real world? I told you from the start that I would pick Wiz over you, and I meant it. Next time *you* come visit, I won't be here." He turned toward the rest of his family. "Peter, Yvonne, if you want to join us on the summer pack trip, I'll pay for your airline tickets. Or anytime you want to visit your grandpa." He turned back to his sister. "Marie, you're never getting another cent from me, so if you were worried about Wiz taking my money away from you, well, you've done that all by yourself. Live within your means and grow up!" He turned on his toe and pointed at the door. "Let's go."

Wiz escaped into the cool evening air, blowing out a big breath of relief. But that wasn't good, either. "Tom, I don't want to come between you and your family. It isn't right."

Tom sighed and walked up the drive. "Come on. I can't stay here." He strode ahead, and Wiz scrambled to keep up. "Look, this isn't really about you. Marie has always been convinced that the world owes her something. And she wants all of *us* to pay her way. This has been coming for a long time now. She's gone after every girlfriend I've brought home. Usually more subtly, so I didn't have to step in. And while it doesn't reflect very well on me, I didn't care that much about any of them. But I love you, and you're worth everything to me."

"No, I'm not. She's right there. There's no upside for you here, Tom." She jogged in front of him and stopped. "I am a freaky little weirdo who needs special treatment. There are days when I can't stand even you touching me, and anything more? I'm not sure it will ever happen." He could do so much better. She was a weight and a burden.

He shook his head, a slight smile on his face. "I don't care. I love you." He held out his hands, and she automatically put hers in his. "And look at this. You didn't even think about it, did you? I put out my hands, and you reached out. You wouldn't have done that a month ago. And if we never get beyond hand holding, well, that's okay." He shrugged. "Not ideal, but I can live with it. I love you, and we'll go at your speed." He tugged gently.

Wiz leaned into him, desperate for the comfort of his embrace. But he couldn't really love her; she was just too damaged.

Tom rocked her slightly. "Shh. It's okay."

She shook like a leaf. "This is ridiculous. Why am I reacting like I was in a real fight?"

"Because you don't like confrontations, especially with people who matter. I don't like them either. Somebody always says something they're going to regret. In this case, it's probably all of us, except you. You have nothing to regret. But trust me, you're not the only one shaking, love."

Tom's body trembled too, so she squeezed tighter. They stood in the middle of the road, holding each other. After a long time, Wiz loosened her grip. Tom immediately let her go but held her hand. They strode up the hill to her driveway, then down through the gates and into her house. Wiz went straight to the kitchen. "Something to drink?"

"Yes." He smiled sadly. "I need it after that. I'll get mine; you get yours." He crossed to the side table in the dining room, which he'd stocked with alcohol and mixers, and poured a small glass of scotch.

Wiz poured glasses of water for both of them and her favorite comfort drink, a bottle of Yoo-hoo. She stopped before she reached the living area.

Tom sprawled on the sofa. He'd started the fire and he stared into the flames. When the designer had picked out the furniture, Wiz had initially objected because it was all so huge; she'd feel lost in it. The designer wanted to match the scale of the room and reminded her that not everybody was tiny. Wiz was glad she'd given in. Tom looked comfortable; the sofa was perfect for a man of his size. He turned to look at her with a smile. "What are you thinking about?"

"That you fit my furniture better than I do." Someday, she'd think before she spoke.

He laughed and looked around the room. "I suppose that's true. Come here; we'll fit it even better together." He raised the footrest and held up his arm. She put their drinks on the coffee table and snuggled under his arm, resting her head on his chest. He wrapped his long arm around her loosely, and she relaxed. "That's better."

"Yes, it is." Wiz reveled in the warmth of his body and the comfort of his embrace. She might not have earned special treatment, but she couldn't bear to reject Tom's love either. They sat there, wrapped together, and watched the flames of the fire. Before too long, Wiz realized that Tom had fallen asleep. Staying with Tom was a much better idea than getting up and working. She nestled closer and closed her eyes.

Wiz woke. A man's arms wrapped around her body, and she moved through the air. Someone was carrying her, someone large and strong—she had to escape! Without opening her eyes, she jabbed her elbow to crush the man's throat. But she'd misjudged, striking muscle.

"Uh!" Before she could strike again, she dropped, landing gently on the floor, and the arms slid away. She bounded to her feet, ran for a wall, and spun to face the threat, dropping into a defensive stance.

"Wiz, it's me. I'm sorry. Wiz, wake up. It's okay."

A large man stood six feet away, his hands raised high while backing away. No threat, unless he had a gun. She grasped the concealed pistol at the small of her back and looked at his face. *Tom. Oh, no.* She'd attacked Tom. She dropped her hands, her heart dropping with them, and collapsed against the wall. "Tom. I'm so sorry. Are you okay?"

Tom stopped and lowered his hands. "Sure. I'll have a bruise on my chest, but I don't think you broke anything." He rubbed the right side of his chest, just below his collarbone.

She could have broken his collarbone or worse, crushed his throat. She closed her eyes but was too stressed to leave them shut. "I'm so sorry. I..." Marie was right. She was too dangerous to be around a real family.

"It's okay. I shouldn't have tried to carry you." He smiled slightly and shook his head. "I didn't think. You were sleeping so soundly that I didn't want to wake you, so I thought I'd just carry you upstairs and put you to bed. It really was stupid of me."

"Tom. I'm sorry." She blinked back tears. She'd been fooling herself. She was too dangerous, too hazardous, and putting those she loved at risk.

"Really, it's okay." He held out his hands. "This was entirely my fault. Of course you'd panic if I carried you. We've talked about this very thing, and I should have known better. Don't you dare feel bad about this."

She couldn't take his hands. She didn't deserve his love. She dropped to the floor, wrapped her arms around her knees, and cried. She was too messed up.

Footsteps caused her eyes to open. Tom, his body wavering through her tears, walked to her and crouched in front of her. He stretched out his arms but didn't touch her. She could have killed him and he offered to hold her. She didn't deserve his love, but she longed for him. Despite her determination, she reached for him. His arms closed around her gently, and she buried her head into his shoulder, soaking his shirt.

"It's okay, love. Really." He rocked her.

"No, it's not. It's not okay at all," she wailed.

"Yes, it is. I'm fine. I shouldn't have done that, and I'm sorry."

"You shouldn't have to be sorry for being nice!"

"Love..." He sighed. "I want to sit, with you on my lap. Is that okay?" She nodded. If she spoke, she didn't know what would come out of her mouth. Bad enough tears were rolling down her cheeks. He sat on the floor with his back against the wall and shifted her onto his lap. "Really, it's okay. I was stupid. And I think you must have realized somewhere that it was me because you didn't hit as hard as you can."

She shook her head violently. "No, no, no, all I thought was that somebody had captured me, and I had to get away."

He pulled her tighter, resting his cheek against her head. "That may be all you *thought*, but I really believe you knew it was me at some instinctive level. I'm absolutely certain you could have hit me harder. If you'd really gone after me, I'd have a broken collarbone or throat. And even if I did, you're still worth it, love."

"No, I'm not. I'm too dangerous. Even a year from now, I could attack you in my sleep or something!"

"Love, you won't." He rocked her again. "A year from now, you'll be so used to me being around that even if you have a flashback nightmare, you'll know it's me. And I'll have learned to move away, rather than moving closer. We're both going to learn new behaviors, rather than relying on instinct and habit."

"Why would you bother sticking around for another day, let alone a year? I'm too broken."

He dropped his arms but slid his hands up to cup

her face, gazing into her eyes. "Because I love you. And someday soon, I hope you'll believe me."

"It's not that I don't believe you, it's just that I can't believe anyone would be able to put up with all my...damage and drama, without hating me in the end."

"Love..." Tom shook his head.

"I don't know if I'll ever be normal." Salt tightened the damp skin on her cheeks.

"Normal is boring. You're you. You're unique." He moved his hands to her shoulders and shook her just a little. "And you're not broken. If you were broken, you wouldn't still be here, you wouldn't be in therapy, and you wouldn't be trying anything new. You're beautiful like kintsugi pottery; the mending makes the piece more unique and gorgeous." He grinned, wrinkling his nose. "Besides, normal is overrated."

"I don't deserve you. You should find somebody who is whole and strong. Somebody who can really be a partner, somebody you don't have to overcome your instincts with." Someone who couldn't carelessly kill.

"I had that, and I was bored. I settled. I didn't have a strong desire to spend the rest of my life with her, or grow old with her, or have kids with her." He raised a hand, waving it. "Not that I'm saying we have to have children; that's up to you. But I know, beyond a shadow of a doubt, that you're the person I want to grow old with, that I want to watch grow with me, that I want to be with, period. I don't want somebody else. I love you the way you are, today and tomorrow."

Wiz looked down at her body and swallowed. She

had to tell him. "Tom, I can't have kids. When my attacker dropped me on the clinic's doorstep, I was evacuated to Landstuhl for emergency surgery. I was in the hospital for weeks, recovering from the damage and the surgery. That's the only reason that I got what little justice I received. The medical community went to bat for me and brought in the inspector general. They'd seen increasing numbers of military members being assaulted by other service members, and the attacks were getting more violent. They drew blood at the clinic, and they knew I'd been given GHB and alcohol. That's why I can't remember what happened. And the fuzzy half-memories make everything worse because I can't remember the details or who did this to me. I only remember hands on me and pain and trying to get away and more pain. It's all shadowed and flashes, and..." Wiz closed her eyes and shuddered. She had no more tears to cry but no energy to do anything but sob.

"Shh. You're okay now. I got you." Tom held her, rocking her gently, and stroked her back.

She felt safe, secure in his embrace. But she couldn't have children, and they were important to Tom, that was obvious from the way he treated his nephews and nieces. She wiped her cheeks with her hands. "Tom, you'd be a great father, and you deserve to be one."

He frowned. "I have nieces and nephews. They're more than enough for me. If you want children, then we can adopt or foster. Plenty of kids out there who need parents. It's not an issue for us. Really. It's not." He pulled her close and held her, but not too tight. "Better now?"

She nodded, her cheek rubbing against his damp shirt. She was a mess.

"Good. And I'm glad you could share your experiences with me. You don't *have* to tell me anything, you know. You don't owe me. I'll take you as you are, if you'll let me."

She shook her head, bumping his firm chest. "I don't deserve you, but I'm too weak to push you away."

Tom huffed and released her, grasping her by the shoulders and meeting her gaze intently. "You are *not* weak in any way, shape, or form. You're a survivor and a fighter. And you deserve far more than some old rancher like me. But I love you, and I'll do my best to make sure you don't regret being with me."

She didn't deserve him. "I could never regret being with you. You're amazing and wonderful, and you're not old."

"Honey, I'm forty-two. That's not young."

"So? It's not old, either."

"No? If we adopted a baby, I'd be sixty by the time they finished high school. That's not young."

"There are guys out there having kids who are way older than you are."

"And I don't think that's wise." He shook his head. "But it's their decision. Just like this one is yours. I love you, and I'll do my best to convince you to stay with me, but in the end, if you can't love me, then I'll let you go. It will suck, and I'll drink myself into a stupor for a week or two. But Dad will still be your father, and I'll smile at your wedding. Because you will get married.

You're too wonderful a person to be alone, and there are too many men out there who will want you as badly as I do." He paused and swallowed. "Well, no, I won't be at your wedding. I'll be getting drunk again. But I'll smile at family get-togethers after that, I promise."

He was being ridiculous to put her at ease. "There is no way I'd be with somebody else. No one could ever care about me the way you do. But I just don't think I'll ever be able to love you the way you deserve to be loved."

He smiled confidently. "Sure you will. You already are, right now."

"How?"

"Because my love for you doesn't depend on you returning it. If you hated me, I'd still love you. I wouldn't act on it, but I'll always love you. Maybe in time, it would fade to friendship instead of relationship, but I'm never going to look for someone else. You're it." He smiled. "Besides, look how far you've come physically. I'm holding you right now, aren't I?"

"What does that have to do with anything?" She was still too dangerous.

"You trust me enough to hold you now, and you'll trust me more in the future. Even if we never go further than me holding you, that's more than good enough." He huffed and shook his head. "With what you just told me, I'm amazed and absolutely thrilled that we've gotten this far. But I have a question."

"Yes?" She tensed.

He ran his hands up and down her back. "You said there was physical damage. Are you okay now, or are you still in pain?"

"I have some nerve damage, and I have to take hormones because of the hysterectomy. And..." Blood rushed to Wiz's cheeks.

Tom pulled her in tight. "And? Can you feel pleasure?"

Not looking into his face made the embarrassment easier. "Argh, this is embarrassing."

"No, it isn't. Love, there's nothing wrong with physical pleasure, but if it isn't possible, then I'm not going to be selfish. That's not love."

She didn't deserve such a selfless man. She'd gotten so much and given so little; she could at least give him that. "The nerve damage isn't that bad. I can feel pleasure."

"If we ever get that far, and there's no pressure to do so, we'll go very, very slow. You've got to tell me if something doesn't feel good. I mean that. You don't have to endure something just because you think I like it. We'll work to find what works for both of us, slowly, together. Okay?"

"Okay. I still don't know why you'd be willing to do all this, but I can't give you up either." She was too weak.

His arms tightened around her, and she felt safe, rather than confined. "You make me the happiest man on earth." He kissed her temple. "Now, it's late, and we both need some sleep. You head upstairs, and I'm going to sleep on your couch."

His low voice rumbled comfortably through her body. "Why?"

"Because I don't want to leave you alone tonight, but I know you probably wouldn't sleep if I was in the same room with you. This way, I'm here, but not too close." He shrugged, and Wiz could hear the amused acceptance in his voice.

"I was able to sleep with you on the couch." But she'd tried to attack him after.

"But that was on the couch. In your bedroom? Your sanctuary?" He pushed her away a little. "I'm not sure about that. We can try, but you need to kick me out if it makes you uncomfortable, especially after all the emotional trauma tonight."

Wiz bit her lip. His arms were so comforting. But her desires were platonic and selfish. "I'd like you to stay, but it's too hard on you." She shuddered. "Besides, what if I wake up and panic again?"

"I'm willing to take that chance. I'd love to just hold you while we sleep. Or just be there for you."

"Really?" Nobody was that selfless.

"Yes, really. I'm sure it will also be a lot more comfortable than sleeping on your very nice couch or sitting on this rather hard floor."

She jumped off his lap. "I'm sorry!" She was so selfish.

"I was joking." He got up, wincing. "Okay, mostly joking. But I'd put up with far worse to have you in my life. I mean that." He put out his hands. "Believe me?"

She put her hands in his and squeezed. "Yes." She didn't deserve it, but she'd accept it. "Oh, you'll need access. Let me get my phone." She ran back to the living room and grabbed her phone, then trotted back and took his hand, leading him up the stairs. She closed and deadbolted the door behind them and pulled him into her room. She closed the bedroom door and locked it too and set the alarm on her phone. Then she granted him access to everything in the house and outside it, even all her emergency escapes and safe rooms. He stood just inside her bedroom door, quietly waiting.

"If you need to get out for some reason, just enter your code in the pad or if you have time, bring up the system on your phone. You've got icons for the whole house. Also, you should know about my escape routes." Taking his hand, she led him to her huge, mostly empty walk-in closet and pulled open the laundry chute hatch on the wall. Reaching inside, she released the hidden door, revealing a narrow shaft with ladder rungs on the far wall. "You can climb down, and you'll end up in the safe room. It's on a separate air handler, and there's food, water, and other emergency supplies. The chute will be a tight fit for you, but you should make it. Lots of guns and ammo down there too."

He leaned over, looking down. "I figured you had an escape route or two. A weapons vault doesn't surprise me. I'd rather not try it, but it's good to know it's there, and I appreciate you telling me." His brow wrinkled. "Are you sure you want me to have access to everything?"

"Yes. I trust you. The second is through the

bathroom window. There's an escape ladder stored in the bottom of the linen closet." She squinted at his shoulders. "That might be a tight fit, too."

He smiled sweetly. "Telling me all this is a huge gift. I won't misuse it, I promise."

She smiled back at him, truly happy for the first time in a week. She couldn't believe such a wonderful man could love her enough to put her first. Maybe, with a lot more therapy, she could become the partner Tom deserved. She was so lucky to even have the chance.

Chapter 17

TOM

Tom woke and blinked at the unfamiliar ceiling. He'd stayed with Wiz. She sprawled on the other side of the king-size, wonderfully comfortable bed. She hadn't skimped on anything in her house, and the mattress was no exception. The lack of windows seemed a little odd at first, but the murals matching the views from the house were lovely, and the airflow was excellent. He'd slept very comfortably once he'd gotten to sleep. The stress of the week had exhausted him, but Wiz's tearful revelations were impossible to forget. He'd had to count sheep to lull himself to sleep. He stretched, determined to not let the fury of the past keep him from enjoying the present.

The invitation to stay had been surprising, access to the entire house shocking, and her insistence on his comfort over hers in bed was doubly so. He'd been fine with sleeping in his clothes on top of the blankets. Fortunately, his boxer briefs and T-shirt were a good compromise. He longed to reach for her, but he knew better. Besides, that might lead to something she wasn't ready for.

Wiz's pajamas weren't intended to be sexy, but the tight little T-shirt and long pants in a thin, soft material didn't hide anything. The superhero print was a bit surprising, but she was so tiny, she probably ordered clothing in teen sizes. Like everything else about Wiz, it was adorable. He absolutely loved everything about her, even all the parts she insisted were broken. She wasn't damaged; she was strength and determination personified.

He should find his phone; he'd probably missed the morning feeding. Without any windows, he couldn't tell if the sun was up or not. Even with the hands taking the day off, Dad wouldn't begrudge him prioritizing his time with Wiz over the ranch. Besides, he probably had Peter out on the tractor. But he should check. He couldn't remember if there was a clock on the nightstand, so he rolled to check. Wiz bolted upright and bounded off the bed. Shoot. He hadn't intended to scare her. "Good morning, love. Sorry I scared you."

She put a hand over her heart. "Morning. What time is it?"

"I don't know. Can't see the sun, don't know where my phone is. Don't really care." He didn't, since she was awake. He stretched out his arm. "Will you come back to bed? You don't have to, of course."

She bit her lip. "Not sure that's a wise idea."

"That's okay, love. Whatever you want." Tom sat up. "Breakfast?"

Wiz shook her head and climbed back on the bed. "Let's see if I can do this much." She swallowed hard enough for him to see.

"Are you sure? We can take this slow." He didn't

want to push her because he wasn't sure where the lines were. And hers might change every second. "I don't expect anything, ever."

Wiz nodded and sat, sliding next to him. "I know. But I do."

"Do you want my arm around you?" He'd move at her pace and try not to assume anything.

"Yes, please."

Tom grinned. "You are so cute." He put his arm around her shoulders, and she slid hers across his back, leaving fire in her wake. Good thing he had a T-shirt on because her hands on his skin would be almost irresistible.

"We can lie down, if you want."

"Oh, I want to." Tom let his head fall back to the pillow. Wiz snuggled into his side, with her head resting on his chest, above his heart, and her hand just below. Right where she belonged. He tried to keep his breathing steady, so his heart rate didn't rise, but his body didn't entirely get the message, reacting like a schoolboy. "You feel perfect here." He turned his head and kissed the top of hers, then relaxed into simple enjoyment of their time together. "Can you tell me what you're thinking?"

"I like this. But I'd like to try more." She pulled away from him, propping herself on a hand, leaned over, and kissed him.

He returned her kiss but clamped the sheets so he didn't reach for her. Her lips were soft and warm, and when she withdrew, his head rose automatically, chasing hers. She came back, and they kissed some more.

A chime sounded, and she pulled away, smiling down at him. "Sorry. I set alarms for this week so I didn't miss anything." Her nose scrunched. "I think your brother and sister are leaving today, right?"

"Right." Tom ran his hand through his hair. "Guess I should go say goodbye." He rolled off the bed and pulled on his clothes. She rustled behind him, doing the same. After he yanked his sweater on, he turned. "This has been the very best morning of my entire life."

"But we didn't do anything." She shook her head, her nose scrunched adorably.

He grinned. "Sure we did." He winked. "We slept together." At her frown, he laughed but sobered quickly. "Seriously, though, that's a lot of progress really fast. I don't expect to spend every night with you, but I'll treasure the ones I get, especially if my presence comforted you."

She sighed. "It did. But I wish..."

"Wish what?"

"Wish I knew if I will ever be able to do more." She hung her head.

That wouldn't do at all. He rounded the bed and sat, holding out his hands. She put hers in his. "Love, we'll get there or we won't. I love you regardless. But, if it will help, I'm happy to talk to your doctor or therapist." He was fairly certain they would get there. "Look, let's enjoy the ride, rather than worrying about the destination, okay?"

She grinned at him. "Is that what you were doing in your city boots on Strawberry?"

Tom huffed. "I'm never going to live that down, am I?"

She shook her head. "Nope."

If it made her smile, he'd get thrown by a spoiled horse every day. "Come on, let's go say goodbye and get some breakfast."

She led him downstairs, poured them both a cup of coffee from her fancy automated coffee maker, and they walked to the neighbor's house across from the ranch. Marie and Scott had left already; Tom wasn't surprised or upset.

Alex and Tara were packing the last of their gear in their rental SUV. Alex hugged him. "Come on out to LA any time and bring Wiz." Tara and the kids followed. Wiz surprised them all by not only hugging the kids but Alex and Tara as well. After repeating their goodbyes several more times, Alex drove away with his family.

They went inside, and Tom opened the refrigerator. "I've arranged for cleaners, but we should clear out any food. Wiz, there's a cooler and a couple of boxes in the mudroom."

"Got it." She turned away.

Dad entered the living room and lifted the couch cushions. "I'll check for toys or clothes. I'm sad to see them go, but they sure bring a lot of noise and fuss. I hope they make it out this summer. Alex said they'd try, and both Yvonne and Peter told me that they wanted to come on our summer ride."

"Really? That's very surprising." Tom figured they'd never come back. At least not Yvonne.

Dad chuckled, shaking his head. "It's too bad you two left right away. Yvonne put Marie in her place but good. She told Marie, in no uncertain terms, that the only reason she was still on the pageant circuit was for the scholarships and that she and Peter were both smart enough to get academic scholarships, so they didn't need Uncle Tom's money. Oh, and they both like Wiz, and Mom should leave her alone because Uncle Tom seemed really, really happy and they both deserved love." He laughed. "It was quite the show. Marie huffed off to her room. Scott told me later that he'd been talking to Marie about her assumptions and that he didn't need our money." Dad shrugged. "I told him that's good because you were going to bankrupt us on some scheme for natural raising soon anyway." He laughed.

Tom was dumbfounded. Wiz snickered. He turned and pulled the boxes out of her hands. "Thanks."

Wiz nodded. "Yvonne's a smart girl. I think she's probably hiding her intelligence a little in exchange for popularity because high school kids are mean. The pageants explain some of Marie's attitude. She's a frustrated stage mother. She probably knows, deep down, that her kid doesn't want to be an actress or a model, and she's disappointed."

Dad nodded. "That might be. She was in some local pageants and plays. We never had the money or time to get her out on the statewide circuit like she wanted. Maybe she's still resentful. Of course, if she'd really wanted it, she could have gotten out there and gotten businesses to sponsor her, but that would have taken a lot of effort, and she was never big on effort. Guess we didn't do that great a job of raising her." Dad shook his head, looking at the floor.

Wiz frowned, crossed to him, and patted his back. "I don't think that's true, Pete. You obviously raised Tom and Alex right. They both understand working for what they want. Some people don't take the opportunities they're offered. And some people want things they're not entitled to. Nature versus nurture, and sometimes, nature wins. I'm sure you did your best." Wiz hugged him.

Dad hugged her back, raising his brows with a triumphant smile over her head for Tom. "Well, we tried, but you're right. Even your kids are just people, and they can do strange things sometimes."

"Yup." Wiz stepped away from Dad and returned to the mudroom.

Tom packed food in boxes. They'd have enough cereal for the next six months, if either of them could stand to eat the kids' sugar bombs or the super-healthy stuff Marie insisted on but never opened. He put that one in the donation box. "I don't understand Marie at all, Dad. There's got to be something else going on there because of course I'll help her kids if I can. Alex's too."

"I don't know. It doesn't make much sense to me. Even if you had your own kids tomorrow, it would be years before they'd go to college."

Tom checked the top shelves but found nothing but a little dust. "Maybe she was afraid there just wasn't enough to go around. Kids are expensive. But I've given her more than enough over the years." Wiz carried the cooler into the kitchen, a tear running down her cheek. Tom took it from her and put it near the fridge. "Wiz, are you okay?" She shook her head and left. "Be right back, Dad."

He followed her outside and stood by her side. She stared across the valley at the Bitterroot Mountains. Dark clouds hung low—a storm was coming. "Hey, what's wrong?" He opened his arms, and she turned into him. He held her firmly, but not too tightly, just in case.

"It's not fair that I can't have kids with you. They took so much from me, from us!" She shuddered and shook. "You deserve kids of your own."

He tightened his hold a little, resting his cheek against her hair. "No, love, it's not fair. But I meant what I said. There's plenty of kids and babies out there who need families. You know that better than most. Blood doesn't mean anything."

"Do we need to tell Pete?" She shivered.

"Not if you don't want to, and if you do tell him, he won't ask for details. He loves kids, but if we don't have any, he won't say a thing. He loves you for who you are now, not the future you."

"I'd rather not tell him. At least not now."

"Sure. No reason to rush. Especially since you haven't agreed to be in a relationship with me yet." He chuckled. "I haven't even asked you. So, when are you going to marry me?" That was a lame proposal—he didn't even have a ring. Or know if she'd wear one. "I don't know if you believe in marriage. I hope you do.

Do you?"

Wiz leaned back, gazing up at him with a quizzical, skeptical expression. "Wait a minute. *When* am I going to marry you? Not *if*?"

His words sounded a little obnoxious and cocky, but hers had triggered the question. "You're talking about wanting *my* kids. But like I said, I don't know if you even believe in marriage, not after what you went though."

"I do." Her eyes widened comically. "I mean, I believe in marriage. I don't think we should get married right now."

He laughed. "I didn't mean right now. An 'eventually' would be good enough for me."

She smiled a little, tilted her head, and her gorgeous dark skin pinked slightly. "Okay. Not right now. Eventually."

"Oh, good." He almost collapsed with relief but hugged her tighter instead. Then he pulled away and took her by the hand. "No, great. You just made me the happiest man on earth. Come on." He towed her back inside the neighbor's house, grinning so hard his cheeks ached. "Hey, Dad!"

"What, Tom?" He leaned into the refrigerator.

"Wiz agreed to marry me eventually. Isn't that great?" He couldn't stop grinning; happiness flowed through his entire being.

Dad stepped back, eyes wide, then smiled, slowly, until he was grinning, too. "That's great, all right. Perfect even. Come on." He led them outside and across the street to the ranch, striding so quickly Wiz had to jog to keep up. In the living room, he pointed at the floor. "Wait here." He trotted upstairs. Tom was pretty sure he knew what Dad was retrieving, but he didn't want to spoil the surprise. He tugged Wiz gently, and she stepped in close, so he could wrap his arm around her.

Dad thudded down the stairs, holding a small black box, the corners worn white. "Tom, Wiz, this might not be to your taste, but this was my wife's engagement ring and my mother's before that. I'd be honored if you'd consider it for yours." He handed it to Tom. Wiz bounded to Dad and hugged him tight.

Blinking back tears, love for his father and his woman scorching a brand on his heart, he opened the box and pulled out the delicate gold and diamond ring. All those years on Mom's hand had thinned the band, but it still shone bright. When Wiz pulled away, she was crying but smiling through her tears. He dropped to one knee and held out his hand. She placed hers in his, and he slid the ring on her finger. It was a little loose; they'd have to get it sized. He looked into her beautiful gray eyes, prettier than any ring, his heart singing with joy. "If you'll marry me someday, I'll be the luckiest person on the planet."

She blinked, her eyes shining and her lips pressed. She sniffed and swallowed. "I will, but I'm the luckiest." Then she looked down at the ring. "It's beautiful." She yanked on his hand so he'd stand. "And even if it wasn't, the history makes it so much better than anything you could get in a store."

Dad wiped his cheeks. "It's not a particularly large

center stone, but it's extremely clear. It's a Chanel. You'll have to get wedding rings of your own. Mine's staying here with Elise's." He pulled out a chain dangling two thin gold rings. "You've both made me the second-happiest guy on the earth." He clapped Tom on the back.

Tom pulled Wiz close. "We'll get some to match and a couple of silicon rings for every day." Wiz nodded, eyes shining brighter than the diamond.

Dad cleared his throat. "Sure wish Elise had been able to see this. She'd have been so happy."

It was his turn to blink back tears. "I'm sure she knows, Dad."

"Yeah." He nodded. Wiz handed him a tissue and dabbed her eyes. She'd come so far from when they'd met. "You said eventually. What does that mean?"

Tom shot him a warning look. "We're not setting any dates. It's up to Wiz and what makes her comfortable, and I'm not rushing her. Neither are you."

"Of course not." Dad smiled at Wiz. "But you've come a long way from the girl I met a few months ago. I don't think it will be long."

"I hope so." Her joyful smile was winning over her tears. He wrapped an arm around her shoulder. He'd take every opportunity he could to hold her and hope that someday, she'd turn to him rather than away during the bad times.

Dad sat in his recliner with a sigh. "I guess I'll be seeing less of you around here in the evenings."

"Maybe. Wiz works long, late hours, so maybe not." He squeezed her slightly. "That's up to her, too."

She pulled away, grimacing. "I do have a lot of work to do. I have to make up for the last week. Pete, you're welcome to come up to my place anytime, even if I'm working. Use your codes." She flashed a smile. "I know you haven't forgotten them."

Dad nodded. "Sure. You know, if you want to, you can call me Dad. Or keep calling me Pete. Either way is good. Or both."

She'd turned to leave, but she stopped. She spun and stared at Dad. Then she ran across the room, throwing herself to her knees next to his chair, and lunged up to hug him. Tears brightened her eyes again when she stood. Tom handed both of them tissues and took one for himself.

Wiz dabbed her eyes and blew her nose. "You two have turned me into a leaky water bottle. I'll see you for dinner?"

"Sure. Tell you what, come down here. We'll get something special together to celebrate." Dad rose from his recliner.

Tom held out his hand, and Wiz grasped it. "I'll walk you out."

Wiz held up her hand, the diamond twinkling. "Thank you so much. I'll treasure this so much and both of you even more." She swallowed hard, then whispered, "Thanks, Dad." Then she dragged Tom out the door. Outside, she stopped and squeezed his hand. "I really do need to get some work done. But I'll see you for dinner. Call me when you're almost ready, okay?" Those big gray eyes twinkled brighter than the diamond.

"Sure, love." She turned, but he didn't let go of her hand. She twirled back, lifting both brows. "Hey, I just wanted to say," he lifted her right hand and kissed it, "I love you. This is the best day of my life."

She blinked, a smile growing across her pretty face. Then she jumped and wrapped her arms and legs around him, kissing him passionately. He returned the kiss, meeting her soft lips with his, and held her tight, hoping he conveyed his love.

Wiz pulled back. "I love you, too." She kissed him softly, then jumped down and ran up the hill to her house.

Tom watched her feet fly, and his heart flew with her. Yep, the best day ever. And it was only getting better.

Chapter 18

 Wiz

Wiz smiled. She was doing that a lot lately, and it felt so good. Like she was emerging from a swamp, washed clean and reborn, a little battered and bruised but stronger than before. She did things she never thought she'd do ever again, and it was all because of the man who had literally landed at her feet. Well, not just Tom. The whole bunch of them. Tom, Dad—it still gave her a thrill to call Pete that—Ryan, Erin, and all the rest of them.

The horses had helped too. Dad had been right. Horses were soothing, and controlling such a large animal was empowering. She stroked the curry comb over Blackie's back. He shivered and leaned into her, so she brushed harder. She'd teased Dad about his unimaginative naming convention, but she had to admit Brownie and Blackie were easy to remember.

"You know he'll keep you doing that for hours. That one just loves to be groomed." Tom peered over the back of her horse.

"I know. I find it comforting."

Tom smiled. "Then continue. But Dad and I are headed in for lunch."

Her stomach growled. "Okay, you win. I'm

starving."

Tom chuckled, untied Blackie from the post, and let him loose in the pasture, where he promptly dropped and rolled in the mud, undoing all her hard work. She laughed. They all did that, but it was still funny.

Tom held out his hand, and she put hers in it. And that gave her such a thrill. She'd believed she'd never touch a man again, or let one touch her, but with Tom, it was almost easy. Perhaps it was that such a big, confident man would give her the lead. He was definitely not a pushover, and very much a take-charge kind of guy, but at the least little sign she was uncomfortable, he backed off immediately. It was so amazing to find a man with the self-confidence to do that for her.

Tom opened the door to the kitchen for her, and she walked in with him behind her. Which was also amazing. She felt so safe with Tom at her back. They both hung their hats up in the entryway. Wiz smiled at hers. Such a wonderful gift; she'd never forget last Christmas.

Pete entered the kitchen from the downstairs bathroom, with Rusty on his heels, panting. "I'll get lunch out while you two wash your hands."

"Thanks, Dad." They shared the downstairs bathroom sink, scrubbing each other's hands while sneaking a quick kiss. She might have kept her lips on his all afternoon, except Tom's stomach rumbled, making her laugh. They dried their hands and returned to the kitchen.

Plates with sandwiches and salad sat on the table

already, with glasses of water. Wiz smiled at Pete, already sitting. "You don't have to wait on me. You must be starving."

Pete mock-frowned. "Now, how many times do I have to tell you, young lady, that we don't do that in this family? Say your thanks, and then we'll eat."

She bowed her head and gave a heartfelt thank you to God for bringing these two men into her life. She was the luckiest woman in the whole world.

They ate while Dad offered ideas to improve her cow herding skills, which she was just learning.

Tom stood and gathered the plates. "I'm guessing you need to work this afternoon on your business, right, Wiz?"

Wiz grabbed the glasses. "Yes. I'm behind, again." She could never seem to catch up. At least she didn't have to feel bad about turning down work—she simply didn't have time to do more.

"But you'll get it done—you always do." Tom smiled.

She sighed. "True. But sometimes it's a struggle. I love the programming. It's the other stuff that takes time and effort and too much work."

Pete wiped the table. "You know, Tom's a smart guy. He could probably do some of that for you. He runs the business side; I just do the grunt work when I want to."

Wiz closed the dishwasher. Pete was right. Tom was certainly intelligent, and he knew business. If she went over her client processes with him, he could tell her what he was capable of doing.

"That look is scary. I wonder how badly this is going to hurt." Tom chuckled.

"Oh, it won't hurt at all. Well, until you're blinking your eyes at zero-three hundred and wondering where you are, then remembering you're doing documentation for my security system." Wiz grinned.

The men laughed. Tom shook his head. "I don't think I'm up to documenting your technical work, but I'm sure I can help with the business end. Research is something I'm pretty good at, and financials are easy."

"If you could help me with initial research, that would be a huge help." Wiz rubbed her chest. The warmth of hope was still unusual, but she loved the feeling. "I'm very particular about my clients, and sometimes it takes a lot of digging to find out if someone's operating honestly. I don't take on clients with dirty money, or criminal enterprises, or immoral ones, like trafficking and prostitution. I'm good at what I do, and my work doesn't require a lot of maintenance other than the automatic updates I do for every client. So, I have to bring on new clients constantly. It's a contradiction, to some extent. I need new business all the time, but it takes a lot of time and effort to check into some people." Wiz frowned. "Some are easy. Anyone Erin's mother refers to me is an automatic no. She's gotten into a dangerous crowd."

Pete shook his head. "It's a shame. Tom followed your advice and moved the majority of our funds into two of the other banks in town."

"Erin, Deb, and Sam have done the same, which makes me feel a lot better." Wiz didn't like speaking ill of local businesses, but the Russians they were dealing with were dangerous, and their methods were brutal. Marcus Bank was playing with fire. She hoped it didn't blow back and burn the whole town.

Tom grimaced. "I know Sam and Deb were grateful for your warnings. Deb was already looking at moving her banking; Ms. Murphy kept sending investors to her that she didn't want. I've warned other people I know, quietly, too. If doing your research helps you stay out of trouble like that, I'm happy to help. Although I have no idea how you dig into somebody's background, and I'm not brilliant with computers, or anywhere near as smart as you are, but I'm sure I can learn the basics." He nodded. "An intellectual challenge would be good for me. And maybe you could work fewer hours."

"And maybe if you keep him busy, he'll quit bugging me about switching over to natural raising." Dad glowered.

They both laughed, and eventually, Dad joined them. Wiz knew he was mostly kidding, but Tom could be a bit like Rusty with a bone, just plain dogged. He needed to back off a bit. So, she could kill two enemies with one round—give Tom something new to work on, and give Dad some time to consider all the factors. "Perfect. So, tomorrow, after our morning ride and lunch, Tom will come work for me for a couple of hours, and Dad, you can do your 'research' in peace. You know, the kind with your eyes closed on the couch. It can even be my couch if you want." Wiz winked at Dad.

Pete guffawed. Tom raised his brows. "Why do I

have a feeling that I'm going to regret this?"

"Because you are. I'm a slave driver when I'm working. And I'm not a nice boss either." She wasn't kidding; she was more like Rusty driving a fractious herd of spooked young steers.

"Oh, I think I can figure out how to make you be nice to me." Tom smirked.

Dad cleared his throat. "I don't need to hear about that. Let's get going. Tom, I want you doing rope work with Strawberry. I've got a possible home for her, but I need to make sure she's not going to throw the girl when she whirls a lasso around." He strode to the mudroom.

"Sure. Let me get my other gloves. These are too heavy for rope work." Tom leaned down and gave Wiz a kiss, then trotted upstairs.

Wiz caught up with Pete. "Thanks for the idea. It's a good solution to all our problems."

He chuckled. "Provided you don't kill each other first. You're both strong-willed and a little stuck in your ways. At first, it will be easy, but once Tom gets the hang of what you're doing, he's likely gonna want to change things. And that may or may not be good."

"We'll see what happens. Even if I end up firing him, it won't impact our personal relationship." Maybe she shouldn't be so sure about that. "Right?"

Tom slapped his gloves against his thigh. "You're already talking about firing me? I'm wounded." He smirked.

She'd been right. "Don't worry, only from the business side, not my life."

"Still, it's an arrow to my heart!" Tom put his hand over his heart and pretended to fall, catching himself on the mudroom door. Wiz giggled. He could be such a goofball sometimes.

"All right, work to do. Let's get going." Dad opened the door and tromped out.

Wiz walked up the road to her house, enjoying the early summer sunshine. It would get hot all too soon, but the winter had been long.

Within sight of her house, she stopped. A car idled in her driveway, and a man stood near the keypad, punching at it. She crouched and moved off the road, hiding behind a small pine, squinting. Jeff, her ex-husband. How did he find her and why couldn't he leave her alone? She didn't owe him anything.

She put a hand on her weapon, nestled in the cowboy rig Dad gave her, then backed down the hill, out of sight, and sidled to her horse fence. She'd use the west side gate and confront him from the other side. But first, she pulled out her phone and brought up her security app. It had already initiated a lock-down. She'd missed the alert because her phone was on vibrate. She pulled up the video camera over the gate, making sure it and all the others were recording. A text came from her alarm company, saying they'd requested the sheriff's office to respond on a non-emergency basis. They were monitoring her video surveillance, ready to upgrade that request if necessary. She sent a text back, acknowledging and agreeing.

Wiz moved off at a fast walk, glancing at Jeff's

increasingly frustrated face on her screen, still uselessly punching in code after code. She entered the horse fence side gate, keyed in her code for the security fence, then sprinted for the opening, because he might have heard the clang of the horse fence latch closing automatically behind her. She yanked the chain link gate shut and secured it, then she turned to face Jeff.

Sure enough, he'd seen her, jumped the horse fence, and ran toward her. She backed out of taser range, just in case he was stupid enough to try, then agreed with the alarm company's text that they'd requested an emergency response based on the trespasser pursuing her. She put away her phone and put her hand on her weapon. She made her voice loud, firm, and unemotional. "Jeff, get off my property. You are trespassing. The sheriff has been called. I don't want to talk to you or see you ever again, and you're not getting anything else from me."

He clasped the chain link, pouting. "But baby, I just want to talk. I miss you."

"I don't miss you. Go away."

"Baby..." He blinked his big brown eyes at her, like a puppy.

Wiz scowled. "Oh, please. You don't miss me at all. You just want my money."

Puppy changed to snarling dog. "You owe me." He shook the chain link.

"I don't owe you a thing. You divorced me, remember? When I needed you, you left and had papers served on me. The divorce decree is final. Now, go away. You're trespassing, and I'll have you arrested if you don't leave immediately. And don't come back."

"You owe me, all right. You hid the money from me. Liar." He jammed his tennis shoe toe into the fence and lurched upward, the chain link rattling.

Wiz drew her weapon. "Jeff, you are being recorded, just as it says on the signs on the gate you jumped. Get down and leave, or I will be justified in using deadly force to defend myself. Do you understand me?" She pointed the gun at the ground, with her finger on the trigger.

"I understand I'm getting what I came for. You'd better let me in!" His lip curled and he climbed farther.

"No." She fired into the ground at his feet, took her finger off the trigger, and bellowed over the ringing in her ears. "That's your only warning. Next one goes into you."

He dropped off the fence. "You ungrateful liar! If you don't start playing ball, you're going to regret it. I'll make sure that what you went through downrange is nothing compared to what we'll do to you!"

"You have just been recorded making threats. You will be served a restraining order."

He laughed. "Like that means anything."

"You're right, it doesn't mean a thing. But you'll never get to me, Jeff. I can have you arrested right now for making threats against me." Tom and Dad galloped up the hill on their horses behind Jeff. She didn't show the relief she felt at having real, live backup. Jeff, dummy he was, didn't even notice them. She'd keep talking. "The sheriff has been called. You're going to end up in jail. And that's clearly where you belong."

Tom entered the code on the horse fence gate and galloped toward Jeff, swinging his rope overhead. Dad cantered higher up the road, then stopped, drawing a rifle from his saddle holster. Wiz kept her pistol pointed at the ground but was ready to raise it. "I don't owe you anything. I earned everything I have after we divorced. One last chance, leave."

"No." Jeff put his hands on the fence.

The lasso dropped over Jeff's shoulders and tugged his arms tight to his body. Tom yanked the rope tight, jerking Jeff off his feet, and wrapped the rope around the saddle horn. Strawberry backed perfectly, just like she was supposed to, keeping the rope tight. "The lady told you to leave. We'll just help you along."

Jeff clambered upright, then Tom backed Strawberry, yanking him off his feet again. After two more attempts, Jeff stayed down. He yelled over his shoulder, "Let me go!"

"I don't think so. You're trespassing, like the lady said. Trespassers aren't treated kindly around these parts." Tom glared—he was absolutely magnificent. Wiz laughed.

Jeff glared at her. "You witch! I'll get all of you!"

She laughed harder. Tom yanked the rope. "There's a lady present. We don't use that kind of language here." He put a hand on the knife sheathed at his waist, and Jeff paled.

Wiz snickered. He was pitiful. "Jeff, I'd recommend you think twice about revenge. Look up the hill. See that man on the horse? He trained at the same school as Carlos Hathcock, the famous Vietnam sniper. You'd better not come back." Wiz let her tone go from gleeful to ice cold.

Tom slapped the rope, twanging it, and Jeff winced. "There's this little phrase we Montanans use that sums up our thoughts on vermin. It's called 'shoot, shovel, and shut up." A menacing half-smile bloomed on Tom's face. "And to paraphrase a famous song, if you disappeared, you'd be a missing person nobody would miss."

"You've just threatened to kill me on video." Jeff's chin raised. "We'll see who's going down now."

"No, I haven't. I've told you what happens to vermin. I haven't said a thing about doing anything to you." Tom shook his head. "You should learn to listen, especially to Wiz."

"You'll regret this." Jeff snarled. "You'll get what's coming to you. You'll all end up dead, but they'll hurt you first." Jeff turned and glared at Wiz. "It'll be worse than downrange."

Wiz's hands jerked her weapon up, but she pushed it back down and kept her finger off the trigger. But it took so much effort—she wanted to shut him up. How dare he use her worst day against her?

"You're done." Tom turned Strawberry and walked away, dragging Jeff behind him. Jeff screamed obscenities and scrambled to his feet, but Tom kept Strawberry moving fast enough so Jeff couldn't get the rope off. Wiz holstered her pistol and pulled her phone, opening the main horse fence gate. Tom dragged Jeff to the door of his car, then expertly flipped the lasso off. Pete adjusted his position to keep

Jeff in view without risking Tom or Strawberry but kept his rifle pointed at the ground.

Wiz stayed behind the chain link security gate and jogged to the driveway. Tom pointed at Jeff, who yelled more obscenities while climbing into his car and left, gravel flying from his tires. Strawberry stood like a rock.

Wiz holstered her weapon, opened the main security gate, and reset her program, texting the all-clear to her monitoring company and asking them to secure several copies of the video for future legal action. They agreed. Tom and Pete trotted to her, and she closed the gate behind them, the chain link rattling.

Tom peered down. "Are you okay?"

"Yeah, I think so." Wiz shuddered. "You were amazing." Dad rode up behind Tom. "You were both marvelous. The look on his face was priceless." She shook her head.

"I'd still like to shoot the varmint. He's going to be trouble, you wait and see." Pete slid his rifle back into the holster.

Wiz trembled. Shoot—the reaction was hitting.

Tom offered her his hand, taking his foot out of his stirrup. "Come on, jump up behind me. We'll head up to the house."

"Okay." Her voice shook, too, but she was safe with Tom. She'd feel even better inside her house, her sanctuary. She grabbed Tom's forearm and hopped, getting a toe into the stirrup. He pulled her up and twisted in the saddle, so she slid on to the horse behind him. She gratefully wrapped her arms around him and hung on until they got to the porch. He maneuvered Strawberry next to the porch, and Wiz slid off.

Dad joined her, slinging an arm around her shoulders. "Come on, let's get inside. Tom's got the horses." He led her to the couch, then brought her a Yoo-hoo. Tom joined her, sliding an arm around her and pulling her into his side. She was so lucky to have such a rock. After contemplating the mountains for a while, Wiz stopped trembling.

Pete sipped a soda. "You ready to talk about this, darling?" Wiz nodded. "Good. The problem is, we scared him a bit, but he was still making threats. He'll be back, and it won't be a straight forward attack. He'll try something sneaky and nasty."

Wiz agreed. "Luckily, he's not very smart. He was trying to get in the front gate with random four-number codes. He should know I'd use more than four numbers and that I'd have it auto-lock after three tries. He's always had an exaggerated view of his own intelligence." She still couldn't believe she'd fallen for him. She'd been so desperate for love. But she'd learned what real love was.

Pete frowned. "He'll still try. Are you going to get Sam to file a restraining order for you?"

Wiz sighed. "Yeah, although I hate to do it because I have to file as myself, exposing my personal information, and I've been really careful to hide all of that, staying behind a corporate wall. Court records aren't sealed, unless you can show cause, and I can't. Not yet. And that worries me because he's working with other people. Unless his threats were all bravado." But he wasn't smart enough to think of that in the heat of the moment, and he'd fallen in with a bad crowd after he'd left the military.

"Can you show me the whole thing? I want to know exactly what he said." Tom squeezed her shoulder.

"Sure." She brought up the video on the TV and played the best views of Jeff's face. Most people didn't bother recording sound on security cameras, but she'd found it handy in distinguishing wildlife from people. Good thing she had because his words were very clear.

Tom and Dad scowled through the whole thing, although they all chuckled watching Jeff's butt bump across the rough grass. Pete shook his head. "He's got friends or he's working with other people. Maybe someone who doesn't like you. This guy is nothing, but a group of people might be dangerous."

He was right. Men could turn savage in groups. She shivered. Tom tightened his hold. "Are you okay, love?"

"Yes, but Dad's right. There are plenty of people who blame me for their problems. They're slimeballs, but I outed their behavior and got them fired, so it's all my fault." Her fear was changing to anger. It might not be the healthiest response, but she didn't care. She was tired of being scared.

Pete scowled. "That's how those kinds of people think."

Wiz sighed. She had no choice. "I've got to file for a restraining order, then. If Jeff found me, anyone can. Or someone did it for him. Eventually, I might have to shoot one of these people, and I'll need the justification." She closed her eyes, trying to control the mixture of fear and fury coursing through her. "This sucks. They should leave me alone."

"Yes, they should. I'm sorry you have to deal with good-for-nothing dirtbags. But I'm glad you're thinking about it, not just reacting or hiding. I don't think either of those would work well in this situation." Tom rubbed her shoulder.

Wiz nodded. "One of my key lessons from the Air Force was to have a plan. It might not survive contact with the enemy, but at least I considered the problem and solutions." She sighed. "I'll send the videos off to Sam and make an appointment. In the meantime, I think you two, and probably your ranch hands, should be armed when you're out. You've made yourselves targets, too."

Pete nodded. "Yes, you're right. Well, nobody blinks twice at a cowboy with a six-shooter, so we'll rig up like we're on the trail every day. One of the hands carries all the time anyway. Let's get together tonight for dinner and make some plans."

Wiz smiled. She was so lucky to have these men in her life. "Sure, Dad. I'll cook. You guys come on up."

Tom rubbed her shoulder again and kissed her temple. "Are you okay to be alone?"

"Yes. I'm okay." She was. She'd check all her security, then cook. That would keep her from uselessly stewing about what she should have done.

"All right." Tom rose, chuckling. "There is one good thing out of all this."

"Oh?" Pete got up, too.

Tom offered her a hand. "Strawberry was perfect. If she can handle an armed confrontation, roping a weird critter, and flying gravel, she's ready for a teenage girl."

Wiz laughed, the two men joining her. He was right.

Chapter 19

TOM

Tom rubbed his eyes, then squinted at the screen again. Nope, not getting any clearer. He sighed and shifted in his seat on Wiz's comfortable office couch.

"What was that sigh for?" Wiz looked up from her laptop.

"I need an eye exam. Computer work is tough on them. I might need reading glasses." Tom grimaced. He wasn't that old, and he'd only been helping Wiz for a month.

"Oh. I didn't think you'd be anywhere close to that yet." Wiz frowned.

"Yeah, I didn't think so either, but I'm squinting. I've been mostly working outside the last couple of years. Now, I'm on the computer all the time." He shrugged. "Not that I mind working with you, so don't take that the wrong way."

Wiz nodded. "I trust you to tell me what you're thinking and feeling." Her head tilted and her brow wrinkled. "Have you increased the font size?"

He huffed. "Well, yes. But I don't want to go too big, or I'll be scrolling constantly."

She gazed at him, her brows rising, then lowering. He'd learned to be a little wary of that speculative look, since it often meant a lot of work for him. Of course, there was a lot of reward, too, but... "What's going on in that pretty head?"

She smiled slightly. "It's time to get you a desk. And some big monitors. I should have done it already, but you seemed pretty happy working on the couch. You should get your eyes checked too, but there's no reason to stress them. I know they make desks and chairs for tall men. Maybe one that can adjust to a standing position. I like mine a lot." She clicked and tapped furiously. He knew better than to say no. When she got on the trail, nothing threw her off. Besides, she was right. He'd be better off with a big monitor on a real desk.

She clicked for a while, then smiled at him. "There. Big adjustable desk, best chair available for tall guys, three twenty-seven-inch monitors, and an ergonomic keyboard and mouse."

She could afford the outlay, but he didn't need all that. "Geez. Seems a bit much."

"No, it isn't. You've been working for my company. The least I can do is equip you properly." Her head tilted. "Actually, I should be doing a lot more for you."

"Oh, I like my rewards just the way they are." As they'd worked together, she'd become more and more affectionate, initiating hugs and kisses often. She'd made real progress, and her therapist was very pleased.

Wiz wrinkled her nose and smiled, then sobered. "Still, I should be paying you a salary; you've more than earned it. Oh! Maybe you should be a part owner.

Yeah, that might work better. Thirty percent?"

Tom held up a hand. "That seems a bit much. I'm not doing that much work."

She smiled and waggled her brows. "Oh, but you are, and you'll be doing more soon, I bet. Thirty percent, with opportunity for growth. Hmm." She tilted her head. "I need to talk to Sam anyway. I'll ask her to come up for lunch this week, and we can revise all my business paperwork and my will and trust."

Wiz had an excellent point. He needed to add a trust for his nieces and nephews; it'd been years since he'd updated his will. "I should revise my will, too. Can you ask her if we could do that at the same time?"

"Sure." She glanced at her screen, then scanned the office. "The furniture will be delivered this week, so we'll have to move some stuff around."

Tom groaned. Last time Wiz rearranged the office, it had taken them hours, and in the end, nothing really changed.

"Don't worry, it will be easier this time. I downloaded an interior decoration program, and I've already put in the existing furniture. I just need to add your new desk, and we'll arrange it virtually first." She winked. "I'll give you a back rub after."

Tom mock-scowled. "The back rub better not be virtual."

She rose and walked—no, strutted, to him. "Oh, there will be nothing virtual about that. Nothing at all." Wiz pulled the laptop from his hands, setting it on the end table next to him, and sat sideways on his lap.

He wrapped his arms around her. Nothing better in

this world than a cuddle with Wiz. Even better when she initiated without any prompting from him. She'd made so much progress. "Oh, yeah. You know I'll work hard for that, baby."

Wiz stiffened. "Don't call me that."

Tom loosened his arms immediately, but he was puzzled. "What's wrong?"

"Don't call me baby. *He* called me that all the time, and I hate it." She scowled.

His heart sank. "Oh. I'm sorry, Wiz. It was an... automatic endearment. I'll try not to use it again, but it wasn't something I thought about." He definitely didn't want to remind her of the idiot ex.

"You haven't before."

"Hmmm." It was tough to think with her perched on his lap. He lifted her, placing her on the couch next to him. She glared. "Sorry." He shrugged. "You're too distracting. I'm a simple guy, remember?" She huffed, but a smile grew. Good, because his explanation was likely to annoy her; it didn't say anything good about him, either. "I think I fell back on an old automatic response. In my former life, I was popular, and women have sat in my lap to get my attention quite a bit. I've never seen you act... sexy, before. Whether you intended to or not, that's how I took it. So, I replied automatically." She glowered at her lap. "Sorry. That reflects badly on me, not you. And trust me, I think you're always sexy, and I love seeing you confident. I want to see more." He absolutely did. While he was perfectly happy to simply hang out with her, kissing and cuddling had become the highlight of his day. The glimmer of something more was encouraging.

"I shouldn't be upset about your old relationships, but I kind of am." She licked her lips, and her shoulders hunched.

He offered his hand, palm up, and she accepted without hesitation. "Maybe you should be. I shouldn't be bringing old habits into our relationship. But I am kind of old and set in my ways. I'll do my best to remember, if you'll go easy on me when I forget. But please tell me, don't let it fester, okay? It's my problem, not yours, and I need to fix it."

She squeezed his hand, finally looking at him again. "You're not old."

He snorted. "Sure I am. I need reading glasses."

She scoffed. "That doesn't mean old. Besides, how old do you think I am?"

Tom chuckled. "You expect me to answer that? No way. I may be old, but I'm not stupid."

She laughed. He loved her laugh, and making her laugh was the highlight of his day. She shook her head. "Tom, I'm thirty-four, not some kid. You're only eight years older than me. That's not that much."

The relief surprised him. Guess he'd worried about the age gap after all. "Well, it's less than I thought." He squeezed her hand gently. "I'm grateful when you're willing to share with me."

She pressed her lips together for a moment. "I didn't want to feel anything for so long that I'd forgotten how to be happy. Sorry."

"You have nothing to be sorry for, Wiz. Nothing. We both know there are going to be things that make one or both of us unhappy. Finding those things and talking about them is a process. A slow process, but as long as we keep talking, we'll be okay." He squeezed her hand again. "Besides, I'm the one who is and should be sorry, not you. But now I know, and I'll try not to do that again. If I do, smack me on the shoulder, and I'll eventually get the message through negative behavior modification." He smiled, hoping he could hold her again soon.

"Okay. I can do that." She turned toward him. "But you might end up with some bruises."

"Oh, hurt me, honey." He froze and swallowed. "Is honey okay?"

"Yes. It's just 'baby' that bothers me. My ex used it as more of a put-down, partly because I'm short." Her nose wrinkled adorably.

"You're not short, you're tiny. And perfect. A perfect little angel." His Christmas angel.

She shook her head and let go of his hand, then lifted his arm and nestled close to his side. "I'm a long way from perfect. And even further from angelic." She rested her head on his chest. "But being small does have some advantages." She twisted, leaning across him, pulled his neck down, and kissed him.

He returned her kiss with interest. She should stay right there, next to his heart, forever.

\#

Sam retrieved the sheaf of papers, her assistant stamping her notary seal on them and finishing the rest of the paperwork. "Okay, so we've got the petition for the permanent protective order and petition to seal records ready. I think, with the documentation you've given me, that this will be a no-brainer. I wish we knew the names of these other people your ex referred to because we can only file against him." Sam glared. "I still can't believe any of this happened to you. It's just so very wrong. I'm sorry you had to tell me, and I'm even sorrier that you're going to have to tell a judge. And serve the papers on your ex. Hopefully the ass won't show up to contest it. But that's the way the legal system works, for better or worse. At least you're well-protected, unlike a lot of the women I do this for."

Tom hugged her closer. As she'd told her story to Sam, she'd hunched her shoulders and pulled her legs up. He'd expected her to run for her bedroom at any moment. But at Sam's last words, she straightened. "Yes. I can protect myself."

"And you have help. Trustworthy help." Sam nodded at him.

Wiz smiled and sat upright again. "You're right. I'm not going to let those jerks back me into a corner again. I'm living *my* life, and if they confront me, well, they're going to lose."

Fierce was sexy on Wiz. He huffed. She was sexy, period.

"Tom, I'm assuming you'll be attending the hearing?" Sam cocked her head.

"Of course." He'd always be there for Wiz.

"You may be in for some trouble." She grimaced. "While I can understand why you acted the way you did, and I think the judge will too, he could decide to charge you, if the ex pushes it. We'll press charges too, but..."

Tom snorted. "I don't care. I wish I'd just shot the braying jackass."

Sam scowled. "*Don't* say that to the judge. Just tell him you're sorry and you'll wait for the sheriff next time."

"Sure. Whatever it takes. But I'd do it again."

Sam shrugged. "And Wiz?"

"Yes?"

"Make sure that if you have to shoot, that it's clear you are in danger, and preferably do it inside your house. Not the yard, your *house*. I can make a case either way, but it's easier in your house."

"Got it." She shuddered. "I'd rather not. I don't want to kill anyone, but if I have to, I will."

"No weapons in the Courthouse." Sam wagged a finger. "I can get a deputy to escort you to and from your vehicle if you'd like."

Wiz nodded, grimly. "Maybe. If you hear that Jeff's showing up for sure, then that might be smart. Although, I can't imagine anyone being stupid enough to try and gun me down on the Courthouse lawn."

"Despite our wild reputation, we try to minimize the Old West gunfights," Pete drawled.

They all laughed. Sam sipped her Diet Coke. "Okay, so what else did we need to do today? Wiz, you said something about modifying your company from single owner to owner and member?"

"Yes."

Tom let Wiz's voice wash over him. He really didn't care about the company ownership, but it was important to Wiz, so he'd do it. Just being in her life was reward enough for him.

\#

A week later, they sat in the back of Wiz's van. Sam nodded sharply. "Well, that went as expected. Excellent."

Wiz fastened the last knife into her arm sheath and pulled her cuff down. "I was surprised at how supportive the judge was."

"I talked to his assistant at length when I got the emergency interim protective order and again, before the hearing, so the judge understood the details I couldn't put in the petition. Unfortunately, even though it's sealed, your ex still has all of this information, and he could pass it on to someone else. He'd be risking contempt of court, but he doesn't seem like the kind of guy to care." Sam grimaced. "Or understand how bad that can be. Anyway, once I get the final order, I'll get the same process server to serve it on your ex, since he found him for the emergency restraining order. I'm glad he's not here." She smiled grimly. "Of course, if Jeff had shown his face, the judge might have tossed him in jail right after the hearing for egregious trespassing and threats involving deadly force."

"I was hoping he'd issue an arrest warrant, but I can understand why he didn't." Wiz fidgeted.

Sam turned and poked Tom in the chest. "And you. After that lecture, you'll leave the physical stuff to the sheriff, right?"

Tom tossed a two-finger salute. "Yes, ma'am.

Although if I feel Wiz is in danger, I will act."

"You'll need excellent proof." Sam poked him again.

He held up his hands in surrender. "I got it. No more Wild West Show justice. Although it was appropriate, and I noticed even the judge cracked a smile when I dragged the guy across the pasture." It hadn't gotten any less funny to watch that part.

"All right." Sam shook her head, a wry smile on her face. "Your wills and business papers are ready. Why don't you drive the Wiz mobile here over to my office, and I'll just get my assistant to come out here to witness and notarize. Will that work?"

"That would be great. Thanks for being so understanding, Sam." Wiz rose.

"Are you kidding me?" The outrage on Sam's face matched her voice. "I wouldn't be half so rational as you are if all that had happened to me. And I know you didn't, or couldn't, tell me all of it. I'm just glad you survived and that you're recovering. Living well really is the best revenge."

Wiz nodded. "I think you're right. A few months ago, I wouldn't have agreed, but now? I have too much to lose to waste time on those idiots."

"Good for you, Wiz. I'm really happy to hear you say that." Dad, with a proud smile on his face, opened the side door for Sam so she could return to her vehicle.

Tom turned the passenger seat around to face the front, while Wiz slid into the driver's seat. She really was recovering, and he hoped desperately that the horrible people who had attacked her had learned their lesson and would leave her alone. He just wanted to marry her and live happily ever after. It really wasn't too much to ask.

Chapter 20

 **Wiz**

As she tied the last knot, sweat ran down Wiz's back. The sun was way too hot for early summer.

"That's not too shabby, Wiz. I think you're getting the hang of this right quick." Dad grabbed the pack saddle and pulled it from side to side, testing the balance of the load. She'd bundled camping gear in lightweight bags, then wrapped the bags in the large sheets of heavyweight canvas customarily used by horse packers, and finally tied each pack to properly hang from the pack saddle. For practice, the pack saddle sat on the Rocking B corral fence rail, rather than on the back of a mule. Making each side the same weight and bulk was critical for the safety of the animal on the trail; an unbalanced load made accidents more likely.

She grinned, then undid the ropes on the pack saddle. Packing was a mix of engineering and alchemy but, like most things, got easier with practice. Fortunately, she'd only have to do the packing in an emergency. Which made it more important to get good at it—because there'd be no time to waste.

She untied the ropes from the saddle and lowered the packs, then unwrapped the canvas and put all the camping gear back. After replacing the last of the items, she left the barn to watch Tom work his horse. But he was turning the horse very slowly, gazing up at the mountains and sniffing. His horse sidled under him, betraying his unease.

"What's the matter?" Wiz searched up the hillside, a hand on her weapon.

"Do you smell smoke?"

Wiz sniffed. "Yes. Do you see anything?"

"No. Tell you what, let's ride up the hill. Smoke makes me nervous. No one should be burning anything right now. It won't be the neighbors; they're all smarter than that, but it could be a camper left a fire burning."

"Sure." She saddled Blackie and mounted while Tom and Dad talked. It had been a good winter, with lots of snow, but that meant the grass had grown tall and thick. Then the summer so far had been unusually hot and dry; they'd had several fires in the lower foothills already. They'd been controlled quickly, but it took so little for a small fire to blow into a conflagration.

Tom trotted up the hill, and she followed. As they neared her house, the smoke went from tickling the back of her throat to burning her nostrils. They halted above her house and scanned the edge of the forest again but didn't see smoke or flames. Wiz pulled out her phone and checked the security cameras on the edge of her property, but she didn't see anything there, either. "Tom, maybe we should check from the observation deck on my house? I've got spotting scopes."

"Good idea. Let's go." He turned and trotted away.

She keyed in the gate codes, and they cantered down the drive. She closed the gates behind them. She had an excellent fire suppression system; if there was a fire, there was no need for the firefighters to waste time on her house. And if it caught, better to simply let it burn. Things were replaceable; people were not.

Tom helped her off her horse and tied both of them in the shade. They ran inside and sprinted up the two flights of stairs, panting a bit at the top. They scanned the hillsides but spotted nothing.

"We could ride along the connector trail." Tom pointed at the rocks denoting the edge of Forest Service land.

Wiz shivered. "I don't know. I'm getting a bad feeling about this. Something's not right here. There hasn't been any lightning, we haven't heard gunfire, there's a ban on burning except campfires already, and there's no campgrounds around us. I just don't like it. Where's Dad?"

"I'll check." Tom pulled out his phone and dialed, while continuing to scan the forest.

Wiz grabbed a spotting scope, set it on the half-height wall, and scanned the air right above the tree tops, searching for smoke.

Tom got off the phone. "Dad's okay. He's with the hands, and they both smell smoke too. They're doing evacuation preliminaries just in case."

"Are they armed?" A shudder ran down her spine.

"Dad says they're all rigged out." Tom patted the

revolver on his hip.

"Good." She scanned. The wind was coming up from the south rather than the west like usual, so she searched farther south. "I think I've got something. Come check."

"Your eyes are better than mine, but I'll look." He crouched next to her.

She locked the scope and scooted away.

Tom put his eye to the scope, then unlocked and moved it slightly. "I think you're right. Let's call 911."

"You call. Let me see if I can figure coordinates for the firefighters." She pulled her mapping program, centered on her house, and triggered the laser range finder on the spotting scope. The haze of smoke was too far away for the laser to lock on, but she'd get a direction and guess the distance. On her map, she snapped a line from the house on the azimuth from the spotting scope, and it intersected with a forest road. She tilted the phone so Tom could see it.

Tom nodded. "Yes, we can barely see the smoke, but it looks like it might be coming from Gold Camp Creek. We'll keep an eye out from here and let you know if we get a better view." He clicked off. "They're sending a fire crew out from Stevensville. Dispatch said they've had a ton of abandoned campfires this year. Stupid, lazy people." He put his phone away. "It's too dry."

Unease crawled along her spine. "Tom, no matter what the cause, you should go help Dad. I'll stay up here. Call if you need me. Oh, and take Blackie back. I'll take the four-wheeler if you need help."

"All right. Text me with any changes." Tom kissed her and headed down the stairs.

"Be careful!" She trotted down to her office, grabbed a laptop and a tablet, then sprinted back to the observation deck. The laptop scanned the outer perimeter security cameras, and the tablet displayed the mapping program. On her phone, she watched Tom mount his horse and grab Blackie's reins. She opened the inner gate, closed it behind him, and then opened the horse fence and secured both of them. Neither the security camera or her eyes saw anyone on the road or near her property line, but something didn't seem right.

She returned to the spotting scope, unlocked it, and scanned north, toward her house. If this was something more than stupidity or bad luck, there might be more fires. Arson happened for a variety of reasons. Or a trailer's security chains might have come off, sending sparks flying as they dragged along a road, or an off-road vehicle malfunction or a person chain smoking, throwing still-smoldering butts out the window.

Another plume of smoke, along the same azimuth but closer. It could be someone riding an off-road vehicle on one of the trails. She called Emergency Dispatch's non-emergency number and updated the operator. They said more reports had come in, and the Forest Service and the local fire departments were dispatching additional crews.

Once she hung up, Wiz brought up the scanner app on her phone. Multiple fire departments were responding, and the Forest Service was requesting air support. They weren't going to take any chances.

She pulled a chair to the spotting scope and continued looking north. A flash of light caught her eye and she focused on it. A four-wheeler bounced along the Forest Service trail, and fire bloomed in its wake. She refocused on the rider—fire started underneath their outstretched hand. A drip torch! The rider was deliberately setting the fires, using the tool wildland firefighters used to set backfires when they had to. She dialed 911 and reported the position and direction, which was too close to her property. Then she dialed Tom. "It's arson. Someone on a four-wheeler is using a drip torch, and they're coming this way. I've reported it, and they're sending law enforcement. But the local fire and police departments are all responding to Gold Creek first for evacuation notifications. The fires are already growing there."

"I heard that on the scanner." Tom's voice was urgent but calm. "We're notifying the neighbors and moving the cows to the river. Are you staying there or coming down to help?"

She tracked the four-wheeler. "I think I'd better stay for a while, so I can tell the police the criminal's location. The 911 operator told me she'd pass my number to the responding officers. And once they're in range, my cameras will record for evidence." Drip torches were common in the area; a lot of ranchers and farmers used them to burn fields in the spring, too. Unless law enforcement caught the person in the act, the arsonist could drop the torch and speed away, never to be found.

"Okay. Be careful, and if it looks bad, don't wait too long. We can replace the house, but you're irreplaceable."

She wanted to join Tom, but she had an obligation to help catch the criminal. The fire could burn not only her place, but the Rocking B Ranch, their neighbors across the street, and well beyond that, if conditions were bad. The sooner they stopped the arsonist, the easier the fire would be to contain. Her house was fairly safe—it would take a tornado of fire to overcome her protections. But those did happen. "Be careful. The cows are replaceable, too. I love you."

"I love you, too. See you soon."

She watched the four-wheeler, fire spewing in its wake. If only she had a way to record from the scope! But she didn't, and in the end, it didn't matter because they were rolling closer with every second.

Her phone rang. "This is Deputy Smith. Am I speaking with Victoria Meadows?" His voice was high-pitched and grated like nails on a chalkboard.

"Yes, please call me Wiz."

The wail of a siren was loud in the background, but she thought she heard a sniff. "Right. Are you still tracking the four-wheeler?"

"Yes, I am. He's just turned from the crest trail on to the connector trail that goes to the Rocking B Ranch Road. I live at the top of the road."

"Copy that. I'm about ten mikes, oops, sorry, minutes out from your location, on the Eastside Highway."

"I understand the military lingo. Be aware that the

Rocking B Ranch is moving their cows to the river, so you may get blocked temporarily. If that happens, please turn off the lights and siren or you'll panic them."

"Yeah, I know the drill. They may not be the only ones, so it may take me longer than my ETA."

"Copy. Did you want to keep the line open, or shall I call you with relevant updates?"

"Text me. I have to notify residents along the way."

"Copy. Out." Wiz hung up the phone, shuddering. The situation was nerve-racking. She didn't like being separated from Tom and Dad, and for some reason, that deputy's voice sent shivers down her spine. She'd heard it before, but she didn't know where.

She watched the ORV get closer, lighting the fires closer together the nearer they got to her property. Was the arsonist targeting her, the Rocking B, or something else? Or was the person mentally disturbed? Or an insurance scammer? She had no way to know, but whatever the reason, the perpetrator was succeeding. Plumes of black smoke billowed into the sky to the south, growing higher and bigger. If the wind shifted, the whole valley could go up in flames. She put her camera to the lens of the spotting scope and snapped some pictures. The person wore a plain black helmet and military camouflage clothing. Neither were unusual here, although a lot of riders didn't wear helmets. But the use of a drip torch implied someone who burned fields or forests on a regular basis. Which could be just about anyone who lived in the local area, since Montanans still burned fields in the spring and lots of people had wildland firefighting experience.

A text came in from Tom. "Cows and horses gathered in the west field. Going back the house for the tractor and emergency packs." Wiz sent him a heart in return. They had all their critical records and keepsakes packed in bins, along with basic supplies in bags. Hers were in fire-safe vaults, but she had a pre-packed bug-out bag. Being ready for an evacuation was part of the price of living in Montana.

Her phone rang—the deputy. "Yes, Deputy Smith?"

"Hey, I'm at your gate. Where's the perp?"

She checked the spotting scope. "Still on the connector trail, up in the forest. Seems to have slowed down." She brought up the camera on her gate. The SUV was the right color and had the right badge on the side but didn't have lights. The deputy's face was shadowed by the interior and his hat.

"Huh. I can't get up there in the patrol car. Can I come up and look?"

The man's voice made her skin crawl, but she didn't know why. She didn't want him in her house but didn't have a good reason to keep him out, either. "I'm not sure what good it will do you. The person is wearing a helmet. I can send you a picture."

"I need to see how fast he's traveling and how he's riding. I know a lot of ORV people, and I know how they sit their machines. You do want to catch this guy, right?"

She shivered. The combination of impatient arrogance and an odd gloating tone set her back up. She had a bad feeling about the man, but he was law enforcement. "Of course I do. I'll open the gates. Park in front of the house, and walk straight through the house toward the kitchen. The stairs are between the dining room and the kitchen. You'll have to climb two stories."

"See you soon." The phone went dead.

She couldn't pin her nervousness down. A stranger in her house was difficult, but her uneasiness went far beyond that. She made sure her internal and external cameras were recording and the video was uploading to the cloud, via her normal internet and her backup. The man entered her house; his uniform shirt strained across his large belly, and his hat shaded his face. He wore a standard police-style belt with a pistol, taser, and a radio. He looked the part, but something was off.

She checked all her weapons and opened the small pistol safe built into the observation deck wall at the far end from the stairs. She turned, facing the stairs, the spotting scope to her right, the open safe behind her, and her weapon loose in her holster. In her left hand, she held her phone a little behind her leg, with two nines entered and her thumb on the last nine.

Footsteps plodded on the stairs, then heavy breathing echoed too. The deputy wasn't in shape if two stories made him pant. She shook out her right hand. Some thought she was paranoid, but she was still alive, and she'd learned to trust her instincts. Or maybe she hadn't; she shouldn't have let the man in.

A pistol emerged from the stairwell, pointed at her, the deputy blowing like a whale, the gun moving slightly with his panting. She'd been right to be nervous. She pressed the third nine and the double star. Metal hissed, snicked, and banged, locks securing and metal shutters dropping into place, including all around the observation deck. Lights flared, compensating for the lack of sunlight, the jerk of the gun in the man's hand relaying his jolt at the noise.

"Well, well, old Jeff was right. It is you." The man sneered. "Drop the phone. Then put your weapon on the floor and kick it over here."

Wiz didn't move. If the man was friendly with her ex-husband, he'd be a bragging jerk, not a competent marksman. "Who are you? I don't know you."

"Don't you? I know you. Biblically, that is." He chuckled. "We had a good time. Well, I did. Oh, that's right, you don't remember it."

The man who assaulted her downrange. Ice shot down her spine. But he'd just confessed on video.

He waved his pistol. "Drop the weapon and the phone, then the clothes." He motioned with the gun again. "I can shoot you in the leg or the shoulder and not ruin the fun." He raised the pistol. "Then the evidence will all go up in smoke. Such a shame."

She didn't bother responding verbally. She dropped the phone, letting it clatter on the floor, and reached for the buckle on her cowboy rig. She unfastened it, watching the man's eyes drop to her hand. She let the end fall from the buckle, his eyes following the snapping end of the belt, then returning to her right hand. She slid her right hand down, slowly, while moving her left up and behind her. She grasped her backup pistol at the small of her back. With a snap, she tossed the gun belt at the man and ducked. Fire erupted from the barrel of his weapon. She drew her backup weapon, aimed, and fired.

Two to the chest, one to the head, just like they'd been taught in training. Just like she practiced every week, right- and left-handed. The man dropped to the floor with a thud she heard over the ringing in her ears.

Keeping her backup weapon trained on the man, she retrieved her phone and belt. She kicked the still smoking gun out of the man's hand, not that it mattered with the holes in his body and the growing pool of red below him, and buckled her gun belt. Then she replaced her backup piece and got extra magazines for both weapons from the gun safe on the wall, jamming them in her back pockets. Only then did she take a moment to consider her attacker's words. The man knew Jeff. Was Jeff driving the four-wheeler and setting the fires, or was her attacker working with more people? She'd assume the worst, that both her ex and others were involved.

She checked the laptop; people were inside her security fence, running to her house, her gates hanging open. The 999 code had locked all access points and notified her security company along with Tom and Dad, but determined people could break through, regardless. She drew her primary weapon and entered the stairs, padding quietly down. The second level door was secured properly. She'd climb into her basement safe room, but since she'd just killed a deputy sheriff, law enforcement probably wouldn't be responding unless it was with a SWAT team, even though the man had clearly threatened her and confessed to his previous crime. And they should be busy with the fires, evacuating people and saving lives. She could save her own and save her property, too.

Tom would have seen the alert, but he was busy with the ranch. And she didn't need his help, even though she desperately wanted him near. She pushed her longing away. She had a job to do. She sent him a text. "I'm safe. Attacker dead. More outside, but I've got it."

Unlocking the door to her office, she jogged to her desk and brought up the surveillance outside the house. Men swore, banging and jerking on the doors. She turned up the sound a little to compensate for the ringing in her ears. She'd never fired a weapon without hearing protection.

A tow truck stood in front of her house, a stranger hooking chains to her front door latch. They must have used the tow truck to pull her gates down, too. Jeff, the tow truck operator, and three more men stood near the truck. The operator got in the truck and drove forward, yanking the latch off the front door. Four men poured inside, only to pound on the inner door. Wiz smiled grimly. With a tow truck, they'd get that one off, too. But getting upstairs would take some work. She'd wait a little longer before going to her safe room.

Her phone buzzed with a text from Tom: "On our way."

She sent one back with a picture of the truck and the five men. "I'm safe in the office. Route to safe room clear."

A metallic screech and bang signaled the removal of the inner entry door lock. Time to make life more difficult for the attackers. She turned out all the lights on the first floor. With the metal shutters in place, it was darker than the inside of a cow. The swearing increased dramatically. Then she pulled up a spooky soundtrack used for haunted houses and played it on all the first-floor speakers at a barely audible level. She chuckled, although her laughter was a little... off. Which wasn't surprising; she'd just killed someone and more were attacking her.

No. Don't think about the past. Focus on the mission. Stay alive. She brought up the infrared cameras on the first floor. She only had a few, but they were sufficient to show the bumbling of men into furniture. The designer thought she was crazy, refusing to leave a clear area between the front and back doors, but her reasoning had just proven correct.

Her phone buzzed with a text from Ryan: "On our way. Status?" Tom or Sam must have told him what was going on because Ryan wasn't on her notification list.

She sent back: "Coordinate with Tom." Then she started a group text with Tom, Ryan, Erin, and Sam. "I'm secure on the second floor. Fence gates and front doors yanked open. Five men on the first floor, lights are out, metal security shutters down."

Tom added Pete to the text group. Surprising; Dad hated texting. "Pete Borde; I've got exterior command. Stage at Borde ranch house; text with ETA, names, weapons. Wait for assignment. I'll coordinate with law enforcement."

Wiz grinned. Dad had just learned the advantages of texting—informing everyone quietly and quickly. Her smile fell. She hated that the older man had been drawn into a battle; he deserved a safe, quiet life after surviving Vietnam. Only her stupid, selfish ex could do such a horrible thing.

Light flared on the monitor, and she switched back to visual cameras overlooking the stairway door. They'd finally remembered their phones had flashlights and they huddled. She turned up the sound level on the closest microphone, but it created some static and the soundtrack interfered slightly.

"…just got to get out, man!" That one was clear; the man was panicking.

"Calm down. Just got to shoot the lock on the stair door, and we'll get her, and she'll give us the money." Jeff's voice was instantly recognizable. She still couldn't believe she'd fallen for the idiot.

"No, man, you can't shoot out a lock, and my chain won't reach this. I'm not using the truck to smash through the place either. My boss would kill me. I'm out." One man dropped something to the floor with a clatter and ran to the front door.

She sent a text. "One outbound, probably in a tow truck." When her house was clear of attackers again, she had to add a microphone so she could talk over her speakers. But if Jeff's phone number was the same, she could call him. She dialed on her tablet, wanting her phone free for texting.

An obnoxious rap song pounded her ears, and she turned the speakers down. Jeff jumped, one of the others smacking his arm. "Why wasn't your phone on vibrate? Dumbass."

Jeff answered. "Hello?"

She made sure her words were clear and cold. "Jeff, you have one chance. Leave now, or you're all dead. Your buddy the deputy is already dead. I've got a team outside, ready to accept your surrender. If you stay, you're clearly a threat to me, and I will take you out. Do you understand?"

"I understand you owe me!"

"No, I don't." She hit the red button, cutting off his demands. She'd tried. Once Jeff discovered she'd hung up, and quit ranting, the remaining men whispered and walked to the kitchen, phones creating beams of bright light. The kitchen surveillance showed two men crouch in front of her commercial range. A gas range. Rats. She hadn't considered the need for an automated propane cutoff.

She texted Tom. "Can you talk?"

Her phone buzzed. "Love, are you okay?"

"I'm fine. But I need the propane turned off outside. They're doing something to the stove, either setting a fire or trying to rig it to blow."

"You're kidding me!"

"No, unfortunately. I've got fire retardant in the range hood, so a fire isn't a threat, but if they empty the propane into the house, they might get enough in there to blow things up a bit. I'll be fine in the safe room, but it will make a huge mess. I can open the security shutters, but the windows aren't automated. The propane tank is buried at the end of the garage. You'd have to pop the cover, then turn it off. Can you do it safely, or are there more enemies out there?"

"There's a guy on a four-wheeler; Dad's got him pinned down behind the house. We'll move that direction, but it may take a while, since they're actually stupid enough to try and return fire. We can use the deputy's vehicle as our cover."

"Thanks. Be careful, especially if law enforcement shows up. I can go to the panic room and stay or take the escape route from there. If they blow the house, it can be replaced. You can't."

"We got this. Be careful. I love you."

"I love you, too." She clicked off.

She brought up the outside cameras and watched Tom crouch and run down the hill to the sheriff's vehicle while Dad fired at the end of the house by the garage. The man with the four-wheeler cowered with his hands over his head, pistol clenched in one hand. Once Tom reached the sheriff's car, Dad drove their old truck down the road slightly, probably looking for a place he could directly target the guy with the four-wheeler.

In the kitchen, the men had pulled all the pots and pans out of the cupboard under the range and were whispering again. Probably trying to figure out how to turn on the propane without killing themselves.

She had to slow them down. She cackled, the sound startling in her office. Swiping through her security programs, she found the sprinkler control panel. They were designed to go off in zones, rather than all turning on at once. Water damage would be easier to fix than being blown up, if it worked. And she could turn it off quickly. Grinning, she triggered the kitchen sprinklers. They blasted down and set the fire alarms ringing. She silenced all of them except the ones on the first floor and texted everyone what she'd done.

The men jumped to their feet, water pounding down and the range hood showering them with fire extinguishing chemicals. The strobe-like effect of the fire alarms made it hard to see the men, but three of them ran for the door, slipping on the wet floor.

She sent a text. "Three outbound."

The remaining man appeared to be Jeff. He walked carefully through the deluge to the stair door. Guess he was determined to die. He raised his pistol, aiming at the door.

-BOOM-

The muzzle flash fuzzed out the IR cameras. He fired three more times. It was unlikely he'd get through the lock, but maybe she should confront him. Get it all over with. She walked to the door going downstairs, opening it but staying on her side of the frame. She left the bottom door locked. She didn't *want* to kill him, not at all. She wanted him to leave. But she wasn't going to die, either. Nor was she going to let her house burn down with her in it. She'd wait for a short time and see what he'd do next.

Jeff kicked the door, then hopped around, holding his foot. He fell and put his injured foot down, stopping his descent, but howling in pain. Then he picked a long, skinny object off the floor. A crowbar; the tow truck driver must have dropped it. He jammed it into the splintered wood near the lock, damaged by his gunfire. He jammed the bar in, over and over, eventually creating a hole large enough to pry the door open, splintering the frame around the deadlock. She should have ignored her designer's insistence on keeping the pretty wood and gone with steel. Jeff stumbled inside the stairwell and landed badly on the stairs, but bounded to his feet and pointed his weapon up the stairs.

Her heart pounding, she stayed out of sight but ready. "Jeff, drop the weapon, or you're dead."

"You owe me that money! And they'll kill me without it." He fired as he ran up the stairs.

Wiz waited. She blew out her breath halfway. His weapon appeared, and fire flashed from the barrel. She fired, hitting the target in the left temple twice, and into the chest as he fell, rolling down the wide stairs. She released her magazine and reloaded. Then she slowly padded to the target and kicked his gun away. His shirt had slid up; a second pistol was tucked in the waistband of his pants, and she pulled that out and tossed it down the stairs.

She stared down at the eyes of the man she'd once loved, staring blindly up at the ceiling. He had to have known he couldn't survive. But he'd said, "*They'll* kill me." Someone else was involved, which meant there might be more attacks. Hopefully, they'd stop with Jeff's death. She closed her eyes and sagged against the stairwell wall. Then she forced them open. She had bad guys to deal with. *Lock the emotions down, deal with them later.* She pulled her phone, skirted the pool of blood, and stopped just inside the stairwell door. Then she pulled up the exterior cameras on her phone.

The remaining men were lined up in front of the house, hands in the air, kneeling on the driveway. Tom was cuffing them to each other. Where did he get handcuffs?

She reset the sprinklers in the kitchen and retracted the shutters, then secured the second floor stairway door. Good thing she'd insisted that one being metal. Then she searched the first floor. She didn't think she'd missed anyone, but better safe than sorry.

She peered out the front door. Smoke rolled and eddied. She'd forgotten all about the fire these morons had set.

Dad stood in front of the men, rifle in his hands, pointed at the ground. Tom was cuffing the last one. Dad beckoned her out. Wiz kept her weapon in her hand and skirted the line of men, careful to stay out of his line of fire.

"Wiz! Are you okay?" Tom shoved the last guy forward, bounded to her, and reached but didn't grab her. The enemy he'd shoved swore but didn't move from his uncomfortable position, face down on the ground, one arm wrenched behind him, connected to the next man.

Wiz holstered her weapon and threw herself into Tom's chest. "Yes. I'm okay."

His arms closed around her. "Thank God. We were so scared."

"Hey, kids, celebrate later," Dad said. "Fire's coming. Let's get out of here."

"You're right." Tom's arms dropped away from her, and she stepped back.

Dad scanned her from head to toe. "Anybody left inside?"

"Two targets dead." She couldn't think about it; they still had to escape the fires.

"Oh, honey, I'm so sorry you were forced to do that." Dad shook his head.

She swallowed heavily. "Yeah, me too. Let's go while we can."

"You're right." Dad motioned up with his rifle. "All right, you scum, unless you want to burn to death, and I couldn't care less if you do, get on your feet and march."

The men struggled to their feet and slogged up the driveway. Pete's old truck was parked on the road, Tom's horse tied to it. Erin and Ryan pulled up next to Pete in their truck.

"Oh, good, prisoner transport." Dad chuckled. "We gotta get the tractor."

As they exited the useless security fence, Wiz reset the security system and engaged the fire protocol. The huge field sprinklers mounted just outside the chain link fence sprayed, making everyone jump. "Sorry. Just getting the house ready for the fire."

Ryan ran down the drive, weapon in his right hand, grasper on the left. "Wiz! You got 'em!"

"Yeah. Can we put these guys in the back of Erin's truck? We need to get out of here with the tractor."

"Sure." Ryan raised his gun. "Okay, slime, one bad move, and I'll plug you without remorse. Into the truck, sit down. Once you get in there, I want to see your hands all the time."

The men struggled to get into the back of the truck. Tom helped, throwing them in.

Erin got out. Ryan stood in the passenger doorway while Erin used tie-down straps to secure the men against the sides and tailgate of the truck, Tom grinning as he helped. There was a lot of swearing.

"Do you want to fall out?" Tom tugged on a strap. "If it was up to me, we'd leave you to die in the fire or put a bullet in your heads, but we'll let the law deal with you."

Ryan opened the back window on the truck and kept them covered. Erin flashed a thumbs up to them and drove away, phone in one hand. Probably calling the police to find out what they wanted done with the men.

Smoke swirled in their wake, and Wiz coughed. It was definitely getting thicker.

Dad climbed up into his truck. "Let's get our stuff and get out of here."

Tom's horse sidled uneasily, but he held her steady and reached for Wiz. She got a toe in the stirrup and swung up behind him. Tom galloped down the road to the ranch house, stopping behind Dad's truck, the door hanging open. Wiz slid off the horse. Tom stood in the stirrups, reaching into his pocket, and tossed a shiny object to her. Beyond them, the tractor fired with a roar, Dad already inside.

"The Volvo's already loaded with the important stuff, just drive it down to the river. The truck can burn." Tom turned his horse, trotting up the drive.

"Got it." She ran for the car, parked next to the house and jammed with totes and boxes. She got in, started the car, and pulled carefully out of the drive, watching for Tom and his horse. They were a few hundred yards down the road, so she sped up. She passed him and got to the highway, just in time to stop for two wildland firefighting trucks, lights flashing, to turn onto their road.

The first one stopped next to her and a window rolled down. A man, soot smeared across his face, yelled, "Anybody left up there?"

"A man is riding a horse down the road behind me, and there's another coming on a tractor. They're the last ones. Don't worry about the fancy house at the top of the road. It's got automatic sprinklers on the roof and grounds. Let it burn!"

"Thanks!" He gave her a thumbs up and rolled up the road. She rolled up her window, coughing, and waited. A few seconds later, Tom's horse appeared in the thickening smoke. She pulled onto the highway and watched for the river bottom gate. Finding it, she pulled in and hopped out to open the gate.

Tom rode through as she opened it, and he pulled up the horse. "Get the car, and I'll close the gate behind Dad!"

She got back in the Volvo and drove through, watching in the rear-view mirror. The tractor finally rumbled in, Tom expertly maneuvering the horse to close the gate behind them. Then he rode around her, letting the horse canter, and she bumped down the rough road. A few hundred yards later, she saw the Rocking B's side-by-side off-road vehicle and the ranch hands with their trucks, along with a herd of cows and horses. Rusty kept the uneasily milling herd together.

She pulled up next to the tractor and got out, leaving the keys in the ignition, just in case. Tom had just gotten off the horse and was tying him to the tractor.

She ran over to him and jumped up into his arms. They held on to each other for a long time, Wiz reveling in the feel of Tom's strong arms holding her tight. She pulled back and kissed him, losing herself in the love between them. Eventually, they released each other, and Wiz slid to the ground. She hugged Dad, grateful he was safe and okay. Tom wrapped his arms around both of them together. She couldn't remember being happier.

Her phone buzzed, and she pulled away, the men reluctantly letting her go. It was Sam. She sighed. "Hey, Sam."

"Oh, I'm so happy you're okay! That was so scary to watch. I'm so sorry." Sam sounded frantic. She sucked in a breath, then blew it out. "Okay, sorry about that. Back to business. I've already spoken to the Marcus County Sheriff, and he's agreed, in light of the video and the apparent identity of the perpetrator as a deputy, that the State Patrol will handle the investigation. But the sheriff says that guy wasn't a real deputy; he's an imposter, that's why they're not arresting you. Still, the State has assured me that they will check the records of everyone assigned to investigate the case and make sure none of them were deployed to your location during the time frame you were there or have a personal connection to anyone who was there, since a lot of them are veterans, National Guard, or Reservists."

"Thank you." Wiz pulled the phone away and put it on speaker so the men could hear.

"Of course. They will delay the investigation until the fire situation is under control. And they will definitely be treating you as a victim, not a criminal. I will call you to set up the interview time, and I'll bring one of my colleagues, who is a criminal defense attorney. Don't go back to your house; it's a crime scene. Erin said you and Tom can use the apartment, and Pete can stay in their guest bedroom. And don't talk to anyone about this until you talk to me. Don't talk to the police unless I'm there."

"Thanks, Sam, sounds like you've got it under control." Sam was Wiz's best attorney yet.

"Of course. Did you doubt it?"

"Never."

She chuckled. "What about the fire?"

Wiz turned to look up the hill. "It looks bad. The whole hillside is on fire, and the trees are torching. I told the firefighters not to worry about my house, so I hope they don't try to save it. Their lives are far more important than my stuff." Helicopter blades thumped, then whirled. "Hey, it looks like the air support is here, though, so maybe they can get it under control. No matter what, I'll be staying with Tom and Pete until we all evacuate together, if it's necessary."

"Okay. Where are you, anyway?"

"River bottom, just below the ranch house. The guys moved the cows and horses down when we spotted the flames."

Dad said, "The neighbors across the river will open their gates for our livestock if we need to evacuate further."

"Good."

"Hey, Sam, what about the guys in Erin's truck?" Tom asked.

"They're already in the County lockup. The sheriff took them himself and made sure that the corrections officers on duty didn't have military backgrounds. They'll be transferred to Missoula County as soon as there's some manpower, just to make sure they don't magically escape or just end up dead."

"Wow. That's better than I expected."

Sam said, "Wiz, this is going to be a long, tough road, and it's going to drag everything out and probably through the mud if it goes to trial. We'll discuss this, but it would probably be better to ask the County Attorney to cut plea deals to minimize the impact on you."

"No," Wiz told her firmly. "I've been hiding and scared long enough. If the defense wants to blame the victim, then they can try. I want this all out and in the open. The more we allow ourselves to be victimized, the worse the whole situation gets. Somebody has to stand up and say this is wrong, and I'm going to do it.

I'm a survivor, not a victim, and I'm going to make sure others don't have to go through this."

"Good for you. It's going to be really tough, Wiz, I won't lie. If it goes to trial, they're going to try and blame you, call you a gun-happy freak who was gunning for these guys and use every other trick in the book. It will become obvious that they were the bad guys in every way, but it's going to be really hard. And there will be wackos out there vilifying you for all kinds of things. You'll probably be a target for quite some time, and you'll have to be very careful."

"I know. But if this lets one other woman be spared what I went through, then it's worth it. And I have the very best backup in the world." She smiled at Tom and Dad and thought about how lucky she was to have such great family and friends.

"All right. We'll talk more later. Be safe out there, guys, and let me know what's going on every now and then, okay?"

"Sure. And Sam, thanks so much. It really helped to know you were there and had my back."

"You're welcome. Stay safe." The phone clicked off, and Wiz stuck it in her back pocket. The men put their arms around her shoulders again, one on each side, and they all sagged against the truck tailgate.

"Holy hanna. I'm too old for this stuff." Dad shook his head.

"I think we all are. I'm just glad we made it out alive." Tom squeezed her tighter.

Bushes crackled and metal jingled. She straightened and put her hand on her weapon.

A man on a horse pushed through the thick underbrush. "Hey, Pete!"

Wiz sagged again, Tom rubbing her back.

Dad raised a hand. "Roger. Good to see you. Thanks for helping."

Roger shrugged. Four more riders appeared behind him. "You'd do the same for me. So, me and the kids are just going to drive your stock across the river and into my south pasture, just to be safe. That way, you won't have to worry about them. We'll drive the tractor over too, and you can get out of here with the vehicles. Sound like a plan?"

Dad held his hand up to Roger, and they shook. "Thanks, Roger, that would be great. We've had a heck of a day, I got to tell you."

"Heard on the scanner that someone set this deliberately and there was some shooting going on." Roger spat away from them. "Tell me later, after they get this mess under control. Y'all can stay with us if you'd like."

"Thanks, but Erin at Coffee and Cars is putting us up. Her apartment's empty right now."

"Good enough. Anyway, we got your stock. You get going."

"Thanks, Roger. Appreciate it."

"No problem. Stay safe!" He rode away. A younger man nodded and climbed up onto their tractor, a girl taking the reins of his horse. Tom untied his horse, tied the reins up on the saddle horn, took the lead rope the girl tossed him, clipped it on his horse's bridle, and gave it to a younger boy. They all rode off. The tractor started and bumped down the track, the man giving them a wave as he drove away.

Tom stood. "Dad, why don't you ride with Wiz in the Volvo, and I'll get the ATV. We'll stay together and meet up at Erin's, okay?"

"Sounds like a plan."

Tom leaned down and kissed her, then got in the ATV. The hands must have already left in their vehicles, probably while she was kissing Tom. She and Dad got in the Volvo, and she followed carefully. The highway was smoky, so they drove slowly. Wiz was grateful for the good air filters.

Pete looked up and out the side window. "Hey, they pulled in the big guns. Looks like the slurry bombers are overhead."

Wiz concentrated on driving. The smoke blew in eddies, some places thicker than others, and they drove slowly. The smoke cleared, and Tom picked up a little speed, then slowed again. A sheriff's vehicle blocked the other side of the road, blue and red lights lighting the smoke. The deputy waved them through. Wiz shuddered. The uniform was a horrible reminder, even if her attacker was a fake.

"Just a little while longer, Wiz." Dad squeezed her shoulder once.

She nodded and concentrated on the road. It wasn't long before they pulled into Erin and Ryan's place. Tom drove past the garage and over to the house, parking in front. As Wiz pulled up next to him, the front door opened.

Erin and Ryan came outside, smiling. "I'm so glad

you're all okay. We were worried. Come on in."

They all followed her into the house, but Wiz stopped just inside the door, looking down at herself. "We're all filthy. We don't want to drag this inside." She had bloodstains on her jeans, and the guys were smoky, greasy, and dirty.

"Who cares? It's just stuff." Erin shrugged. "But why don't we go out to the patio? We'll have some beers, and you can shower. We'll find you something to wear. It won't fit very well, but we'll get your stuff in the washer, so you can make do. Sound like a plan?"

"I could use a beer. Wiz, you go first, okay?" Dad pointed.

"Okay." Normally, using someone else's house would freak her out, but she was beyond that. The reaction was setting in, and she was exhausted.

Erin crooked her finger. "Wiz, you can use our shower, and the guys can use the upstairs. We've got plenty of water."

"Great." Tom squeezed Wiz's shoulder. "Dad, you go first before the adrenaline all runs out, okay? I'll grab your bag from the car."

"I guess that's probably a better idea." He nodded and plodded up the stairs.

Wiz followed Erin into the master bedroom and into the bathroom. Erin handed her a towel and a washcloth. "Use whatever you want and take your time. Got a tankless hot water heater. I'll find some clothes for you and close the bedroom door behind me. You can lock this one."

"Thanks." Wiz forced a smile. "I won't take too

long, or I'll probably fall over."

Erin nodded. "Yeah, that's how it takes me too." She closed the bathroom door.

"Thanks." Wiz locked it and peeled off her clothes. Her shoes were caked with dirt and a rusty brown—blood. Sure hoped she hadn't tracked anything into the house. *Oh.* "Hey, Erin?" she called.

"Yeah?"

"Don't wash my clothes. The cops are going to want them. Do you have a big bag we can put them in?" Wiz unlocked the door.

"Sure. Good thought. Here." A hand reached in through the door with a camisole, T-shirt, and a pair of shorts. "These will be too big but better than a robe."

Her bug-out bag wasn't doing any good at all, sitting in her bedroom closet. She'd just wanted to get out of there so badly she hadn't even considered taking anything with her. Wiz put Erin's clean clothes on the hooks on the back of the door, leaving hers on the floor. She sucked in a big breath and looked in the mirror.

She didn't look different. Hair escaped her braid, but no blood spattered her or anything else that screamed she'd just killed someone. She swallowed and started the shower, unbraiding her hair as it warmed.

She stepped inside, the water sluicing across her, soap wiping the dirt and sweat away but not washing her clean. She sank to the floor of the shower and cried. She should feel good. She got the bad guys, and no other woman would be hurt by them. But instead, she felt guilty for cutting their lives short. Jeff would never run another video quest. That deputy would no longer catch bad guys or do whatever he did if he was a fake. She was still here but so broken she might never have a real relationship again.

A knock sounded on the bathroom door. "Wiz, it's me," Tom called. "Are you okay?"

"No." She put her head in her hands.

"Can you get dressed and come out here, please."

She did, not even caring the clothes were two sizes too big and her hair was still soaking wet. She opened the door, and Tom flung his arms out. "Come here, I got you."

She stepped into him and bawled her eyes out again. Tom cradled her gently, turning her and pulling her in tight. He held her on his lap, rocking her and running a towel over her hair. "Better?"

She nodded against his chest, too tired to cry more.

"Want to join everyone or just go over to the apartment?" His voice rumbled through her, comfortingly.

"I'm okay. We can join everyone else."

"You sure? They understand you had a really bad day."

"I'm okay." Wiz looked up at him. "And I'm done hiding."

"That's my girl." He lifted her from his lap, then stood and looked down at her. "You sure? It gets to be too much, Erin's already given me the keys and the codes. They'll understand."

"It's okay. Let's go have that drink."

He smiled down at her and took her hand. She squeezed it for a moment, then let go to gather her weapons. The cops were going to want both of them, so she'd have to get another one, and she probably wouldn't be able to get to her safe. Well, Tom and Dad had theirs, but she wanted one of her own.

They entered the living room, Erin waiting for them. "Wiz, I'll put all your clothes in a bag. The police are going to want your weapons, so you can borrow mine. I have a backup, and Ryan's got his, so we'll be fine." Erin pointed to a black semi-auto pistol on the coffee table, two magazines sitting by it.

"Thanks, Erin. And thanks for everything else." She was so lucky to have such wonderful friends.

"Nothing you wouldn't do for me." She nodded at the couch. "Have a seat. I'll get you beer and water, and there's pizza coming. Pete's upstairs, said he needed a nap worse than food." Her mouth compressed for a moment. "We could sit outside, but the smoke is blowing over here."

"Thanks, Erin." Tom guided her to the couch and sat, tucking her in next to him. Ryan was on the chair at the far end, and he raised his beer toward her in a salute.

Wiz turned to Tom. "Is Dad doing okay with this? He didn't have to kill anybody, but..." Tom nodded to Ryan.

Ryan grimaced. "Pete and me talked a little while you two were in the shower. He's more concerned about you, but he promised to talk about this with his buddies." He shrugged. "I think he'll be okay. But maybe ask him to do a joint counseling session?"

Tom squeezed her shoulder. "Good idea. Wiz, you can talk him into that, I'm sure. Just say it's for you." She nodded and relaxed into him again.

Erin brought them beers and waters, then sat, holding her bottle up. "Here's to survival."

They clinked bottles, a water glass in Wiz's case, and drank. "Survival and living well. It really is the best revenge."

"Amen to that." Erin rose and went to the patio. Ryan raised his bottle to Wiz again and drank. She relaxed into the comfort of Tom's embrace. She'd done it. She'd survived everything they'd thrown at her, and now, she was going to live life to the fullest. No more hiding or being scared. No, she was going to live every minute like it was the last and never look back again.

And she would start tonight. She yawned. Well, okay, maybe tomorrow; as soon as she got some food into her, she was going to crash. But tomorrow morning, nothing was going to hold her back from celebrating life with Tom to the very fullest. It was time to show him just how much she loved him in every way possible. She took another sip, squeezed his thigh, and smiled up at him.

He smiled back, sweetly, and kissed her. She heard Ryan get up and go to the patio, but she really didn't care if he saw them. She was safe, and she had Tom, the love she'd looked for all her life. She was the luckiest woman in the entire universe.

Epilogue
TOM

Wiz rocked comfortably in the saddle on the horse in front of Tom. She'd taken to trail riding like a cow to corn. These days, she took to everything with happy enthusiasm. She'd changed so much from their first meeting, just over a year ago. She turned and smiled at him. He mouthed "love you" and she promptly returned the sentiment. Then she twisted back, paying attention to the trail winding through the beautiful Anaconda-Pintler mountains.

After their backcountry trip, they'd start pre-wedding counseling for an early December ceremony. Wiz had wanted to do it sooner, but he'd asked her to wait. She was changing her life so fast, determined to enjoy every second, and take every opportunity to do something new and different, but he suggested she needed to catch her breath and enjoy the ride. Wiz seemed to think the opposite—that he needed the time—but the end result was the same.

Despite Montana's favorable laws, it had taken too long for the wheels of justice to turn. While Wiz's actions were investigated, she'd struggled between determination to enjoy her life, guilt, and terror. Anticipating the last, he'd asked her to stay in the

ranch house while they got her house cleaned.
Exhausted by fixing her house, working the ranch and
her business, she'd fallen to sleep easily, but he'd
rocked her through nightmares at least once a night for
a couple of weeks. Therapy and the comfort of family
had worked wonders, but after a month, Wiz had
needed a little space and moved back into her house.
While they officially lived separately, they almost
always ended up in the same house every evening.

Wiz was eventually cleared of all wrongdoing, but
Sam had been right, the aftermath of the incident had
been very difficult. Initially, someone had put a
significant amount of money and effort into painting
Wiz as a crazed, gun-toting vigilante. They'd had to
hire a security firm to guard the ranch road, and even
Sam needed a bodyguard during the trial. The State
police shooed paparazzi with telephoto lenses trying to
take pictures from the verge of the highway, but local
law enforcement wasn't very responsive. Even though
Wiz's attacker wasn't a real deputy sheriff—he'd
bought the uniform online—the state had still run the
investigation. Even though he initially agreed, the
Sheriff had deeply resented the state's intrusion,
especially when they expanded the scope
unexpectedly. The state found several inadequately-
investigated cases and some reports that hadn't been
looked into at all. The Sheriff claimed lack of personnel
and funding made it impossible to do everything. In
the end, only some retraining was required. But still,
any requests for assistance from Wiz or the Rocking B
dropped into a black hole.

Nutcases still bothered them occasionally, and they'd stopped two snipers and an attempt to firebomb Wiz's house using a drone. The forest fire had cleared the undergrowth above her house, so she'd brought the drone down with a weighted net fired from a slingshot—purchased after the first paparazzi drones overflew her house—and the snipers had been easy to find. She'd used her own drone to drop "leave or die" messages on their hideouts; they'd packed up and left. On the dark web, professional hitters had marked her as too big a risk for the pay. Amateurs tried occasionally, but after one disappeared entirely, abandoning his car at a trailhead, they'd been more cautious. A hunter had found that man's remains the next fall; he'd slipped and fallen into a creek before he'd gotten more than a mile from his vehicle. Wiz had never seen him; Montana's weather and geography had proven deadly.

Troubled by her ex's last statement that "they were going to kill him," Wiz had investigated Jeff's life since their divorce. He'd built huge gambling debts, owing several criminal organizations, including the Russian mob. Some of those organizations had attempted to extort Jeff's debts from Wiz. She'd started a website and posted every attempt publicly, encouraging other business owners in the area to stand up to the criminals attempting to infiltrate Marcus for their money-laundering and protection rackets. She'd found some troubling ties to Marcus law enforcement and Marcus City Bank, but nothing concrete.

In an effort to fight back against the smear

campaigns, Wiz had agreed to participate in a documentary film highlighting the ongoing prevalence of sexual assault in the military. No immediate changes had been made, but every bit of attention drawn to the problem helped, and she was thrilled to assist. Unfortunately, since the perpetrator was dead, the military had declined to reopen the investigation into Wiz's assault, despite her lingering suspicion that he hadn't acted alone.

Even with all the furor, Wiz's business thrived. Tom had become the public face of the company, making many potential clients more comfortable. With her strident stance against organized crime, few of those people attempted to contact her anymore. Tom chose their clientele carefully, and immediately dropped those who moved into dangerous or illegal dealings, as stated in their contracts.

Since he and Wiz were settled, Dad had opened to change as well. Wiz had bought into the Rocking B Ranch. With her funding, they'd swapped over to raising their beef entirely on grass. They'd hired more ranch hands and marketing help; the local community was happy and supportive. Dad was casually dating some of the ladies who'd been after him for years, taking them out for dinner and dancing. None of them were serious enough to invite on their backcountry trip, but that could change.

A few minutes later, their next campsite appeared, Warren Lake shining a bright blue, the surrounding cliffs reflected in the still waters. Dad, Yvonne and Peter were already stringing the highline for the pack string. Since it was their third night out, setting up camp was easy and fast. In less than an hour, the kids ran into in the lake to swim. Tom was settling into his chair when Erin and Ryan hiked in, dropping their daypacks and accepting a seat and a beer.

Ryan clinked cans with them. "I love backpacking, but this pack string thing has some real advantages!"

Erin tapped hers to Wiz's sparkling water. "Here, here. Strolling with light packs in the depths of a beautiful wilderness is a wonderful experience."

Wiz smirked. "You know, you could be riding."

Ryan shook his head violently. "No way. I'm not getting on a horse with just one good arm!"

"People do, you know. All the time." Dad winked. "They don't even bother with the fancy grasper." They'd had the same discussion every afternoon.

"Yeah, yeah. I like my own two feet, thanks."

Erin sipped. "What are we cooking tonight, Pete?"

"Chicken and sausage gumbo, with corncakes and pineapple upside down cake for dessert." Dad rubbed his hands together.

Tom's stomach rumbled, and Ryan groaned.

"Good thing I'm walking, or I'd never burn off all the calories." Erin lifted her beer.

Tom laughed at her statement. "Riding burns plenty."

"Maybe so. I'm happy walking. But this is an argument we'll never agree on. So, can somebody tell me where our stuff is, and we'll go set up our tent?"

"Already done. I'll show you." Wiz rose.

"Oh, good. And thanks. You really don't have to do

that." Erin followed her away from the lake.

"I know. But the faster we're set up, the quicker we can jump in the lake."

Tom finished his beer, intending to join Wiz; he never missed an opportunity to see her in a swimsuit. "Dad, you coming in today?"

He shook his head. "Nah, might wade a little, but you two go ahead. You got more energy than I do."

Tom and Ryan both snorted. Dad could ride or walk them into the ground. Tom led Ryan to their tent sites, passing Wiz and Erin, already changed and on their way back. He put on board shorts and sandals, grabbed a towel and headed back to the lake. Wiz's brutal workouts were good for both of them; he felt younger than his years, even after riding all day.

As he neared the lake, screeches rang loud. Rather than wading into the massive water fight, he plopped into his chair.

Dad handed him a water bottle. "Not gonna jump in?"

"No way. I'll go in when they've got it out of their system. More fun to watch from here." They exchanged smiles, and watched until the furor died down. Tom waded out and as he expected, everyone threw water at him. But it didn't last long, because the kids got chilled, and Erin and Ryan had to cook.

Tom dove and swam, washing all the trail dust off, popping up next to Wiz. "Going back to shore?"

She smiled. "Sorry. Getting cold."

They swam together. When he touched the bottom, he snagged her around the waist, pulling her close, and kissed her. "I missed you. On a horse, you're too far away."

She leaned back and shivered. "I missed you, too. But it's still chilly out here."

He grinned. "Well, let's get you warmed up. Climb on." He slid her to his back, and she wrapped her arms and legs around him. He walked up and out of the lake, moving carefully on the slippery rock. He didn't want to drop his precious load. At the cook site, he paused by Erin. "How long until dinner?"

She smiled and winked. "Oh, thirty minutes or so. Maybe a little longer if you need it."

"Good. Don't wait on us." He set off at a jog for their tent, Wiz bouncing on his back, laughing. He set her down at the tent, and turned to hold her close. "That's my favorite sound in the entire world."

"What is?" She leaned back against his arms, smiling up at him.

"Your laughter." He caressed her soft cheek. "For so long, I thought I'd never hear it. Don't ever stop laughing, Wiz."

"Don't worry, I won't. I've got too much lost time to make up for." She jumped and wrapped her arms and legs around him, kissing him.

They might be late for dinner, but Tom didn't care. He had the best life in the world: cows, computers, and most importantly, Wiz's love.

The End and Happily Ever After!

Want more stories from Marcus, Montana? Deb's book is next! Watch for *Bitter Sweet*!

Sign up for my newsletter to get notifications about new releases, plus bonus stories like *Love, Ranchers & Raptors*, and extra scenes! https://sendfox.com/amscott

Author's Note

Marcus, Montana isn't a real place, but it's based on Hamilton, Montana, where I live. You can find pictures on my Instagram at annemscott_author. Sadly, there isn't a Rocking B Ranch, or a Coffee & Cars, but we have lots of real cattle ranches and great espresso shops. We also have a lot of huge, fancy timber frame houses, mostly behind locked gates. Wiz's home isn't based on any particular house, but you can find lots of examples on local real estate websites.

On the other hand, the MPG Ranch is real. Follow them on Facebook for amazing wildlife research, pictures, and video! Mannix Family Beef is only one of several natural and/or organic beef producers in Montana, and they all raise delicious beef. If you visit the Bitterroot Valley, try one of our great steakhouses. And if you're looking for a cowboy hat, there really is a custom hat maker in Darby, MT along with several custom leather shops in the area. Most of them can be found online, as well.

The Sapphire Crest Trail is also real, as is Gold Creek Road. There is lots of great camping, hiking, and riding in the less famous Sapphire Mountains, along with a lot of off-road vehicle trails. But please, make sure your campfires are dead and cold before leaving; it takes very little for a wildfire to start.

The story about Pete's Vietnam sniper rifle is based on real life. The first snipers bought their own rifles, and they were handed from person to person in country, and the last owner brought them home. In later years, some were able to find their original rifles. While this may seem like a macabre memento to non-military members, those rifles kept not only the sniper and his spotter alive, but also many, many others. The rifles are extremely important to those snipers.

Wiz's story isn't based on any one particular person, but sexual assault is far too common. If you are a sexual assault survivor, there are resources available to help you. In the US, RAINN is one of the largest; call their hotline at 1-800-655-4673 (HOPE). There are similar organizations in many countries. Get help now; don't wait, please.

If you experience suicidal thoughts for any reason, please reach out for help. Don't give up—we need you! In the US, the National Suicide Prevention Hotline is 988; you can call or chat. The number for military veterans is the same. There are similar hotlines in many countries; again, don't wait, reach out for help, please.

Biography

After twenty years in the US Air Force, Anne M. Scott traded her sword for a pen. Well, a laptop. She writes about strong women and men, love that grows slowly in small western towns, with a little suspense, action, and adventure—anything more than kisses and hugs happens behind closed doors. Anne is lucky to live, hike, and ski in the Bitterroot Mountains of Montana. On the rare occasions she leaves, Anne volunteers with Team Rubicon, a veteran-led disaster response organization. She also writes exciting science fiction as AM Scott.

Check out her closed-door, small town, slow-build Montana romances at: https://www.amscottwrites.com/romance/ and sign up for her newsletter at: https://sendfox.com/amscott for a free ebook.

Find her:
Facebook: facebook.com/AnneMScottAuthor
Instagram: Instagram.com/ annemscott_author
Merchandise: LightwavePub.redbubble.com
Email: romance@amscottwrites.com

Acknowledgements

Thank you, lovely readers! Without you, I couldn't afford to publish. I appreciate you reading my stories very much and I hope you enjoy them!

God has been very good to me, sending me on this wonderful writing adventure, with the full support of my wonderful husband, The Amazing Sleeping Man. Love you!

Another big thank you to my sister Lia Huni, rom-com writer. She's my first/alpha reader, and her feedback made this a much better book.

My sprint group is super supportive too. Thanks to Lia, Irene Micheals, Sara Ivy Hill, Marcus Alexander Hart, Tony Slater, Lou Cadle, and Kate Pickford, along with all their pen name alter-egos! I appreciate the focus, dedication, professional advice, and fun. Y'all are the best!

Thanks also to my Team Rubicon friends. They've supported my writing journey and kicked disaster ass!

I also want to thank my Doomscribbler Bombshells: SD Clayton, SM Shaffer, and Katy Hollway. Thanks for sticking with me through the whole journey! It was longer than any of us ever thought it could be, but I think it was worth it.